When it comes to family, love, tradition and pride are a powerful brew...

"In the South you grow up steeped in tradition. It's not that you find the South particularly quaint or interesting. You simply have no choice. By the time Miss Eulayla Overstreet, or her equivalent, places the metronome-from-hell on the family piano, you know four very important things that will shape your life. You know who your people are, where the home place is, and that you will never, ever like the piano.

"You also know precisely how much sugar to put in a gallon of tea.

"True sweet tea is a sublime syrupy DNA test for family identity. You either belong to the syrup subset of Southerners or you belong to the carpetbaggers who moved down from up North. Sweet is sweet, and you can't cheat. No hostess of any stature would be caught dead sweetening her iced tea at the table.

"More than once I've asked myself how a modest beverage gained so much power. The simple answer is that sweet tea is the dividing line between us and them."
—*from Sweet Tea and Jesus Shoes (Debra Dixon)*

"The trouble with growing up rooted deep in a family, tucked safely in a pretty valley south of the Mason-Dixon, is how your future lies in front of you like a clean sheet just off the line. Ask me. You'll take it for granted.

"All my life, I knew when the first crocus would come up by the back step of Mama and Daddy's house. I knew when the first hay would come in from the field, when the scent of a wood burning fire would curl out of the chimney, and when the sunflowers would stand taller than a man. And I knew that on the first fall weekend I'd clean out Mama's perennial beds so they could bloom again the following spring. There's something about that kind of security that will make you believe you have all the time in the world."
—*from Sweeter Than Tea (Kimberly Brock)*

The Sweet Tea Story Collections

Sweet Tea and Jesus Shoes
More Sweet Tea
On Grandma's Porch
and now . . .
Sweeter Than Tea

"The Sweet Tea books clearly define what it means to be Southern with a Southern family."
—*Newnan Times Herald, Newnan, Georgia*

"If you don't recognize a family member or can't recall a story that could be a twin to one in here, you're a Yankee. That mystical union of Southern pride, sensibilities, and practical faith traipse in all their glory through these stories."
—*VABooks! Center for the Book*

"[Sweet Tea and Jesus Shoes] is rich in storytelling and makes me long for those Southern days as a child listening to the stories of the past."
—*Barbara Dooley, author, radio talk show host, and wife of University of Georgia Athletic Director, Vince Dooley.*

"Miss Julia would feel right at home on the front porches and in the living rooms and kitchens where these delightful stories originated."
—*Ann B. Ross, author of* Miss Julia Speaks Her Mind.

"Storytelling is back with all its Southern habits and charms, thanks to six women who are making it easier to get it in print. The stories are so good you'll be hungry for more."
—*Liz Carpenter, acclaimed author and former press secretary for Lady Bird Johnson.*

"A brilliant compilation of Southern women's stories in the tradition of Anne Rivers Siddons."
—*Harriet Klausner, Midwest Book Review.*

"Sweet Tea and Jesus Shoes is a feast for any reader."
—*Lisa Knighton, editor, Georgia Women Speak*

Sweeter Than Tea

by

Deborah Grace Staley
Valerie Keiser Norris
Susan Sipal
Misty Barrere
Kimberly Brock
Jane Forest
Willis Baker
Clara Wimberly
Kathleen Watson
Tom Honea
Martina Boone
Deedra Climer
Darcy Crowder

To Stacy + Charlie –
If you make me laugh til you're
forever. I'll always treasure
your friendship. Love, Valerie

Valerie Keiser Norris

BelleBooks, Inc.

This is a work of fiction. Names, characters, places and incidents are either the products of the author's imagination or are used fictitiously. Any resemblance to actual persons (living or dead), events or locations is entirely coincidental.

BelleBooks
PO BOX 300921
Memphis, TN 38130
Print ISBN: 978-1-61194-135-7

We Dedicate These Stories To...

To all those, past and present, who have served in our nation's military so we can enjoy our freedoms, and particularly the men in my family: James R. Jones, Sr. and James R. Jones, Jr.—WWII, Joe K. Jones, J. Edward Jones, and J. Eugene Jones—Korea. My father, Sherman L. Grace, Korea. My fathers-in-law, Fred E. Staley, Sr. and William P. Davenport—Navy. And my nephew, Christopher C. Staley, currently serving, U.S. Air Force. A heartfelt thanks and much love to my boys, Fred and Ethan, who have given me a family and home. Because I feel safe and secure in your love, I can do what I do. And for my niece, Hannah, who allowed me to borrow her name.
—*Deborah Grace Staley*

To my mother, Suzann, who loved for her grandmother, Stella, to read her tea leaves.
—*Misty Barrere*

For Sylvia. A life-time's worth. And as always, to John, Brenna, Wil and Brittani—I love you.
—*Darcy Crowder*

To Mama, whose glorious gardens are only overshadowed by the abundant love she's nurtured in so many lives, and to Daddy, whose mountains of roses may one day lift us all up to heaven.
—*Kimberly Brock*

To my Family—my husband Wayne; to Wayne Jr. and Tina, Lindsey, Lucus and Lily: to Mark and Jenny, Hannah and Meadow; to Suzanne and Doug, Emory and Ethan. You are my everything. I love you all very much.
—*Clara Wimberly*

To my mom, Mickey, who was born in Mobile, Alabama and has remained a southern belle all her life. Mom taught me to love reading—she took me to my first library and found me a story about Siamese cats. I haven't stopped reading since.
—*Jane Forest*

To my grandmother, Myrtis McDaniel Honea . . . Who taught me to clean my tools before I put them away. Who told me, *"A ten cent tree in a ten dollar hole is better than a ten dollar tree in a ten cent hole."* . . . And, who always had tea cakes on the table when any grandchild came to her house late on a summer afternoon.
—*Tom Honea*

To my mom, and all the wonderful moms in my life: Mindy, Dee, Nita, Holly, Janet, Gina, Tracey, Deonne and Hazel.
—*Kathleen Watson*

To the members of the Greenville East Chapter of the South Carolina Writers Workshop, for all their help and encouragement.
—*Valerie Keiser Norris*

To Karen Hall—a real-life, modern-day Minoan snake goddess, whose home is a sanctuary for all living things, whether beast, fowl, or child.
—*Susan Sipal*

To my family of true Southerners, through whose lives continues to flow another kind of tea, spiritual, sweetened by such eternal intangibles as love and respect, faith and family.
—*Willis Baker*

IN ORDER OF APPEARANCE

Deborah Grace Staley—Made With Love

Valerie Keiser Norris—All Foam, No Beer

Susan Sipal—Running Raw

Misty Barrere—The Agreement

Kimberly Brock—Never Promised You A Rose Garden

Jane Forest—Bedeviled Eggs

Willis Baker—Not Through My Window

Clara Wimberly—Circle Of Life

Kathleen Watson—Lessons on a Paper Napkin

Tom Honea—A Pig Roasting

Martina Boone—Bringing Lula Home

Deedra Climer—Lavender In Blue

Darcy Crowder—Chasing Sunset

Made with Love

Deborah Grace Staley

The kitchen was the heart of Hannah Goode's home. It was a big, loud, messy place filled with heavenly aromas and great conversation. Momma firmly believed idle hands were the devil's workplace. If that was the case, the cure was to keep everyone busy cooking. Yep, the yard had more weeds than grass, and inside, dust could be found accumulating on furniture and in corners, but the kitchen was well stocked and well appointed.

In the kitchen, each family member had a job. Momma did entrees, Daddy desserts, Lara made side dishes, and Hannah was in charge of breads and sweet tea. Not that Helen Goode didn't mix it up on occasion. Momma was known to change everyone's jobs without notice, just so each person learned how to make everything. But Hannah loved the breads, and, of course, sweet tea was a southern staple.

It's not so surprising that Hannah grew up wanting to be a baker. When the time came, she applied to the finest schools. She and her parents had spread the acceptance letters for culinary schools across the scarred kitchen table and talked about which she should choose. Momma had cried, and Daddy had looked proud. Hannah squeezed Momma's hand and said, "It's okay. I'll be home on holidays, and it's only a two-year program."

Momma took Hannah's hand in both hers while she and daddy shared a look.

"What is it?" Hannah asked, not sure she wanted the answer.

Daddy laid his big, warm hand on top of hers and Momma's. "The doc says I need surgery, but I don't want you to worry—"

"Surgery!" she said in unison with her sister.

"Now it's nothing to worry about. I'll just go in, have it done and be good as new before you know it. Now, which of these schools is good enough to deserve my little girl?" He'd wrapped his arms around her shoulders. "I'm so proud of you."

She chose a school, and then Daddy had had surgery and begun chemotherapy. The prognosis was good. Hannah left for school that fall. When she'd come home for Thanksgiving, her daddy had been so weak, so feeble. She didn't know which broke her heart, that or him asking for help with the pumpkin pies. He sat on a stool and supervised, but as always, Hannah cherished time in the kitchen with her family.

Christmas that year, the Goodes had baked more than ever before because everyone had wanted to spend every second together doing what they loved. There were decorated cutout cookies, cakes, pies and dessert bars. They'd covered everything that had gotten in their path with chocolate. They even made rum soaked fruitcake—Gran's recipe.

It had been Daddy's idea to ship most of it to the soldiers overseas and away from home at Christmas. The rum cake stayed. It had to come with the warning, "Do not operate heavy machinery after consuming."

Hannah laughed, remembering. She could just imagine soldiers driving tanks around the Middle East tipsy on rum cake.

It was that Christmas Hannah had first gotten the idea to sell their baked goods. Momma and Daddy wouldn't say, but with Daddy unable to work, things were tough financially. Christmas Day, she'd stayed up all night making cupcakes. The next week, she had taken them to every restaurant and corner store she'd come across. When she'd returned home, she had orders from three restaurants and two delis.

Hannah didn't go back to school. Daddy hadn't been happy about it, but she was determined to spend her days baking with him. Momma had helped with deliveries while Daddy had rested.

Business was good. Great, in fact. The orders had soon outgrown their kitchen's capabilities. They needed more ovens, commercial mixers and storage. Hannah found cheap equipment online from closing businesses and took out a one-year lease on a shop front with good foot traffic downtown. For the first month, Hannah had just filled commercial orders. Toward the end of the month, Daddy had felt so much better that he'd come in and helped them. Lara had done what she could after school, but none of them had wanted to take her away from sports or her schoolwork.

Things went so well that the family found themselves with spare time in the afternoons. That's when they put some tables and a coffee bar in the front of the store. They began opening midday to sell cupcakes. By then, most of the baking was done, and Momma was making deliveries. The first week, they'd sold out by three. As word spread, they sold out sooner.

"Hannah, honey," Daddy said, "I think you're going to have to hire some help."

"I don't know, Daddy. I want to keep it a family business."

"Then talk to your cousins. Your Aunt Christy said the girls have been looking for a job, but haven't had any luck."

"Can they bake?"

Daddy laughed. "We'll do the baking. Let them take orders and wait on customers."

She hired Ginger and Gracie, who, thankfully, started right away. Hannah was so busy she was dead on her aching feet most afternoons. The shipping company had just picked up treat boxes going to the soldiers overseas. Sending them had become something like a tithe for the Goode Family Bakery. God had blessed the business so much, they all wanted to do something to help others. Supporting the troops was another way to honor Daddy, who had spent the years before he married Momma in the Army serving in Desert Storm.

The years passed almost without Hannah noticing.

Daddy got a clean bill of health and had been in remission since. Thank God. Lara went off to college, and Hannah had bought a loft downtown to be close to the business. Hannah liked being able to walk everywhere she went. With Maryville, Tennessee being a small town, it was pretty quiet, so the routine was a bit monotonous. She'd like to say she was too busy to get lonely, but if she was being honest, sometimes she wondered what might have been if she'd stayed in cooking school. Would she have moved to a big city and become a chef? Would she have met someone? Had a family of her own by now?

Hannah shook her head. Thinking about what might have been served no good purpose. She had no regrets. She loved her work and spending time with her family. It was afternoons—the time when all the busyness of baking had passed and she had time to think—when her mind wandered. Or more to the point, her mind wandered when she should have been trying to make sense of the jumble of paperwork cluttering her desk and clogging her inbox.

Hannah grabbed a cup of coffee and a cupcake and sat at a corner table with her laptop and overflowing inbox. Instead of sorting through it all, she wound up doing some mindless Internet surfing. The bell on the front door signaled the arrival of a customer. She didn't even look up, just tapped away on the mouse pad and sipped her coffee while deleting junk emails.

"Welcome to Goode's," Gracie said. "What can I get you?"

"A double-chocolate buttercream cupcake and a bottle of water, please."

She looked up to check out the owner of the rumbling, deep voice and found a man wearing fatigues with an American flag and several bars on the sleeve that indicated his rank. The insignia indicated he was Air Force. He was average height, but nothing else about him was average. Like most soldiers, he was in great shape and powerfully built. Tanned, clean-shaven, close cut dark hair. She propped her chin on her hand and irrationally wondered what color his eyes were.

"For here or to go?" Gracie asked.

The man inhaled deeply. "The smell is so amazing, I think I'll sit awhile and enjoy."

Gracie smiled. "Have a seat, and I'll bring it right out to you."

"How much do I owe you?"

"It's on the house. Memorial Day is this weekend, and cupcakes are free to members of the military."

He nodded, twisting his cap in his hands. "Thank you." He reached into his pocket and dropped a few bills in the tip jar, then sat at a table not far from Hannah. He caught her eye and smiled a greeting. Hannah smiled as well, then looked back at her computer screen, but soon, she was sneaking another peek at him. He had a compelling face that kept her looking past what should have been polite glances. There was something about his eyes, which were the color of rich, velvety chocolate. He couldn't be much older than her, but his dark eyes held a sadness that said he'd seen more than a man so young should.

He looked up then, and their gazes locked.

Caught again. Hannah swallowed hard, but didn't look away. Instead she smiled. Good thing she wasn't standing, because his smile literally made her knees weak.

Gracie set his cupcake and the bottle of water in front of him. "Let me know if you need anything else."

The man looked up at her. "Actually, I was wondering if the owner of the shop might be in."

Gracie looked over her shoulder at Hannah, unsure if she wanted to speak with anyone since this was her first break of the day. Hannah stood and walked over to join her cousin. "I'm the owner," she said, holding out her hand. "Hannah Goode."

The soldier stood and took her hand, smiling. "Lieutenant Sam Evans. It's a pleasure to meet you, ma'am. If you don't mind me saying,

I wasn't expecting someone so young and pretty."

Add charmer to his growing list of attributes. Her hand in his tingled at the contact, and unsure of how to respond to his comment, she just smiled, then pulled her hand back to rub it against her jeans. "What can I do for you, Lieutenant?"

"Sam, please. I wanted to come by and personally thank you for what you do for the troops."

"Oh." Hannah frowned. "How did you know?"

"My company in Afghanistan received more than one shipment of your baked goods."

"Really?" Her family had received a number of letters from soldiers since they'd started the shipments all those Christmases ago, but they'd never met any of the soldiers in person.

He swept a hand towards a chair at his table. "Would you care to join me? That is, if you're not too busy. That looks like a lot of paperwork over there, and I don't want to interrupt your work."

"It'll keep. I was just taking my afternoon break." Still smiling, she pulled out the chair he'd indicated, but he moved around the table to hold it for her while she sat. Something in her midsection softened. She was a sucker for courteous men. His good looks and the uniform didn't hurt, either.

"You were stationed in Afghanistan?"

"Yes, ma'am."

"You're starting to make me feel ancient. Please, call me Hannah."

His smile drew her in. "Hannah." The way he said her name in his deep, slow, southern drawl had her moving closer to the edge.

"My tour just ended, so I'm on leave before reporting back to base."

Hannah frowned. There weren't any Air Force bases near Maryville. Just the Air National Guard Base, but they didn't have any troops presently deployed. Their baked goods were a local delivery. "Where are you stationed?"

"Georgia."

"You have family here, then."

"No, ma'am," he said, but caught himself. "Sorry. Hannah."

"What brings you to East Tennessee?"

"I came for you." He flushed. "I mean, it's like I said, I came to thank you in person."

"That's very nice of you, but surely you have family anxious to see you now that you're home."

He took a bite of his cupcake. "Mmm." He licked icing and crumbs from his lips. "Delicious. I didn't think it was possible that they could taste better."

She was completely distracted by both his obvious enjoyment of the dessert and by his lips. They looked soft and moist from where he'd just licked the icing and crumbs away. Her wayward mind conjured an image of them looking just like that after a kiss.

"I made those fresh this morning," she said. "Getting them halfway around the world takes a bit longer."

"They tasted like heaven. The airtight packaging you used kept them pretty fresh. Having the icing in a separate packet was a great idea." He spoke so softly that Hannah leaned in, not wanting to miss a word. His voice was low with the most beautiful, easy cadence. She could have listened to him talk all day.

"Don't get me wrong, the mess hall made baked goods for us, but what they gave us was nothing like this." He took another bite. "These," he held up the cupcake, "were like a taste of home." He set the cupcake down and wiped his mouth with a paper napkin. "My mom made me cupcakes when I was growing up. They're my favorite dessert."

She crossed her arms on the table, smiling. "What flavor do you like best?" Hannah was thinking she would whip up a quick batch of a dozen or so that he could take with him, since he'd gone to the trouble of finding her shop and delivering his thanks in person.

"I've yet to find a flavor I don't like."

"You have to have a favorite," she pressed.

His smile was wide and unrepentant. "The one I just ate is always my favorite."

A baker could die happy cooking for this man. This thought, combined with the other strong feelings swirling through her, should have set off warning signals, but instead, everything about him intrigued her.

"You never answered my question—about your family? I hope you're not delaying your homecoming on my account. It's very nice that you came here to personally thank us for the baked goods, but you could have sent a card or letter. That's what most of the soldiers do."

The shadows clouded his eyes once again. "There's no one for me to go home to."

Just then her father walked out of the kitchen, and seeing her sitting with a stranger, approached. "Who's your friend, Hannah?" he asked.

She stood. "We actually just met." Sam stood as well. "This is

Lieutenant Sam Evans. Lieutenant, this is my father, Frank Goode."

The two men shook hands and took one another's measure.

"Daddy was in the Army, Sam."

"Is that right?"

Dad slid his hands in his pockets. "I volunteered right out of high school. Did five tours overseas before settling down with Hannah's mother."

"Daddy was in Desert Storm," she proudly added.

"Schwarzkopf is a legend," Sam said. "Amazing that campaign was so short with no casualties."

"I wish the same could be said of the current conflicts in the Middle East," Daddy added.

Sam simply nodded.

"So, you live in Maryville, son?"

"No, sir. I just wanted to thank your daughter for the care packages she's been sending the troops. I'll be heading back to base soon. Since I'm just returning from a tour, I have a few weeks off. I plan to get on my motorcycle and just ride with no particular destination in mind."

A smile spread across her Daddy's face. "You came here just to see my Hannah, then?"

"Yes, sir."

"Well, that was mighty considerate of you." He looked from her to Sam, and back to her. Hannah could see the wheels churning. "You know, we're having a little family gathering at my folks' house tonight. Why don't you join us?"

Her eyebrows rose in surprise. Little gathering? "Daddy, don't you think—"

Daddy held up his hand. "Now, I insist. We can't have this young man sitting alone in a hotel and eating restaurant fare when there's going to be more home cooked food to consume than he's likely seen in some time."

Dread pulled at me.

"Oh, I wouldn't want to intrude on a family gathering," Sam said. Please, God . . .

"I won't take 'no' for an answer. Hannah, Mom's birthday cake has been iced. It just needs decorating. I'm going to go pick up your mother and head on over to your grandparents' house. See that the cake and the lieutenant get there. Four sharp. You know Mom gets cranky if she has to eat too late."

Resigned, Hannah said, "All right, Daddy."

He held up a hand to them both and then left.

Several customers entered and walked up to the counter to place orders.

"If you don't think it's a good idea for me to come along," Sam said, "you could just make my excuses to your father."

Hannah sighed. "No. He'd never forgive me for letting you get away. But you should know, if you do come, you're willingly walking into a circus."

Sam smiled and folded his hands in front of him. "Well, now you've piqued my curiosity."

She shook her head. "Don't say I didn't warn you."

"If you don't mind, I'd like to go shower and change. I came straight here after we landed," he admitted.

"I can't believe you came here just to say 'thank you' when you could be home right now."

"It was important to me to let you know in person how much what you did meant to not only me, but to everyone in my company. Little touches from home are so important for morale when you're away for months at a time under such difficult circumstances."

If giving him a cupcake every day for the rest of his life would chase the shadows from his eyes, she'd gladly bake for him. "It's my pleasure. You and your colleagues have sacrificed so much. In comparison, it's such a small thing for me to send treats."

He stepped closer, into her personal space. The air around them crackled with awareness. "Thank you," he said softly.

Sucking in a breath, she swallowed hard. "You're welcome."

After a moment, he took a step back, breaking the intensity of the moment, though the feeling of them having shared something profound lingered.

Sam picked up his cap from the table. "Should I meet you back here at 3:30?"

"You're sure you want to do this?" she asked, reluctant to open the door and willingly allow this stranger to walk into what was sure to be one family embarrassment after another.

He gave her a long slow look that left no doubt as to where his interests lay. "I don't believe I've ever been so sure of anything in my life."

Hannah made a quick trip home to shower and change as well.

Family gatherings were typically casual, so she chose jeans and a dark green V-neck shirt that complemented her hair and eyes. Blast her dad for inviting Sam and, as a result, making her a bundle of nerves and anticipation.

Get a grip, Hannah. It's Gran's birthday. He's a soldier passing through. Tomorrow, he'll be on his way, and you'll be back to your routine, which leaves you in your life—a good life, even if men are not presently part of it.

She should join a dating website. Desperate times had apparently arrived. Measures would be taken, but first she had to get through tonight.

Looking at herself in the mirror, she smoothed her hands over dark, wavy hair. She wished she had time to curl or flat iron it, but it was probably just as well that she didn't because she was so out of practice at styling it. Normally, she just threw it up in a ponytail and wore a ball cap in lieu of a hairnet in the kitchen. Practical, but not very attractive.

Hannah checked her watch. Barely enough time to get her car out of the garage and meet Sam at the bakery. She grabbed a leather jacket, her keys and purse, and locked up.

The sun glowed a deep, burnt orange as it sank behind the mountains, painting the sky in lavenders and grays. She pulled up curbside in front of the bakery. Since they'd closed up early for tonight's family gathering, Sam stood out front, waiting. He wore faded jeans, a collared shirt and a dark jacket that fit snugly across his shoulders and clung to his sides, stopping at his waist. She found everything about him appealing.

Their gazes collided. An easy smile transformed his face and eyes. Good thing he was leaving tomorrow. This man could quickly become more addictive than her cupcakes. She got out of the car and walked around to step up onto the sidewalk.

He approached slowly. "Going my way?" His voice was low and smoky and skidded up and down every nerve in her body.

"Sorry you had to wait outside. I hope you haven't been here long."

"No worries." He moved closer. "Wow. You look great," he said, giving her a slow look that missed nothing.

Tongue-tied, she just managed to say, "Thanks. *Um*, we'd better get going."

He took her arm and walked around the car to open the door. Wow. "Thank you."

"My pleasure."

Oh, Lord . . . did he have to bring up pleasure? It had been so long . . . Hannah worked at getting ahold of her runaway hormones as he walked around and got into the passenger seat, but then he filled up the interior of the cozy Honda CRV with his size and scent. His cologne smelled so good, Hannah had a wild fantasy of nuzzling his neck and breathing him in.

He buckled his seatbelt, then seeing that she hadn't done hers yet, reached around her and secured it. His hand brushed her hip in the process, and more heat infused her body from head to toe.

Instead of moving back to his side of the car, he stayed close, his gaze lingering on her mouth. "Hannah . . ."

Could a person explode from feeling too much at one time? She pulled her lower lip in to moisten it. What was happening?

Unable to stop herself, Hannah touched his face. His cheek was smooth, like he'd just shaved. He eased his hand around Hannah's waist and touched his forehead to hers. Their noses brushed, lips so close their breath mingled.

Sam said, "This is crazy. I didn't mean for this to happen—"

She swallowed hard. "Me either."

"But it's a pleasant surprise."

"Yes," she agreed, although unsure about how "pleasant" his leaving would play into the scenario.

He threaded his fingers into her hair, and Hannah sighed, closing her eyes as he pressed warm, soft lips to her cheek. Feeling exploded like fireworks against a black velvet sky on a hot summer's night.

"Still, there's always a choice. We don't have to give in to this feeling."

Hannah looked at him then and thought, what a waste that would be. Feelings like this didn't come along every day. "There's not really time to debate the point," she said, not sure if she was talking about Gran's party, his leaving or both.

He leaned back a bit, but kept his hand cupped around the back of her neck. "Right."

She slid her hand around his wrist, and he stroked her cheek with the backs of his fingers. This felt so good, so perfectly right.

And then he broke the contact all together. Without his warmth, a cold surrounded her that had nothing to do with the temperature. That should have been a warning that anything happening between them would be a mistake, but she didn't know if resisting the pull was possible. Earlier, she'd been feeling lonely and like life had passed her by. Was Sam the universe's answer to her musings?

They completed the short drive in silence, Sam's mind a whirl of surprise and confusion. He'd come to Maryville to thank a baker for caring about the troops, but had found a beautiful, intriguing young woman. Hannah Goode had those girl-next-door looks that he'd always been a sucker for—long, dark, reddish brown hair, soft curves, hazel eyes and freckles that had him longing to explore her body so he could find and kiss each one. He passed a hand over his short-cropped hair and tried to breathe normally. Not working. He was about to meet her entire family. It wasn't a date, but the whole scenario felt damned intimate.

Stop it, Evans. They're just being nice to a stranger, alone in town for the night. Nothing more, nothing less.

When Hannah pulled into the drive of a small, brick rancher, several cars were already parked out front. Inside, Mr. Goode and an older version of Hannah bustled around the kitchen. In addition to her, there was another woman, close in age to the elder Goodes, and two pretty blondes, one he recognized from the bakery.

"Here they are. Right on time," Mr. Goode said. He offered his hand. "Glad you could make it, Sam."

"When are we eating? I'm hungry," a woman called from the living room.

"In about an hour, Mom," Mr. Goode said, chuckling. "She's been a little demanding since she broke her hip. She was always so self-sufficient; it's hard for her to let others take over.

"Come on, let me introduce you to everyone." He put a hand on Sam's shoulder and gestured to the woman who looked like an older version of Hannah. "This is my lovely bride, Mary. That's my sister, Christy Lane, and her two daughters, Gracie and Ginger."

"It's a pleasure to meet you all. Thank you for allowing me to intrude on your family dinner."

"Welcome to the chaos," Mrs. Goode said.

The women all smiled at him, but kept working at their various food projects. Classic rock played from somewhere in the kitchen, competing with the television in the next room.

"I'll introduce you to Mom and Dad in a bit," Mr. Goode said. "Dad's still having his afternoon nap on the couch."

"Hannah, find your young man a job," Mrs. Goode said.

Hannah blushed and gave her mother a look. Sam just smiled and asked, "What can I do?"

"I'm sorry."

He couldn't resist teasing. "Why? Because I have to pitch in or because your mom called me 'your man'?"

"The latter, both, take your pick."

The devil made him lean in close and whisper, "I don't mind being 'your man' for the evening." Or longer . . .

She took a step to the side, but her eyes said she was tempted. Let the dance begin.

"Everyone has kitchen duty in our family," she explained. "Want to help me with the appetizers?"

"Sure."

"I'm making sausage puffs. They're Gran's favorite." She handed him a couple of tubes of crescent rolls. "Open these and spread the sheets of dough out on the cookie sheet while I get started on the filling."

"Sure. Just point me to the restroom so I can wash up."

"We're informal around here. Just use the kitchen sink."

After washing his hands, he did as she asked, all the while, watching her as she moved to the stove, chatting with her mom and aunt. Everyone joked and had fun as they tended to their tasks in preparing the meal. It was a tight space, but no one seemed to mind. Moving around each other was like a well-rehearsed dance. Hannah's dad reached around his wife to snatch a piece of meat, and she playfully slapped his hand. "Ow!" he complained, but everyone laughed.

Hannah returned with a bowl of creamy meat sauce and checked his work.

"Be sure to smooth out those perforations in the dough. We don't want any filling to seep out while these bake."

Again, he did as she asked, and when she was satisfied, she handed him a knife. "Good. Now cut the dough into two-inch squares. No, three. It'll be quicker."

Having her stand so close had all his overwrought senses on hyper-alert. Her fragrant hair fell forward, and she flipped it back over her shoulder. It smelled like fresh fruit. He remembered what it had felt like earlier, and he wanted to brush it back from her face just so he could feel its texture and touch her face again.

As he cut the strips, she spooned in the filling, pulling up the corners of the dough and pressing them closed. "What's in the filling?" he asked.

"Sausage and cream cheese."

She scooped some up with her finger and held it to his lips. He opened his mouth, and when she would have tipped the blob of cream cheese onto his lips, he surprised her by taking her finger into his mouth and licking it clean. Eyes that were an intriguing mix of blue, green and gold captivated, reminding him of long lazy days on the beach. "*Mmm* . . . Delicious." Spicy sausage mellowed by smooth cream cheese. A perfect combination.

Her gaze focused on his mouth, and Sam wondered if she was wondering what a kiss between them would taste like. It would be so easy to lean down and kiss her. Then the sound of the television in the other room increased, breaking the sensual web forming around them. At first, Sam thought they must be making too much noise in the kitchen. Maybe Hannah's grandmother had turned up the volume so she could better hear whatever she was watching. Then it got louder.

"Here we go," one of the teenagers said above the din.

"Wow," Hannah said.

"What's going on?" Sam asked.

Mr. Goode stepped into the living room. "Ma! The TV is too loud!"

The older woman had to shout to be heard. "I'm trying to wake your father. He needs to get up. He's been sleeping all afternoon."

"He can't hear the TV, Ma. He's deaf. Remember?"

The volume on the television went down. Sam couldn't help laughing.

"Vernon! Wake up!" she shouted. "Vernon!"

"Huh?" a man mumbled. "What is it?"

"Get up! Everyone's here, and you're taking up too much room. There's nowhere for anyone to sit."

"Oh. Oh. Okay."

"Go brush your hair, for heaven sakes," she said. "You look a fright."

The man mumbled as he moved away, or was that a grumble?

Mr. Goode returned to the kitchen shaking his head and humming a circus tune.

Hannah laughed along with everyone else. "Welcome to a Goode family get-together. I wish I could say it's not usually like this."

If Sam could have dreamed up a big family gathering brimming with people and love and laughter, it would not have been as nice as this. Growing up, it had always been just him and his mom. And then, after she'd died, just him and no one. The military was the only family he had. That had been enough, until now.

Hannah took the filled tray in front of him and popped it into the oven. She returned with an armload of ingredients that she set on the counter in front of them.

"What's this?" he asked.

"Now we make the rolls."

He smiled. "Sounds good. What else is on the menu?"

"The appetizer, ham, six or seven sides, yeast rolls, and birthday cake, of course."

"Of course."

"All of Gran's favorites."

They should all weigh three hundred pounds. Allowing his gaze to slide over Hannah, he appreciated that her curves were just right. A hunger stirred inside him that had nothing to do with food.

"Do y'all eat like this all the time?" he asked.

"My family has dinner together several times a week, and we eat here every Sunday. It's just something we've always done. But we don't usually have this much food. It's a special occasion."

"Christmas dinner must be awesome at your house."

Hannah smiled. "If you call twice as much food and three times as many people in this tiny house awesome. What do you do at the holidays?"

"I usually spend it at the base, or volunteer at a homeless shelter if I'm off duty."

"That's nice," she said, but she was giving him the same look of sympathy he'd seen from his co-workers—the ones who always tried to get him to come home with them for the holidays.

"It's not so bad. I never had a big family to spend holidays with, so I don't have anything to miss."

"I can't imagine holidays being anything but loud and full of activity and family. A quiet holiday might actually be nice."

He'd always thought his holidays were good, but being here with Hannah and her family set off a longing in him for something different.

"When are we eating?" the older Mrs. Goode shouted from the other room. "It smells so good, you're staving me to death!"

Sam elbowed Hannah. "What, and miss all this?"

Mr. Goode said, "Mind if your grandma helps you with the rolls, sugar?"

"Not at all. We can pull up a stool for her," Hannah said.

"Come into the kitchen, Ma. I'll give you a nice snack to tide you over, and you can help Hannah with the rolls."

"Hannah's here?"

"Yes, and we have a guest."

"Who?"

A metallic tapping preceded the entry of a sweet-faced, white haired lady. She pushed a walker that was more of a prop than a walking aid.

"Ma, this is Lieutenant Sam Evans. Sam, this is my mother, the birthday girl, Evelyn Goode." An alarm went off on the oven. "Hannah, your sausage puffs are ready."

"Coming."

"Sausage puffs?" Gran said.

"Here you go, Ma. You can sit here with Hannah and Sam. They might need you to help with the rolls."

"She might need me to taste those sausage thingies." The older woman cackled. "Welcome, young man. So handsome. And a soldier? My Vernon was a soldier."

"Happy birthday, ma'am."

"So polite. Where's your uniform?"

"I don't wear it when I'm off duty, ma'am."

"What a shame. I so love a man in uniform."

"Ma, you're such a flirt!" Mr. Goode teased.

"It's my birthday. I can do what I want."

Hannah cleared a space and set the pan of sausage puffs on the counter in front of them. "Don't let her fool you," she said to Sam. "She always does what she wants."

"So sassy, but she's right. Life's too short to not do what you want."

Sam looked at Hannah, clarity forming his thoughts. "I couldn't agree more."

Hannah lined a large bowl with paper towels and began transferring the puffs from the baking pan. "Ow, ow!" she complained as she burned her fingers. "Toasty balls, toasty balls!"

"Yum," Gran said.

"Hannah," Mrs. Goode exclaimed.

"They're hot," she said unnecessarily.

Sam nearly choked.

She looked up at him then, got the double meaning, and flushed bright red. He couldn't remember the last time he'd had so much fun.

The rest of the night passed in much the same fashion with plenty of food, conversation, and good-natured ribbing. Everyone made him feel right at home—like he was part of the family. Being a person who wasn't used to being involved in large family gatherings, he'd wondered if he'd feel uncomfortable, but instead, he could really see himself enjoying being part of something like this. Exactly like this.

He glanced at his watch. It was much later than he'd thought. After being on airplanes for much of the last couple of days, he needed some sleep. "I should be getting back."

Hannah rose. "Me, too. Four-thirty comes really early. No one wants to see me without the proper amount of beauty sleep."

A vision of waking up next to Hannah bloomed in Sam's mind . . .

"I should get the girls home, too. It's a school night," Christy said. "We'll walk out with you."

"Thank you so much for having me over," Sam said. "I thoroughly enjoyed myself."

Mr. Goode stood as well. "Will you be leaving first thing tomorrow?"

"Yes," he said reluctantly. "I need to get back to the base."

"You be sure to stop by the bakery before you leave. We'd like to give you some treats to take back with you. Right, Hannah?"

He looked at Hannah, gauging her reaction to the invitation.

"Yes. I can give you enough to share, if you have room to take it."

He nodded. "That'd be great."

"Good. We'll see you in the morning, then," Mr. Goode said.

"Goodnight."

Sam walked out to Hannah's car, opening her door for her. Holding his stomach, he moaned, "I can't remember the last time I've been so full."

He loved her laugh. It came easy and natural, like she did it often.

"Gran would say you could use some fattening up."

Shaking his head, he said, "That would be misery in the desert."

She gripped the top of the car door's window. "Are you going back?"

"Not for a while. I'll be stateside for most of the next year, unless something extraordinary happens."

"Here's to it being an uneventful year, then." She got behind the wheel. When they were on their way, she asked, "How long have you been in the Air Force?"

"Nine years."

"So, you're career military?"

"Yes. Well, I mean, that was the plan."

"Was?"

"I've been thinking about doing something else."

"Like what?"

He looked at Hannah, her face illuminated by the car's panel lights. "I'm thinking that I'd like to settle down. Live in a house, maybe put down some roots. Hell, I might even get a dog."

She nodded, glancing at him and then back at the road. "Sounds nice. What would you do?"

"I have a degree and experience in logistics, so something to do with that."

She sighed. "I could use that kind of help. I don't have the patience for it. Have you thought about consulting? I'm sure a lot of small businesses like mine could use someone with your background to help set up systems for ordering, shipping, and delivering goods."

That wasn't a bad idea. In fact . . . "I noticed that you seemed a little covered up in paperwork when I came in today."

She raked a hand through her hair. "Yeah. I need to go through orders, try to figure out what supplies I need, work on the delivery schedule at some point, and I have to do the commercial invoicing." She looked over at him as she pulled up in front of the bakery. "There are never enough hours. I should have been working on all that tonight. I'm going to be even further behind tomorrow, but then, I'm always behind, so . . ."

"Sounds like you don't have much time for fun."

"Fun?" She laughed. "What's that?"

That was something they had in common, but looking at her, he could come up with half a dozen ideas, like her on the back of his bike, her arms wrapped tightly around his waist as they drove over to the Atlantic coast to spend a week or so lazing on the beach, soaking up the sun and catching some waves. They could stop in Asheville on the way and spend the day window-shopping and letting someone else do the cooking.

In short, Hannah Goode was in desperate need of having someone take care of things for her for a change. It surprised him how much he wanted to be the person spoiling her. It also surprised him how right it felt to want to be with her. He also wanted to get to know her better and see where the attraction between them would lead.

He needed time to come up with a plan—and to develop an appealing way to present it so she couldn't refuse.

She turned to him and said, "Goodnight, Sam."

He smiled. "Yes. Goodnight, and thanks again. For everything." He leaned in and kissed her cheek, lingering to breathe in her scent. "Sweet dreams," he whispered near her ear. Her quick intake of breath said she felt something, too. Learning back, he opened the door. "See you in the morning."

Sam didn't show up at the bakery the next morning. Hannah tried not to show her disappointment as she went through the day's baking to fill the commercial orders. The fact that he'd left without saying goodbye weighed on her thoughts. He hadn't seemed like the kind of person whose word meant so little. It just didn't make sense.

To make matters worse, her dad hadn't come in either. Instead, he sent her mother, who'd kept up a steady stream of conversation about everything and nothing since she'd arrived. Thankfully, replies requiring multi-syllable responses were not necessary. Never let it be said that Mary Goode couldn't carry on a one-sided conversation.

It felt like the baking had doubled by the time she found ten minutes to grab a drink and escape the kitchen late that afternoon. She popped into her office to grab her laptop and her overflowing inbox, determined to make headway with it. She took one step into her office and nearly had heart failure.

"Mom! What happened to my office?"

Her mother rushed up and peered over her shoulder. "What's wrong, dear?"

"Someone has been in here. All the orders and receipts that were . . . were . . . everywhere—are gone." She held up her inbox. "It's empty. And my desk has been cleaned off." And something else was missing. "Oh, no."

"What?"

"My laptop is gone. We've been robbed!"

"Oh no, honey. I'm sure there's an explanation."

"We have to call the police. How could this happen?" She pulled her cell phone out of her pocket.

"Now, just take a breath, dear. Maybe your dad came in earlier and took everything. He's been talking about trying to help organize things for you."

"We've been here all day, Mom. No one else has been back here but us. And besides, I can't make sense of the paperwork. What in the world could Daddy do with it all?"

"I'm just saying, let's give him a quick call before we jump to any conclusions." She touched Hannah's arm. "Why don't we go out front and sit. It's been a long morning. Getting so upset when you're tired and hungry is so bad for you, dear."

Her mother opened the swinging door to the dining room and propelled Hannah into the front room. She was about to protest when she saw that her dad was seated at a table with Sam, her laptop in front of him and all of her paperwork stacked in neat file folders. Pink file folders, the signature color of the shop.

Sam stood and said, "Hi."

"What's going on?" she said cautiously, trying not to overreact.

Sam pulled out a chair at the table. "Sit with me, and I'll show you."

"I'm not sure I feel like sitting. Dad, what is this about?"

"Now, Hannah, please don't be angry. Sit, and Sam will explain everything."

She did so, reluctantly.

"Yesterday, you told me a bit about how you struggle with the paperwork associated with the business as well as making out the delivery schedules. Like I told you last night, my degree and work with the military is in logistics. Since you've done so much for the troops, I wanted to do something to help you. I called your dad last night after I got back to the hotel and enlisted his help."

She didn't know what to think. Did not know how she felt about this stranger presuming to involve himself in such a private matter. And damn it, she was angry that he'd deceived her and occupied her thoughts all morning. At length, she said, "Go on."

"I loaded a software program on your laptop that will help you manage every aspect of the business. Accounts payable, receivables, invoicing, cost control, ordering supplies, and scheduling deliveries. You can do it all with just a few clicks of the mouse and by maintaining some daily data entry. The program will even gather information from the dates you input to generate the delivery schedules. You can then print them out to post on clipboards in the back."

"Sounds complicated and time-consuming."

"Someone will have to stay on top of the data entry and printing out the invoices and schedules, but it's a user friendly program. I've already trained your dad. One of your nieces could do it when they're not busy."

"How will I know they're not making mistakes?"

"They can generate reports for your review, daily—weekly. Your choice."

"Just think of it, hon," her dad said, "you can focus on the baking that you love, and your mom or I can handle the paperwork so you don't have to worry with it. You could even take some time off."

Hannah laughed. "Time off. What's that?"

"How long has it been since you had a break from this?" Sam asked.

"There is no break from it, and I'm not asking for one," she said flatly. "The business takes all my time, but I love it."

"You burning out is no good for you or the business," Sam said.

Okay. That was crossing a line. She'd known the man one day. He didn't know anything about her or what she could or couldn't take. If she was being honest, she had to admit this had needed doing for some time. She'd even considered hiring an accounting firm to do this kind of thing for her, but she hadn't found the time to do the research to hire someone. Still, she hadn't asked for Sam or anyone else to step in and handle this or anything else for her. It was her responsibility, no one else's. And she didn't appreciate Sam swooping in to save her from herself, nor could she overlook the part her parents had apparently played in it all.

"Someone should have spoken to me before you did this."

Sam's smile was slow and sensual. "But that would have ruined the surprise."

Hannah's dad backed his chair up and stood. "Mary, take me home, would you? My recliner's calling my name."

"I'll deal with you later," Hannah promised.

Her dad kissed her cheek. "I look forward to it, honey. Sam." The two men shook hands.

"Thank you for your help, sir."

Her dad chuckled. "Don't thank me yet."

Sam sat, and the stare off began. Principle dictated that she couldn't just let him off the hook. He'd invaded her domain, and they were barely acquainted.

"Why did you do this?" she asked.

"It's like I said," he started. "I wanted to do something nice for you. You've done so much for so many people."

Great. Her dad had clearly been chatty. "Why do I get the feeling that you're not just referring to the care packages I send the troops?"

Sam sighed. "Your dad told me about his illness, and how you dropped out of school to start the business and help support your family."

"Perfect." She looked away. Embarrassed.

"You're an amazing woman, Hannah."

His softly spoken words had her looking at him again. She could get lost in that look that had her thinking about things happening between the two of them, things she couldn't afford to consider. Not with him leaving.

"So, that's all there is to it? You wanting to do something nice for me?"

"Well . . ."

Now they were getting somewhere. He wanted something in return. She crossed her arms and waited.

"I have two weeks off."

"Right. The cross country motorcycle tour is now delayed a day because of this."

"I'm not worried about that."

"Good, because I intend to pay you for your trouble."

"No. Absolutely not."

"Okay, Sam. Spill it. Clearly you had something in mind when you did this."

He surprised her by taking her hand and leaning across the table towards her. "To start, I hoped you'd let me take you to dinner tonight."

She hesitated, distracted by his nearness. "To start?"

"Then I'll come back tomorrow to finish this up and train your mom."

Still circumventing her. "When were you thinking you'd train me? It is my business, after all." She would be completely annoyed with him if it weren't for the distraction of this wild attraction between them that had no hope of ever becoming anything.

"When we get back," he was saying.

She raised an eyebrow.

"Hannah, I want to spend time getting to know you better. If you feel the same, I'd love for you to come with me to Georgia this weekend to pick up my bike. It should be nice weather for the ride back."

"And then?"

"I don't have plans beyond the weekend, but I'm hopeful that we'll decide we want to spend more time together. What do you say?"

A ray of hope lifted her spirits. "Let's see how dinner goes."

His smile was huge.

"I mean, we haven't even kissed yet. There might not be anything there."

He leaned in closer. "Only one way to find out."

He tugged at her hands, pulling her closer. His lips touched hers, soft and warm, teasing them with the question of when he'd take the kiss deeper. She heard herself moan when he traced the seam of her lips with the tip of his tongue.

"Wow, like, get a room," Gracie said.

Sam smiled, breaking the contact, but rubbed his hands up and down her arms.

"Take a break, Gracie," she said.

"Gladly."

When her niece had walked into the back, Sam asked, "So, what's the verdict?" between feather-light kisses that had her head spinning.

"*Mmm* . . . I think you need to finish what you started."

This time when their lips met, it was a hot hungry expression of need that left no doubts as to the explosive attraction they felt for each other. When they broke the kiss much later, both had trouble catching their breath.

"Wow, that was amazing," he said.

All Hannah could do was nod her agreement.

Sam smiled, and her stomach did flip-flops. "I think dinner should go just fine."

When she finally found her voice, she said, "Thank you for organizing all this paperwork and for setting up the program on my computer. I've needed to have this done. I just haven't had the time to deal with it."

"You're welcome." He released her hand and stood.

Hannah allowed a bit of excitement and anticipation, as well as the aftermath of that kiss, to lead her to consider possibilities for the two of them.

"I'll just put all this back in your office, and then I'll go get ready," he said. "Where should I pick you up?"

"I live in a loft a block away. If you want, we could walk to a nice restaurant that's here, downtown."

"Perfect. Is an hour too soon?"

Probably, but she didn't want to waste any more time when they had so little. "See you then," she said.

He kissed her and was gone, leaving Hannah with the unmistakable feeling that she was about to fall in love.

Dinner went well—had, in fact, been amazing. The trip to Georgia and ride back to Tennessee, even better. The next two weeks, they divided time between the bakery and being together. The more she knew about Sam, the more she wanted to know. The feeling was very mutual.

Hannah's mom and dad took over the bakery part of the time during those two weeks so she and Sam could take a few short trips. She'd never imagined herself on the back of a motorcycle, but she had to admit, she loved it—mainly because she was with Sam in the spring sunshine, relaxing and enjoying life. After so many years of focus on the business, it felt good to be carefree and exploring a new relationship.

When Sam's two-week furlough ended, Hannah knew the future would hold many trips between Georgia and Tennessee, because Sam had another year on his commitment to the Air Force. Each time they parted, sometimes for weeks at a time, being apart became harder. The separations were hard, but she couldn't just leave her business and her obligations to the community and her family.

Summer came, making the baking long, hot work. She walked out front, and grabbing an ice-cold bottle of water from the cooler, pressed it to her neck. Outside, temperatures were in the nineties, but it had felt like it was twice that with the ovens going full blast.

Hannah sat. She was so hot and sticky she was having daydreams about standing under the oversized showerhead in her condo with cool, clear water sluicing over her body. Maybe she could get away for a few minutes to shower and change clothes. But first, she'd just rest her head on her hands for a moment. Her late night talking to Sam on her cell, combined with the heat, had sapped all her energy.

The bells on the door jangled, but she didn't have the energy to look up to see who it was. Her niece could deal with it.

Sam . . . she missed him so much, she could smell his cologne. It had been almost three weeks since she'd seen him. Too long.

"Hannah?"

She sat up startled. "Sam!"

Launching herself at the man kneeling beside her, she clung to him, so happy to be in his arms, but then backed up almost immediately. She must look awful with her hair plastered to her face and neck and her T-shirt all damp and clinging to her body.

"I'm sorry." Hannah smoothed a hand over her hair. "I know I'm a sight."

"A sight for sore eyes." He soothed her hair back towards her ponytail with a gentle hand. "You're beautiful, and I love you," he said softly.

She touched his cheek, tears misting her eyes. "I love you, too, but what are you doing here? Why didn't you tell me you were coming?"

Sam urged her back into the chair but remained kneeling beside her.

"I have a surprise for you."

"I don't know if I can take more than you materializing out of thin air. You're more than enough."

He smiled, but pointed to something outside. A large truck sat in front of the bakery.

"What's that?" she asked, frowning.

"A moving truck filled with my stuff, which makes this next thing I have to say critical."

"I don't understand."

"I accepted a position with the Air Base here in town. A position came open. I talked to them, and they wanted me so badly, they were able to work something out with the Air Force to let me out of my commitment early. But that's not what's really important."

"Not important!" She framed his face with her hands. "You mean you're here to stay?"

He nodded.

"You're going to live in Maryville?"

He nodded again.

She was so happy she couldn't speak.

"If you're through asking questions, there is one more thing."

"What could possibly top the fact that you're here to stay?"

"If you'll let me say it—"

"Say it already so I can kiss you senseless!"

His smile lit up her soul. "Hannah Goode, I love you with all my heart. You're the most amazing woman I've ever known." He held up a velvet box, and opening it, revealed a sparkling, round diamond surrounded by smaller diamonds set in white gold. "Will you marry me?"

Hannah pressed her hands to her lips, nodding and laughing and crying all at once.

"Is that a yes?"

"Yes, oh yes!"

She launched herself into his arms again, clinging to him as they kissed to seal their commitment to one another. How could she be so lucky? When she'd opened the bakery, she'd done it out of love—love of baking and love for her family. Her family had worked together here, sharing their love with the community and the troops through the baking. All these ingredients had combined to not only fill her life with love, but had also brought her Sam.

When he'd walked into her bakery, she could never have imagined that eight months later, he'd be sliding a diamond on her finger and promising to love her forever. One thing was sure, the cake they would make together for their wedding would be a perfect expression of their love, but it certainly would not be the last. Just like her parents, she and Sam would love and bake together for the rest of their lives, passing the tradition on to their children and grandchildren.

Theirs was sure to be a future made with love.

All Foam, No Beer

Valerie Keiser Norris

When I was twelve and Daddy ran off with the preacher's young wife, Mama never shed one tear. She gathered up the clothes he'd left behind and lugged them to the big oil barrel in back to burn with the trash.

"No way am I donating any of that mess to the church rummage sale," she declared. "Already given those hypocrites more than I planned to."

Mostly, she didn't talk about him. She seemed more annoyed that he'd gone off without fixing the next-to-the-bottom basement step than that he'd left with another woman. Within a week she purged the house of everything of Daddy's. She hauled his worn recliner to the dump, sold his guns, and got rid of every last one of his NASCAR hats and die-cast model cars, right up to the current 1964 versions. The unattached garage would have to be gutted to strip it of Daddy's things, so Mama just ignored it, parking the car in the driveway like always. Photos and personal stuff she tossed into a carton labeled "Joyce and Angie's father," and gave it to my older sister and me. "Just keep it out of my sight," she warned us.

I stored it beside the vacuum in the hall closet. Mama, tall and broad-shouldered, loved yard work, but wasn't much for house cleaning.

One thing Mama didn't get rid of was the beer-brewing equipment in the basement. "I'm the one who always ended up taking care of it, and I make pretty good beer. Which you won't know until y'all are legal age." She fixed Joyce and me with her steely-eyed glare.

"Yes, ma'am," I said, but she didn't need to worry on my account.

Joyce, two years older than me and worlds more sophisticated, had no such qualms. Barely fourteen, she and her friend lifted a half-dozen bottles from Mama's stash and drank them in the garage. Since Mama had sworn not to go into the garage ever again, Joyce felt safe. I don't know what she planned to do if Mama kept count of her beer—no one ever accused Joyce of being the brainy sister. After her little party, she stumbled into the living room, fell onto Mama's lap, and gushed, "Mama, you're so beautiful."

Mama looked down at her and sighed. "Joyce Louise, could you be a little less like your father?"

They say girls act out when their fathers disappear from their lives, but even when Daddy lived with us, he was pretty much indifferent to us. Joyce had gone boy-crazy at twelve and drove Mama wild with her behavior. After Daddy left, though, Mama seemed to lose the energy to police Joyce. Whenever the school called about Joyce's truancy or her failing grades, Mama got after her, but that was it.

I don't think Daddy's being there or not made much difference in me. I was the good kid, the one who came home after school, cleaned house, and made supper. When Mama got in from her job as a trucking company dispatcher, I was usually at the kitchen table, homework spread out, with supper simmering away on the stove. Joyce would slink in just before or even after Mama arrived. You couldn't miss the swollen lips, the dark hickeys peeking out above turtlenecks, the dried grass clinging to Joyce's sweaters, but Mama never said a word.

By the time Joyce turned sixteen and officially started dating the boys she'd been sneaking around with, Mama was finally herself again, less prone to hide in her room of an evening. She wasn't keen on any of the specimens Joyce brought home. "Like brew gone bad," Mama said. "All foam, no beer."

When one stayed in his car at the end of the driveway, honking for Joyce to come out, Mama grabbed Joyce's arm as she raced to the door. "Oh, no you don't. Either he comes to the door to meet me, or you don't go."

"But Mama—"

"No, ma'am. If he can't behave like a gentleman, y'all ain't going out."

We listened to the honking horn awhile, and finally a car door slammed. A few seconds later came a knock on the front door. Mama answered, me peeking from behind her. Many of the boys in Joyce's class were wearing Beatles' bangs, but this boy's hair was oiled and formed into a front curl, and his socks were white. Greaser.

Mama glanced to her left, giving Joyce the look that could reduce me to a pile of mush. Out of sight of the boy, Joyce crossed her arms against her new orange A-line dress, her face set in the pout she'd mastered before I was born.

Mama turned back to the door. "Can I help you?"

"Joyce?"

"No, I'm Mrs. Peterson."

He rolled his eyes. "She here?" he asked, scratching at his sparse goatee.

"Yes, she is."

A silence. Mama looked prepared to stand there all day, one hand holding the door open, the other firmly pulling the screen door shut.

"Well, we have a date?" He widened his eyes, as if Mama was a mite slow.

Oh, you poor fool, I thought.

"Oh? And who might you be?" Mama asked.

"Just tell her it's Turk."

"Turk. Hmm. Why don't I tell her it's that little Fadden boy who used to pick his nose and eat it?" Mama said.

Three feet away, out of sight of the boy, Joyce's whole body slumped. She cast an anguished look at Mama.

For a moment Mama and the boy stared at each other. "I'm Derek," he finally said. "That was my brother."

"Oh? I never heard there were two Fadden boys." Mama opened the screen door enough to stick out a hand. "Nice to meet you, Derek Fadden. I'm Joyce's mother."

Warily, he held out a hand and let her shake it.

"Would you like to come in?" Mama didn't let go.

"Uh, no, just send Joyce—"

Mama pushed the screen door completely open with her shoulder and pulled him forward. "Come in, come in. Have a seat. Let me get to know the young man my daughter thinks enough of to date."

Joyce glanced my way, misery etched in the thick coat of base makeup covering any hint of a pimple. "I'll never get another date in my entire life," she muttered.

By the time I was eligible to date, two years later, Joyce had dropped her sights lower, dating boys who looked even more dangerous. When they actually came to the house, Mama tried to put the fear of God into them, but Joyce was wily, meeting boys when she was supposedly off with a girlfriend or at a school-sponsored event.

With my sister paving the way for me, I was automatically designated "that kind of girl." Only boys who wore pointy shoes and smelled of cigarette smoke asked me out, to keg parties or drive-in movies, so I never dated. And that was okay—I agreed with Mama. Boys just weren't worth the trouble. The greasers were beyond contempt, and the other boys were immature—shoving each other in the hallway, making crude comments, infatuated with the cheerleaders—I wasn't any more interested in them than they were in me.

Joe Pelham sat on the bus with me, and we did homework together, but the one time he asked me out I told him, "No. And don't ever ask again, or I won't study with you, either." I concentrated on my classes, earning all A's and hoping for a scholarship to get me out of town. Maybe a college campus would widen my dating pool.

Mama wasn't dating, either. "Oh, no," she told her friend Sandy. "Most of the men I know are like the sludge left in the bottom of the beer fermenter, the stuff I'd feed to pigs, if I had any."

"They're not all that bad," Sandy protested. She and Mama sat at our kitchen table playing poker and drinking Mama's beer.

I'd always found it strange that Mama and Sandy were friends. Sandy wore bright lipstick and nail polish, dresses, and stockings. Mama tended toward jeans and flannel shirts, nightly applications of Pond's Cold Cream serving as her entire beauty regimen. Sandy was married but had no children, and spent her days watching soap operas and experimenting with new hairstyles from magazines she kept fanned out on her coffee table. Mama worked and spent her spare time brewing beer and reading murder mysteries. They'd been friends for as long as I could remember.

"Name me one good one," Mama said. "Angie, run down and bring us up two more beers, would you?"

"Sure, Mama," I said from the living room. I didn't put my book down and race down the steps, though. I wanted to hear who Sandy thought was worthy of Mama's attention.

"Well, Dave, of course," Sandy said. Dave was her husband, a skinny, quiet, glasses-wearing man who looked at Sandy just like Muttsy, our Golden Retriever, looked at Mama.

Mama politely agreed that Dave was fine.

"And Charlie. You met him at my party."

"Charlie? Really, *Charlie*?"

"What's wrong with Charlie?" Sandy asked. "He's sweet, and he knows how to dance."

"First of all, there's the comb-over," Mama said. "If you're going bald, you're going bald. Don't part your side hair just above your ear and plaster it across the top of your head. Has that *ever* fooled *anyone?*"

Sandy waved her hand dismissively. "Easily fixed."

Mama grimaced. "He wears English Leather cologne."

I completely agreed with her on that one. Joe Pelham had come to school reeking of the stuff, and I told him he smelled like perfume mixed with outhouse. He never wore it again.

"Again, easily fixed," Sandy said.

Mama threw in the clincher. "He's a steady church-goer."

Sandy gave up. Daddy had been a steady church-goer.

I headed for the small refrigerator in the basement where Mama kept her beer chilled. Grabbing two cold ones, I started back up the steps, but stopped when I heard Sandy and Mama's hushed voices.

"No, thanks," Mama was saying. "Muttsy keeps me warm at night and doesn't steal the covers."

"There's more to a good night than staying warm," Sandy said. "And for that you need a man, not a dog."

Mama was quiet for a moment, and I almost took the next step. Then she said, "A Golden Retriever will never break your heart."

While I finished high school and prepared to go off to college on an academic scholarship, Joyce dragged home loser after loser. She had recently dropped out of beauty school and started waitressing at a truck stop near the expressway. When I asked why, she said, "Have you ever been to beauty school? All females, all day long. You'll find out, living in a girls' dorm." She continued to date bums, but in August she came home triumphant, a ring on her finger. Mama and I were in the kitchen, her cooking a batch of beer, me looking through the Sears catalog for a new winter coat.

Joyce waved her hand at us. "I'm engaged!"

Mama set the spoon down, carefully lining it up with the side of the stove. "Funny—I don't remember anyone asking my permission."

"That's so old fashioned. Besides, you ask the father, not the mother, and he's not here."

I'm sure Joyce was hoping to deflect the blame to Daddy, but I also knew it wouldn't work. "Who's the lucky man?" I asked.

Joyce went into offensive mode, chin jutted out, eyes flashing warning signs. "Buck Bonnett."

"A Bonnett?" Mama's eyes bugged out. "Have you lost your mind?"

"I thought all of them were in jail." I closed the Sears catalog. Coat shopping could wait.

"No, they're not *all* in jail," Joyce snapped.

"Which one is this?" Mama said. "The one set fire to the police station? The one shot his cousin's eye out shooting rats at the dump? Or wait, the one broke into the elementary school and peed on the principal's desk and chair?"

Joyce faced her sullenly, refusing to answer.

"It's the little pisser, isn't it?" Mama nodded and crossed her arms over her shirt with the Western-style stitching.

"That was years and years ago. He's changed." Joyce's face turned red, and her lip began to pooch out.

"Into what?" Mama turned back to stir the beer mixture, the wort, on the stove. "You going to move in with him out at that, that *compound* they live in? Because if you do, don't expect me to come out there and babysit y'all's children. I wouldn't set foot out there. Those people ain't right."

The Bonnetts lived communally, with hovels, trailers, and sheds dotting any of the landscape that wasn't covered by junk cars and other heaps of rusting metal. A tall fence made mostly of roofing tin surrounded the property, and thin, ill-tempered dogs roved in packs, threatening anyone who dared to come near.

"Wasn't it the Bonnetts who stole the hoses off the town fire truck after the parade last year?" I asked.

"There's no proof it was them," Joyce snarled, vicious as the Bonnetts' dogs. She turned back to Mama. "We'll live in an apartment until we can get a house. We'd never live out there."

Mama counted on her fingers. "His mother lives out there, and all his brothers and half brothers and stepbrothers and cousins. The first time Buck gets thrown in jail for being drunk in public, loses his job, and can't make the rent, y'all'll move into a shed in the midst of all that squalor."

"That will *never* happen. Buck's not like those others. He's got plans. He's going to get his GED and go to work for a friend of his." Joyce blushed and bit her lips inward, maybe wishing she could take back that last part. She leaned against the doorframe and turned her head, as if suddenly fascinated by the corner of the kitchen.

Mama pointed the wooden spoon at Joyce and demanded, "What friend?"

Joyce shrugged. Her gaze slid past Mama to the window.

"Pumping septic tanks for Alvin Poole, that's his big plan?" Mama asked. She shook her head and turned back to stir the wort.

I started to laugh, but Joyce smacked the back of my head.

"He'll only do that for awhile," she said. "Then he'll move up in the company."

Mama whirled around and snorted. "There's no 'up' in that company. You think Alvin has a flock of managers prancing around in white shirts? It's him, his wife on the phones, and a couple of drivers."

"You don't even know him, and you're judging him."

"Yep."

"Mama!"

"First, he's a Bonnett," Mama said, counting off items on her fingers once again. "As far as I'm concerned, that's plenty. But okay, second, he hasn't even made it through high school, although I think he spent a fair amount of time enrolled. Third, driving a honey wagon for Alvin Poole is not going to earn enough money for a family. And right now, he doesn't even have *that* job."

Joyce turned the too-big ring around her finger and stuck her bottom lip out farther.

"Let me see that ring. No, not on your hand. Take it off." Mama held out her hand, and Joyce gave her the ring. Mama turned the ring so she could see the inside. "What is this?" She gave Joyce a wide-eyed look. "'Diane, All my love, David.' Who are Diane and David?"

Purple-faced, Joyce grabbed the ring. "Well, he isn't made of money. He must have bought it used."

"Bought it. Well, I guess that's possible," Mama said. "But I'd be careful about wearing it in public. Whoever he 'bought' it from might want it back."

Joyce was stubborn, like I said, and clung to Buck Bonnett like a tick. She tried to get Mama interested in the wedding plans even though there wasn't a set date, and she forced us to spend time with him.

He came for supper, and since he was of legal drinking age, Joyce offered him a beer. I caught the irritated look Mama gave her—Mama didn't like to share her home brew with anyone she considered unworthy. "Let them drink Dixie Beer," she'd say.

"Mama brews her own," Joyce said. "Come down and see. There's some down there now, fermenting."

They traipsed down the steps.

I called, "Watch out for the second step from the bottom. It's loose." Mama had tried to fix the step, but it was still wobbly. We'd gotten used to just stepping over it.

They were down there for a while as Mama and I finished making supper. She went to the stairs and said, "Supper. And be careful of that step."

They came up, Joyce all flush-faced and Buck with a full beer, which I figured meant he'd finished one already, and I'd have to go fetch the empty to wash it out.

Mama interrogated Buck about his plans. No, he wasn't working right now. He was planning to get his equivalency degree. Yes, he had a firm offer from Alvin Poole. One of the drivers was retiring in a few months, and Alvin was going to take Buck on. No, they hadn't set a date for the wedding yet.

"Where did you buy the ring?" I asked, aiming for an innocent tone.

Joyce's glare could have cut through the stone in her ring, if it was even real.

"Bought it from a friend," he said. He turned to Mama. "This is really good beer. Mind if I have another?" He was already on his feet and heading for the steps.

"Go ahead," Mama answered, darting a glare of her own at Joyce. "Be careful of that step," she reminded him.

We finished eating while he was downstairs, and Joyce got up to go after him. She met him on the stairs. "What happened to you?" she asked.

"Nothing. Just looking at the brewing equipment. Never seen anything like it before." He returned to the table, a full beer in his hand. *Two* empties in the basement, I figured.

Once they left on their date, I went downstairs to fetch the bottles. Sure enough, two. As I grabbed them I noticed something odd. The heavy old safe, which came up above my knees, sat just beyond Mama's brewing gear. The safe's dial, set to seventy for as long as I could remember, was now set on zero.

I came back up, careful of the loose step, and set the bottles on the fake butcher-block counter with the two Buck had finished in our presence. "Mama, have you opened the safe lately?"

"Not in a couple of years." Her hands became still in the dishwater. "Why?"

"It's been set on seventy," I said. "Now it's on zero."

"Are you sure it was set on seventy?"

"I'm sure."

Handing me the last pan to dry, Mama wiped her hands on her

jeans. "I knew that boy was all foam." She headed down the stairs.

Later she came into the living room where I sat with a library copy of *War and Peace*, my chosen summer reading. I'd renewed it once but was going to have to return it in defeat.

"Is your sister still out?" Mama asked.

"Yes."

"Okay. Buck will wait until he knows we're all going to be away from the house, and then he's going to come back here and steal that safe." She laughed. "Like we've got a million bucks in it instead of insurance policies and birth certificates."

"You really think he'll risk it?" I asked. "He's got to know we'd suspect him first."

"This is the boy who peed all over the principal's desk and bragged about it to half the school," she reminded me. "He's an idiot."

"Okay, what's the plan?"

She plopped down on the couch, her arms draped across the variegated orange and brown afghan. "We'll let him know we're all going to be away on Saturday. I'll set my trap, and we'll come back and catch him."

"What trap?"

"Just wait," she said, an evil glint in her eye. "And stay out of the basement."

The next evening when Buck came by to pick up Joyce, Mama and I were on the front porch. Not trusting us alone with Buck for even a minute, Joyce had forgone her usual last-minute primping to sit on the porch with us. The porch ceiling fan was trying its best to fight the heavy August heat, but I had been thinking about standing in the open door of the fridge awhile, or painting myself with ice cream. Now that Buck was here, I was thinking only that Mama had some devious plan to expose him. Even though I knew he was no good, and I wanted to get rid of him as bad as Mama did, I felt an urge to throw myself at his feet and confess. Instead I put my hand over my mouth.

Buck got out of the car and came up the steps. Mama still didn't allow Joyce to run out to meet him in the driveway.

"Do y'all want to go with us to the state fair on Saturday?" Mama asked.

Joyce snorted. "The fair? It's a hundred degrees out there. Besides, I have to work."

"That's too bad. You always used to enjoy the fair," Mama said. "We'll be gone most of the day. I want to see the quilts and shows and everything."

Pulling my hand away from my mouth, I lied, "I want to see all the exotic chickens." I'd seen them a dozen times and could live without seeing or smelling them ever again.

"Have fun," Joyce said. "Y'all'll sweat to death."

Buck just stared at Mama, looking as close to brainless as possible without actual drool. She stared back.

The trap was set.

On Saturday morning, Mama and I dressed in what we'd wear if we were truly going to the fair—me in cut-off jeans and a tie-dyed top, her in another Western shirt and ten-year-old Capri pants. I felt like a criminal as we headed out in the old Pontiac. Mama just hummed. About a half-mile down the road we pulled into a dirt driveway that led to an abandoned farmhouse. Mama parked out behind the barn, and just as I reached for the door, it flew open.

"Aaaahhh!" I yelled.

"Shhhh!" Mama and Sandy shushed me, and Sandy pulled me out of the car.

"Hush, girl," she said. "Want to scare the Bonnett boy off before we catch him in the act?"

I turned to Mama. "You told *her* the plan, but you didn't trust me?"

"Honey girl, you walked around looking guilty just knowing that I had a plan. If I'd actually told you, you'd have gone to Buck and confessed."

I could feel my face turning red. I'd probably cross myself like a Catholic when I did it, too.

Mama gestured us into a small huddle out behind the gray barn. "Okay, here's the plan. I tied invisible threads to bottles of beer on the bookshelves behind the safe and glued the threads to the bottom of the safe. As soon as he picks it up, the beers fall off the shelves and break around him. And he's busted."

A beer trap. Perfect.

We walked on the edge of the road, poised to run and hide in the trees along the road if we heard a car coming. When we got near our house, we hid in the garden amid the browning corn stalks.

We didn't have to wait long.

A strange pickup pulled into the driveway, and Buck went to the door. The other two men, probably Bonnett brothers or cousins, waited in the truck.

When knocking didn't rouse anyone, Buck waved for them to follow him around the back of the house. They pulled the truck around to the back door. We had left the heavy door open with just the unlocked screen between Buck Bonnett and his goal.

"Muttsy's in there," I whispered.

"Muttsy loves everyone," Mama said. "If Buck didn't already know we had a safe, Muttsy would probably lead him straight to it."

Sandy, dressed in all black like we were on a midnight stake-out, asked, "When do we go in?"

Mama said, "In a minute. I want them to have plenty of time."

We waited, fighting off gnats, and then headed for the back of the house. Quietly, we went in through the screen door and stopped when Mama held up her arm like a cop. She put her finger to her lips, and we all stared at the open basement doorway, listening.

"Grab that side," Buck ordered. "This thing weighs a ton."

"What's with all this beer? What are they, alkies or something?" a strange voice asked.

"We should take the beer," said another.

"Let's us get the safe first," Buck said. "Then we can celebrate with a beer or two. Or twenty."

They all laughed.

"Oh, y'all'll have a beer or two—or twenty," Sandy whispered.

"Shh!" Mama waved a hand at her.

Buck said, "On three. One, two, three."

Crashing, cussing, even a few explosions. We ran downstairs, guiding Sandy past the loose step.

The three men were soaked, foam licking their pointy boots.

"Well, well, well." Mama surveyed the three with her arms crossed over her chest. "All foam, like I said."

Buck went to jail, and Joyce gave up on him. She and Mama drove me to campus and helped me make my bed and unpack. When they were leaving, Joyce said, "It's a new start for both of us."

"Really? Are you going back to beauty school?"

"No. I'm going to take a business course and get a job in an office. Meet a better class of men."

Mama rolled her eyes at me, but didn't say anything. I walked them back to the Pontiac and waved until I couldn't see the car anymore.

No one on campus knew me or my sister except Joe Pelham, and there weren't too many greasers at college, so normal-looking guys started asking me out. But I kept my distance. I was there to get an education. I'd think about dating after I got my teaching certificate. Besides, even though these were college boys, they were still boys, horsing around in the hallways, staging panty raids, acting like fools. Joe and I still studied together, and once again he approached the idea of dating.

"Forget it," I told him. "I'm not here to find a husband. I want an education."

The four years passed quickly. I spent my summers at home, working to earn more money for the next year to supplement my scholarship. Joyce got her business certificate and worked in a law firm in Atlanta. After I graduated and finished student teaching, I came home to a bedroom all to myself for the first time in my life. Joyce had moved into an apartment and hadn't brought anyone to meet Mama in months.

"Which is fine," Mama said. "Haven't seen one I liked yet. Bunch of culls."

"Even the lawyers?"

"She's only brought junior clerks and summer interns home, no lawyers," Mama said. "And they weren't the cream of any crop I could name."

But two weeks later, Joyce did bring a man home for Sunday dinner. He seemed fine, good-looking, well-dressed, looked Mama straight in the eye and smiled when they met.

I brought in beers as Mama leaned forward on the couch. "So, where did y'all meet?"

Joyce blushed, but Bill said, "In a bar." He grinned at Joyce as if it were the biggest joke in the world. He tasted Mama's beer. "Hey, this is really good. I'd love to have your recipe. I brew a little beer myself."

Right, like Mama was going to give him her recipe. She guarded it like it was holy.

I could almost see the wheels turning in Mama's head. Met in a bar, brews beer. Although Mama had brewed beer for as long as I could remember, she seemed to have a low opinion of others who brewed or even drank the stuff.

Mama turned to Bill. "Would you like to see my little operation downstairs? Be careful of the second to the bottom step, though. It's loose."

Mama, Joyce and Bill went downstairs where they spent a long time while I finished putting dinner together: pot roast, mashed potatoes, green beans, corn pudding. All that early childhood servitude came in handy—I could cook like a country granny. When I went downstairs to call them to supper, Bill stood near the bottom of the stairs. He watched me come down and reached out a hand to help me over the loose step.

Mama stood next to the safe. She leaned down to swipe at the top. "Oh, goodness, I need to dust that thing off," she said. She gave me a meaningful glance and said to Bill, "Would y'all like to go to the movies with us tomorrow night?" She and I hadn't talked about going to a movie, but I immediately knew what she was up to.

"I have to go to that baby shower tomorrow night," Joyce reminded her.

"Oh, too bad. Well, some other time." Then she added, sounding like a really bad actor, "It's a long one—I don't know *what* time we'll get back."

So transparent. Joyce would know in an instant what Mama was up to.

I glanced at my sister to see her reaction. Nothing. Joyce gazed at Bill so raptly I expected cartoon hearts to leap from her eyes, stars to dance rings around her head. Of course, she hadn't witnessed her boyfriend soaked and standing in a puddle of beer. Maybe that made it easier to forget.

The next evening was almost a rerun of the Buck Bonnett show, with Sandy joining us down the road, and me jumping when she popped up at my elbow. Undergrowth and recent rain made our trek through the trees much worse. Wet limbs and leaves slapped us, soaking us all. We hid at the edge of the trees beyond the empty garden, which was stripped of even its cornstalks for winter.

There came a pretty little white car with a black hood, foreign-looking, which pulled into our gravel driveway, raising a cloud of dust.

"That there's a Mercedes Benz," Sandy breathed in awe. "Looks like a brand new '75 model. This guy has money."

"Probably one step ahead of the repo man," Mama whispered.

"He'll have a rough time putting the safe in the back of that," Sandy said. "Is there even a back seat?"

"Shh!" I warned, as Bill stepped out of the car. He carried a tool belt which he slipped on, and then he grabbed a gym bag from the trunk.

"What's the tool belt for?" Sandy wondered. "And the gym bag?"

"His safecracking kit," I whispered back.

This time Mama shushed us.

When no one answered the front door, he went right in. We waited a moment, then rushed to the back and eased the screen open. Mama had left the big door open despite the chilly day—didn't want to tip off Bill with our entrance.

We listened for a few moments and heard only a slow, measured banging.

"Is he trying to beat it open?" Sandy asked.

"Shh!" Mama and I said.

Muttsy came in from the living room and woofed, happy to see us.

The banging continued, then a pause, then more banging. We waited another minute before we rushed inside and down the steps. Maybe we'd catch him before all the bottles smashed, before we were faced with a huge cleanup.

"Stop!" Bill yelled. He knelt on the basement floor in front of the steps, hammer in one hand, a piece of two-by-four in the other.

We crashed into each other but managed to stop halfway down.

"Get off! Get off the steps!" he said.

As we stood there in confusion he dropped the hammer, stood up and pushed the air with his hands, motioning us back up. "The whole flight needs to be replaced, but I was reinforcing the worst ones right now. Get off before the whole thing collapses. But slowly, one at a time."

Obediently, we headed back up the steps singly. The stairs groaned and creaked ominously. Sandy and I glanced at each other, she looking as embarrassed as I felt. We crowded around the door to watch as he put braces under steps and tested each stair. He was slow and methodical, and soon Sandy and I got bored and sat at the kitchen table to see how this all played out.

Eventually he finished and hollered up the stairs, "I'm coming up. Anyone want a beer?"

We all did.

"Be sure to bring one for your own self, too," Mama called. I would have assumed he would, anyway.

Soon he came up with four beers and his gym bag. He unhooked the tool belt and stuffed it into the gym bag.

"Sorry I just came on in. Joyce said it would be okay. I was pretty worried about those stairs," he said, and tipped up his beer to take a quick sip. "Didn't want anyone to get hurt." He leaned back against the counter.

Mama stood near the basement doorway, her arms crossed over her chest. Sandy and I still sat at the kitchen table.

"Sit down," I said.

"Thanks, but I've got to go soon." He turned to Mama. "This beer is excellent. You sure I can't talk you out of the recipe? I'd pay pretty well for a beer this good."

"Pay?"

"Well, yes, of course. If we could agree to a price, I can get the papers drawn up."

"Papers?" Mama asked.

"The contract. For the recipe."

She tipped her head and frowned. "What are you talking about?"

He hesitated, glancing at Sandy and me for help, as if we had a clue to what he was talking about. "That's how I do it," he said, speaking slowly, as if to a dangerous crowd. "I don't want to get sued. Not that I think you're going to sue me, but . . ." He trailed off.

Mama straightened. "Why would I sue you if I gave you the recipe?"

Again, Bill glanced around at us. "Because if it was a hit, you might decide I owed you."

"A hit? At hit at what, your backyard barbeques?"

"At my brewery." At our mystified expressions, he said, "Joyce didn't tell you I own a small specialty brewery?"

"No, Joyce didn't mention that part," Mama said.

"Oh. I'm a brewer. I had a taste-testing and invited my lawyer and his assistants and secretaries. That's how I met Joyce. She said her Mama's beer was better than any we were testing that day. She was right." He held up the bottle. "Good stuff."

"So you want to buy my recipe?"

"Yes, if you're willing to sell."

Mama frowned. "I'll have to think about it."

"Sure, I understand. You really need to get those steps replaced," he urged. "I'd be happy to do it, but I'm not that good a carpenter."

"Yes, yes, I will," Mama agreed, walking him to the door. When she shut the back door behind him, Sandy and I began to laugh. After a moment, Mama joined in.

"So," Sandy said. "You were wrong. He's a good one."

Mama lifted her chin. "Just because he didn't try to rob us doesn't mean he's good."

"He came over because he was worried. He fixed y'all's stairs. He wants to buy your beer recipe. He doesn't sound like an all-foam sort of guy to me. Sounds like a keeper."

Mama held out her bottle at eye level. "Hmm. My beer, famous. What do you say we call it 'Keeper'?"

The beer was a minor hit, and Bill was indeed a keeper. After I taught for a year I called Joe Pelham and asked him out, and we married two years later. And Mama? She's dating Comb-over, who took her suggestion and shaved his head naked to celebrate their first year together. And he loves the Brut cologne she bought him.

We still say "all foam," at times. After hearing the new preacher, for example. Sometimes we even mean it in a good way. After Mama's recent biopsy, she came out of the doctor's office saying, "All foam!" We cheered and danced around, and didn't enlighten the others in the waiting room. They could tell it was a good thing, though, and that was enough.

Running Raw

Susan Sipal

George Jones' lively rockabilly, "White Lightning," toned from my cell, the ring I'd assigned to my best ridge-runner. Grinning, I checked my rearview mirror for any sign of a tail, then pulled into the entry of a gated community. The security guard skeptically eyed my mom's old Camry wagon with its dents and sagging bumper, and I flashed him a snarky salute.

Beyond him, neatly ordered lines of upscale townhomes were followed by suburbia's obligatory McMansions. Their tiny yards displayed perfectly manicured lawns dotted with trees selected for their bright orange and red fall foliage, all at the peak of the season. Runners and bikers, in tight, designer athletic wear, raced along a paved greenway surrounding a man-made pond. A cookie-cutter development of the one where I'd lived until ten months, one week, and three days ago.

I motioned to the guard, waving my hands about crazily, that I was just turning around, and then pulled a bootleg one-eighty to the exit lane and put my liquor car in park. Tugging my pink Fedora lower over my left eye, I slumped in my seat while I reached for the buzzing cell, but kept my gaze peeled on the road in front of me. When you run 'shine, you must always be on the alert.

The text on my screen glowed: *Have arrived. No sign of the boiler here. What's your ETA?*

I quickly texted back: *10 mins. Watch out for that blue Ford in case he followed you.*

Setting my cell back on the passenger seat, and making sure I'd not picked up any tails, I pulled onto the residential road, picking up speed slowly and carefully so as not to jar my precious cargo. It was too risky to drive on the Raleigh Beltline with the cache I was hauling. Going fast to blend in with the speeding traffic had left me many broken jars and lost profits.

Careful not to draw attention with a granny-crawl either, I entertained myself and kept my anxiety at bay by imagining myself in a pair of Daisy Dukes, giving the law a spin around the courthouse. Finally, the red bull's-eye atop the mega shopping Mecca appeared before me. I circled the jam-packed parking lot once . . . twice . . . three times. But that last was just to indulge my obsessive-compulsive tendencies. There was no sign of a blue Ford or lone driver lurking in his vehicle.

With a relieved sigh, I spotted Tammy in her Elgrand minivan, her two youngest strapped in carseats waving out the rear windows, waiting for me at the far end of the grocery side. My second to last stop of the day.

"Next week we'll have to meet somewhere else," I said as I hopped out of my car and met her at the back of my wagon. "If he was waiting at our usual meeting place, he must have detected my pattern."

Tammy grimaced and pulled her jacket tighter about herself. "Liz, dear, you know when it's my turn to drive I don't mind all the cat'n'mouse stuff. But a couple other members of the co-op are starting to get antsy. Afraid they might get into some legal trouble themselves."

"Nah. He's not after the buyers. He's after the bootlegger."

Tammy chuckled and rolled her eyes. "Well, just remember, if you get caught, I only suggested the business. You're the one who grasped hold of it with both pails swinging."

As if I'd had much choice. But I didn't say as much to her. As my best friend of seven years, she knew. She'd listened to me moan and complain after my severance package had been spent up and run out, and I'd been forced into this new venture.

I looked to the curly-haired imp in her backseat, whacking her twin brother over the head with her sippy cup. "How are Gracie's allergies?" Her skin appeared less red and splotchy than the last time I'd seen her, and I hadn't heard the hacking cough yet . . . wails from the brother she'd hit, yes, but no coughing from her.

A bright smile lit Tammy's face, making her appear less the worn-out mother. "So much better, thanks to your raw—"

"Shh!" I hissed reflexively.

"Sorry." She lowered her voice. "Goodness, Liz, he's really put the fear of God into you, hasn't he?"

"Fear of the revenuers more like," I said on a nervous chuckle.

Taking a last sweeping glance of the parking lot, I popped my trunk and opened the larger of two coolers half full of filled jars.

"Ruth's so excited to get your delivery," Tammy said as she switched a dozen half-gallon Masons into her own cooler while I kept watch. "Said she hasn't been able to find a supplier since moving up from South Carolina."

"And you're sure she's cool?"

"Bit weird, maybe, but not a snitch." Tammy shrugged. "She's one of those homeschoolers, homesteaders, keep the government out of my business types, but not enough acreage for a cow."

Lord, I met all kinds with my customers. I didn't understand home-schooling. But, hey, she'd ordered five gallons of my secret recipe and had already asked about hooking up one of her friends to buy as well. My old crowd, the upscale hipster foodies, would cancel their order whenever something more important came their way. Like a weekend trip to the Outer Banks. Which I used to take, too. I'd sigh at the thought, but I was long sighed out.

"And you gave her the password?" I asked Tammy.

She held up her empty hand as if in a pledge and recited, "The cream always rises to the top."

Aunt Jessie's voice echoed in my mind even as Tammy repeated her oft-quoted adage. But with my Aunt Jessie, it was usually delivered with a note of accusation over how I'd abandoned the farm and forsaken my family. I'd not risen properly.

As I helped my friend transfer the now heavy cooler into the back of her minivan, Tammy continued, "I'll text Ruth and let her know you're on your way."

"Thanks," I said. I was running late and needed to race home to give Mama her pills and start her supper. All this cat'n'mouse as Tammy called it, or struggling for survival as I was forced to think of it, made my daily runs twice as long as they used to be. When I'd first started this new career that had been forced upon me, I'd not taken the legal threat seriously . . . until that dad-blamed Department of Agriculture agent had developed a special interest in my white lightning, as I liked to call it if for no other reason than to aggravate Aunt Jessie.

A banging drew our attention. Little Gracie was now whacking her sippy cup against the window rather than her twin's head. Her bottom lip pouted out in a pose I thought adorable.

Her mother must have viewed it from a different perspective. With an aggrieved sigh, she opened the back door and grabbed the empty cup from her darling daughter's balled hand. "Okay, but you won't get any more until we're home," she said to Gracie, whose eyes were now alight, watching her mom open a Mason jar and pour the white liquid into her cup. She reached for it with greedy, wiggling hands as Tammy rattled on, "I've got two stops to drop this stuff off, and I won't be refilling your cup every time."

I chuckled, my heart warmer, lighter despite my friend's irritation. As Aunt Jessie loved to remind me, my own biological clock was approaching midnight. I'd repeatedly pressed snooze on it and all family obligations to single-mindedly pursue my career. I'd over-timed and over-achieved my way to the position of director of finance with an international pharmaceutical company. But my labor became a casualty of the Great Recession, and I'd been running on empty for a long time.

As I watched little Gracie chugging the wholesome, fresh milk, I wondered why something that brought such health and happiness to this family was considered a criminal offense. Why any government agency would spend their very limited revenue persecuting raw milk providers rather than violent criminals or corporate tax-evaders was beyond me. But it seemed like in the last three weeks, I'd become Special Agent Strate's personal scape-cow.

Tammy closed her rear hatch door, and after giving me a quick hug, hopped into her minivan. "Now, Liz, you stay safe, and don't you be giving them revenuers a wild ride," she ended on an exaggerated Southern drawl.

Yeah, she could laugh. But Tammy'd been the one to lure me into my now criminal ways. I'd worried as she'd agonized over Gracie's allergies and asthma and complained about how raw milk really helped, but was so hard to find. And here I now was, sitting on a dying farm with four cows and loads of pasture, but no equipment to work it, all just an hour's drive from the state's capital. And thus my milk-shine business had been born.

Tammy's engine became a distant hum, and I corralled the gloom which had settled in with my friend's departure. Try as I might to keep the difficulties of the run humorous and my spirits up, this was no game I was playing.

I retrieved my cell and checked my GPS for the last stop, a new customer Tammy had met at her CSA. To fill up her now free time, thanks to our company's cutbacks, Tammy had become active in her local, community-supported agriculture farm. While her layoff had probably been influenced more by twins on the way with two already in school, mine had been simple politics. I'd challenged the CEO on too many questionable accounting practices, and he wanted to reward a more loyal underling with my salary, if not my title. Though that would probably be handed over in a couple of months, once my lay-off had reached a years' mark.

"Fancy meeting you here again, Lizzie Bet."

The low, masculine voice behind me sent a frisson of stress sizzling up my spine. I whirled, finding myself eye to chin with the man determined to make my new life miserable.

I crossed my arms over my chest as I cocked my head back to glare him in the eye. "How'd you find that out?" No one except Aunt Jessie had called me by my birth name since I'd left home after high school. Not even Mama, but then, in the last few months she'd rarely remembered my name at all.

"Well, see," Special Agent Strate squinted at me through his half-lowered eyelids, "it's like this . . . When one's going to issue a search warrant, and one must insert the searchee's legal name on the form, one must find out what that legal name is." He smirked, that snarky attitude I remembered from our last encounter.

"Search warrant?" I screeched, my composure forgotten, my heart thumping wildly against my rib cage. "For what?"

"Your car." He jerked his head to my still open trunk and waved a paper in my face.

My gaze shifted to the two coolers in the back. I had five tubs of raw butter left. Thank God they were under the false bottom I'd constructed to separate the butter and cheese below from the melting ice above . . . long before Mr. Nosy Boiler-pusher had taken an interest in my enterprise.

"Go ahead," I taunted him, mustering all the bravado I had learned from years of sitting across a corporate Board table.

He simply quirked one dark bushy eyebrow, his gray eyes alight beneath. Was that the thrill of the hunt, or was he toying with his prey?

Leaning against the side of my car, I crossed my arms and ankles. I did my darndest to pull off both an innocent, beleaguered glare and an expression of so bored, couldn't care less, have nothing to hide. I refused to turn and watch, but listened to the unmistakable click of the cooler latch releasing, the swish and clink of his fingers running through the melting ice at the bottom. (God, let it be freaking cold!) No squeak of a pushed aside false bottom.

But I didn't grin, and I didn't release the breath I'd been holding.

Then, finally, the thump of the second lid closed sharply. Frustration perhaps? I hoped so.

"Move aside, please." His "please" was a bit tense this time as he waved me away from the passenger rear door.

I watched this round. Couldn't help myself, or the amusement I allowed to spread across my face as his movements became jerkier, finding nothing. As I knew he wouldn't. I'd learned early on not to carry records with me. My detail-trained financial mind had to come in good for something with this new enterprise.

He finally faced me, his arms cocked on his hips, a tic throbbing in his cheek. "You won't get so lucky every time."

"You consider me lucky?" My amusement fled abruptly.

Strate looked me up and down, from my Foxcroft satin tank to my slim Audrey pants to my Gucci ballet flats, all over three years old, but I still had my pride after all. Nothing else but that. I gave back as good as I was getting, however, letting my gaze wander disdainfully from his crisp business shirt to his dark pressed pants back up to his clean-shaven squared jaw and unsmiling face.

"Why else would someone like you," his gaze narrowed on my black freshwater pearls, "be selling illegal raw milk unless it was some sort of game?"

I felt myself flush, but bit back a retort. My mother's face, her confused dark eyes, floated in my mind. A sudden surge of emotion gripped me at the wasted years, years I'd spent away at college and building a career, when those eyes had been filled with determination to carry on without asking for help. And now that she desperately needed help, she couldn't ask. I blinked hard.

"You found nothing," I said, controlling my voice through gritted teeth. "Can I go now?"

He didn't say anything for a long minute. Just watched me beneath lowered lids, his head quirked to the right. "Yeah. But you'll be seeing me soon." He lowered himself into his car, then looked back at me over his shoulder. "Soon as I can get a warrant for your farm."

As I watched him drive away, George's "Moonshining" trilled in my pocket where I'd tucked my cell, but I no longer felt the sense of fun with the game I'd been playing. Desperation flowed hotly through me like that white lightning I'd pretended to haul. Agent Strate's home invasion could do more than land me a hefty fine. It could wipe away all the slim security I'd provided for Mama over the last few months.

I clenched my fists. Somehow, someway, I'd beat him at his own game, because the loss was just too great to take. Aunt Jessie would help. After all, aggravation was her specialty.

"Evie, I've already told you a hundred times," Aunt Jessie screeched as if Mama wasn't standing only three feet away, removing jars of cream from the cooler which Aunt Jessie had just packed. "We've got to get all this milk and cream out of here before the feds show up. You're slowing us down. Now go set back in your rocker."

I stopped myself from fussing at Aunt Jessie for fussing at Mama. It did no good. Plus, to see the woman who'd once singlehandedly converted a poor dirt farm into a thriving dairy and ice cream business wander aimlessly through the house, asking us the same questions over and over, made me feel like I'd stepped in the nastiest cow patty.

"Why are you moving all my milk?" Mama asked again from the sitting room as she shuffled past the old cracked butter churn on the hearth and jostled it, making it rattle. "Shouldn't you be tending the store?"

"You ain't run an ice cream parlor in two years, Evie."

Aunt Jessie's nagging only drew attention to Mama's confusion and made her lip tremble, reminding me of Tammy's little Gracie. On Mama, however, the look was heartbreaking.

Instead of letting myself slide into that emotional waste lagoon, I reminded my aunt, "I've already told you, Aunt Jessie. He's not going to be looking for the milk itself. We're allowed to drink our own. He's going to be hunting for any kind of record showing that I've been selling it."

"Which is what dozens of milk jars will tell him, Lizzie Bet, if he has half a brain." She eyeballed me where I was bent over inside the closet under the stairs, boxing up empty jars and lids. "And from what you've told me, he's got more'n that. Have you hid that computer away?"

I nodded and wiped my forehead on the sleeve of my flannel shirt. "It's up in the attic in an empty Christmas tree box."

Mama had drifted from the sitting room back into the kitchen and was hovering over the old chest freezer I'd converted to a cooler, looking at the jars of milk Aunt Jessie was drawing out to transport to her house a half mile down the road.

"But what will I give my families?" Mama asked, her mind back in the past, where it seemed to remain most clear. She'd not had to supplement her farm workers' pay with milk and eggs since way before I'd left home, though she'd continued to pass produce out freely whenever she knew someone was hitting on hard times.

"You don't have any workers anymore," Aunt Jessie screeched back. "And we've left you enough to have with your grits along with some store-bought butter since Lizzie Bet has sold all I'd made." Then she mumbled under her breath as to how that pasteurized mess wasn't fit for man nor beast.

"Good thing we don't have any men or beasts in this house then, isn't it?" Mama replied in one of her unusual moments of clarity.

Her hearing was perfectly good. It was the mind attached to it that was not so sound.

Two years ago, with one flourish of her dementia-guided pen, and me off in the Research Triangle Park focused on another rung in my career ladder, she'd sold off all the major machinery and pasteurization equipment for a fraction of its value. A fact Aunt Jessie would never let me forget, and had used mercilessly to draw me back to my "responsibilities." "'Bout time you put all that financial learning to good use, for once," she'd say, as repetitive as Mama.

My primary responsibility, as Aunt Jessie saw it, was keeping Mama out of a nursing home and in the home where she'd been born, raised, married, widowed, and worked all her life. A farm that had been in their family, my family, for over two-hundred years.

"Now go on, Evie." Aunt Jessie ushered Mama to her favorite rocker by the bay window in the front sitting room, drew off her favorite crocheted afghan from the back of the chair, and covered her lap. "You watch out and let us know when that officer drives up."

My mother would never pass the warning. She'd forgotten the second after Aunt Jessie made the request. But old habits died hard. Mama had raised her younger sister and brother while Grandma worked in the nearby shirt factory as Grandpa tried to churn money out of a rock farm. Now Aunt Jessie was returning the favor by playing mom to her older, widowed sister.

For the most part, Aunt Jessie was good to Mama. She spent long hours rocking beside her, looking over old photos, sharing memories of the time when Mama's mind was the most clear. Shame I didn't have time to sit and jaw, but I was run raw trying to milk four cows twice a day and keep the farm afloat.

After loading Aunt Jessie's car, I watched her drive away from the front porch, staring past the aging pecan tree, absently noting the heavy limbs with the browning nuts that had started dropping. Soon, they'd need to be gathered and shelled. My gaze drifted to the mule-drawn hay-rake off to the side of the gravel drive, the grass grown so high it nearly camouflaged the rusted machinery. With my milk runs taking twice as long now, I'd not had time to mow.

Sighing, I mentally clicked off the check list of what I must get done before "he" showed up. The cows were milked and the equipment sterilized, ready for the evening shift. I'd given Mama her morning meds and fed all the animals. And lastly, I'd picked a pot of collard greens to cook for lunch. Menial physical chores I'd once ran away from were somehow now oddly comforting, like Mama's bowl of warm grits on this crisp fall morning.

Shaking myself mentally, I opened the front door and stepped into the sitting room. Mama rocked faithfully by the window. I scanned the room, from the heart mantle my grandfather had carved for my grandmother as a wedding gift, to the mass of pictures cluttering the top of the upright piano Mama had tried to teach me to play as a child, to the row of her old magazines cluttered along the edges of the stairs. I'd left no incriminating evidence behind. Of course, I wasn't even certain Special Agent Strate would show today, but an old colleague, one who'd made the transition from layoff to government employee down at the state capital, had tipped me off that his paperwork had been approved late yesterday. So I expected Mr. Boiler-Pusher any minute now.

I'd stayed up to the wee hours of the morning, reading online about raw milk raids in California, Wisconsin, Kentucky. About the thousands of dollars of someone's labor in the form of raw butter, milk, and cheeses confiscated along with computers, even animal feed. About the families, even children, held under guard while their homes were searched.

Ridiculous. Surely it couldn't happen to me.

"Wonder why the cat's running scared like that?" Mama asked from her front window perch. "Sure is strange the way ol' Tom's skedaddling up the tree."

My curiosity pricked, I turned to see and heard the knock. Drawing in a deep, and admittedly rather shaky, breath, I reached for the glass knob and opened the door to those gray eyes I'd been getting much too familiar with lately. Aligned behind him were two police officers, a man and woman, both wearing bland we're-here-to-do-a-job let's-get-on-with-it faces.

Seeing those blue uniforms, and the badge and search warrant Agent Strate held out for me to read, made me feel like a criminal. The coldness that froze up my chest must have whitened my face, because a flicker of regret . . . doubt maybe . . . tightened the corners of Strate's eyes and lips.

With minimal effort and well-trained efficiency—he'd have done well as a CEO—he directed his team while keeping my mother and me company, or under guard, in the front sitting room. He didn't seem eager to talk, his sharp eyes taking in everything around him. Mama, however, kept plaguing him with questions, convinced he was the son of the local district attorney from years ago. Within the first half hour, she must have asked him a hundred times how he'd liked life in New York City and what had made him come home. He never once let her know she'd already asked him that and was actually rather charming and cordial in his replies.

Me, however, he ignored. I watched the officers from my perch in the side window seat as they searched everything from the bottom of Dad's old wardrobe, now stuffed full of canned veggies from the garden that I'd sweated over, to the barns—empty of equipment but filled with piles of apples and pears I was planning to preserve, to the old pack house with its eighty years of rusting farm machinery, back to the house to the attic. At which point, I busied myself with preparing Mama's greens, with her puttering along behind me helping out, putting things away just as soon as I set them out.

"Won't you have something to drink, little Enos?" my mother asked, holding out a cup of milk to Agent Strate.

Craning my head back to look into the next room, I eyed the cup, my eyes narrowing, my muscles tensing. With the thick yellowish cream floating to the top, it was obviously raw. But what could he do? It wasn't being sold, and we were allowed to drink our own production as well as offer it to any pseudo-guests.

He took a sip, then nodded his thanks to my mom.

"Wait just a dad-blame minute." I stomped to the doorframe between the two rooms. "You're going to drink that?" I felt my eyes bugging out of my head.

He merely quirked an eyebrow at me. "I was raised on a farm. Drank raw all my young life."

I couldn't believe the hypocrisy I was hearing. Stepping into the sitting room, I thrust my balled hands on my hips. "Then why do you chase after me so?"

He leaned back against the mantle and placed one palm casually over the paddle of that old cracked churn. His gaze, however, pierced mine with his accusing glare. "Have you ever seen a child sickened critically by some quack's greedy, unsanitary practices? Lying in a hospital bed as her little body's wracked with diarrhea and nausea?"

The dark look in his light eyes made me feel as if I'd been kicked by a cow. Gracie's rosy cheeks flashed in my memory. What if she'd gotten sick from my milk instead of better?

But no, I was always scrupulous about sterilizing the bottles, cleaning each of the cows' teats, filtering the milk immediately, and testing it regularly. But I couldn't say that to him. There could be no open acknowledgment that I did anything to prep for sales.

I returned to stony silence in the collard-smelling kitchen as I finished preparing lunch for Mama, who promptly resumed questioning Agent Strate about his "daddy," the prosecutor.

At some point, I'm not even sure when, Aunt Jessie slipped back into the house and kept Mama company, and thankfully focused on the past, by looking through an old photo album together. As the time dragged on, I joined them, pulling up a footstool between Mama and Aunt Jessie. I stared blankly at black and white images of Mama and Aunt Jessie as girls jumping into a mound of cotton, of Mama dressed in coveralls riding the old tractor, and with the turning of pages, of colorful images of me under the grapevine, my mouth stuffed full as purple juice stained my lips.

"See that. That's my Lizzie Bet," my mom's voice rang out. I turned and saw her standing at Agent Strate's elbow, holding out an old photo of me at graduation. She thumbed at the picture. "She graduated top of her class and then went on to Duke. Got a fine job in the city. All I ever wanted for her, even if I didn't see her so much."

Aunt Jessie snorted. "She should have come home more often." And she cut me a sharp glance from the corners of her eye. "Maybe you wouldn't be in this pickle if she had."

I didn't respond to the lure, but Mama spun on her. "Don't you even think that, Jessie. Look at what I gave up for Mama and you and Gabe. I didn't want my daughter tied down here like I was. I fought to make this farm pay so Lizzie Bet would have her choice."

"Mama . . ." I said, the words coming out a croak. But I'd never heard her say that before. Somehow, realizing how she'd never forced me to stay made me wonder why I'd been so wild to escape all those years ago.

She turned to me, and her eyes sharpened for one brief moment, then her voice dropped back to the slightly vacant mumble I'd grown accustomed to these past months. "My fault. All my fault," she said, shaking her graying head as she plopped back in her chair. "I signed the wrong papers. Gave away the machinery, everything. Forced you back here."

I hurried to her side and knelt by her rocker. "It's okay, Mama," I said, gripping her hand, her skin paper-thin, her fingers gnarled beneath my own. "I wanted to leave that life. Needed to come home." And as I said it, the release spreading throughout my body told me it was true. The life I'd been living, the job I'd given my soul to, hadn't filled me with the sense of belonging and accomplishment I'd expected and longed for. "I feel good about turning the farm to a new venture, just like you did, starting a fresh legacy."

Mama looked straight at me and said, "My fault you had to cart your equipment up to the attic."

My heart swelled against the tight confines of my chest. "I don't know what you're talking about, Mama." My voice sounded faint to my own ears, and I sensed Agent Strate's eyes boring me in the back.

"You know, sugar. That computer you bought with what little you had left over from the court case and buying back this house."

I whirled to face Mr. Strate. He looked at me, his gray eyes meeting mine over his glass of milk. For a long moment, he studied me, his steady gaze inscrutable. Then he set down the glass with a thud on the mantle.

I braced myself for the cold feel of metal around my wrists.

He squeezed past me on his way to the base of the stairs and called up to the officers above. "Hey, Byron, Sheila, time to go. We've exceeded our warrant's time limit. There's nothing wrong going on here."

And as he was walking out the door in the wake of the officers, a hint of a white mustache atop his lips, he turned to me and said, "Maybe next time we meet it will be under more pleasant circumstances, Ms. Duke." He nodded toward the mantle and hearth where he'd waited for so long. "I know a thing or two about fixing cracked churns."

The intense look he gave me left me wondering with an odd fluttering in my stomach . . . just which cracked churn was he planning to fix?

Behind me, I heard Mama's voice murmuring to Aunt Jessie, "Such a nice man, that Enos. But then his daddy always was a fine attorney."

"They'd make quite a match, wouldn't they?" Aunt Jessie said back in a raspy voice meant to be a whisper. "That smart Agent Strate and your Lizzie Bet?"

As I tried to choke down an involuntary snort at the ridiculous notion, Aunt Jessie's next words came through loud and aggravatingly clear: "It's like I always said, the cream always rises to the top, but only when it's been run from raw."

The Agreement

Misty Barrere

When Mimi came to help with Mother I was in first grade, and I learned addition by playing Blackjack. On Independence Day, Mimi steamed oysters. We drenched them in hot sauce and took them on a platter to the front porch. We sat, swinging our legs over the edge and waiting for the fireworks to start over the water.

Because of Mimi, my biggest problem back then was not saying "busted" when I reached twenty-two in math drills.

She kept a change jar in her closet and let me grab a handful to buy toys and treats every time we went to the downtown Mobile CVS to fill Mother's prescriptions. She never questioned why I bought the things I did, not even the last time. Somewhere she'd read that snakes in my tea leaves could mean I had a secretive soul, and she didn't want to mess with that.

I was at the pier with Daddy when she died.

Yep. They said it was lung cancer. They said she hadn't wanted anyone to know because Daddy needed her. They also said I was too young for a funeral. It would be a bad memory, and life has enough of those.

So, I didn't go.

Daddy played basketball in the driveway, and he smiled when I interrupted him to help me with math. He promised to steam oysters, like Mimi. He promised to take me to the oyster beds in his boat, just like he and Mother did when they first started dating. He said it should be a tradition.

"How 'bout it, Tibby?" he asked my mother.

But she just closed her door, and he left, heading off to Biloxi for a few days.

They said it wasn't right to leave me like that.

Daddy claimed it was the wind chime that kept Mother off the porch, so when he came home, he took it down. But nothing changed.

I wasn't awake when Daddy left for good.

Nope.

He waited until after I went to bed.

They said he couldn't take it anymore, so he called his little sister—that's Lexie—and made a deal. Now, Lexie's creamy hands put away the cereal and milk.

They say Lexie doesn't bother to clean down to the nitty-gritty, that our window sills are covered in dead bugs and that nobody better send us a peace lily since Mother lost the baby, because Lexie's no green-thumb, either.

"You're all ears, Sophie Crandall," Lexie says when I repeat their gossip. Her boobies are small, but her stomach is bigger than Mother's ever was. Lexie hands me a Giant Mystical Sea-Life coloring book and a new box of Crayolas. "The Aunts are all talk," she adds. "I'm not going anywhere."

I don't call her Aunt Lexie, because she looks nothing like Them. They wear big hats on Sunday and heels and want to read my tea leaves like Mimi, but I say *No, Thank You* because no one can replace my big-eyed, tan-skinned Mimi, even if they are her sisters.

Losing a baby that was never born is not like losing a Mimi that you knew.

There's no funeral.

Just a lot of silence and casserole.

On a humid August morning, two weeks before second grade starts, Lexie has the TV turned up loud so we know it's Tuesday. The morning news people say the heat is pressing toward ninety, and it's not even nine a.m. We are supposed to go clothes shopping if it's a good day. I've done everything I can to contribute because I want Daddy to come back home.

On other good days, Mother will click off the news to quote things from her favorite book, which is all about pirates and this queen named Elizabeth. "It's all true," she says, while sitting in her favorite chair, painted yellow. Except she's picking at the paint, showing that it used to be red. She rakes her fingers through her brown hair.

"This isn't a sappy romance novel, Lexie. Those Tudors were fighting for their lives. Elizabeth had guts."

Then she'll ring up Daddy on the phone and call him Sir Francis Effin Drake. I don't think this helps because Lexie grabs the phone from her and says, "Sorry, Peter."

So, I've done what I can.

Right now, Mother's medicine has kicked in, and she's in the bathroom. She's usually not in there until Sports Highlights. I'm already dressed, on my belly in my bedroom, coloring mermaids when she shrieks.

"Snake! Snake! Snaaake!" Mother slams her bathroom cabinet shut.

The thrill of possibility courses through me, and I drop my crayon and crawl across the floor, peeking under my door.

Still in her old maternity night gown, the bottoms of Mother's bare feet slip on the waxed floor.

"Tabitha?" Lexie calls from the kitchen.

I open my door with sweaty palms to see her stumble down the hall. Her fingers touch the chair rail, but she stumbles, trying to get as far from the bathroom as she can.

My heart is leaping, bounding, squeezing.

She might actually do it this time.

I step into the hall. My tongue burns to tell her, "Go! All the way to the grass." But, I keep quiet.

The porch would be good enough.

The porch would be a gold star.

My hopes reach the front door, but Mother's hand jerks back as if the knob is on-fire-hot. She whimpers and paws the wood like a puppy, then pounds it with her fist.

"Snakes in the soap," she says. "In the bathroom. Snakes in the soap."

"Tabitha?" Lexie asks. "Have you been watching *Animal Planet* again?"

Lexie's soft voice reminds Mother that the boards under the house have been checked and rechecked, as if she is reminding me that puddles breed mosquitoes. But scolding does nothing to help my mother. She scratches her eyes, screams that she wants to blind herself so she will never see the sight again.

I cover my ears and back into the hall. Out of their view, I lie low, thinking if she blinds herself, I will never see her eyes again, which are blue like mine. I want her to stop. Now. But no sound comes out of my mouth.

Lexie tries to hold Mother's wrists and pull her close at the same time. "Stop it, Tabitha," she says, irritated now. "You're hurting yourself. I'll have to call Peter."

"Peter?" Mother stops fighting at the mention of Daddy and

collapses like a lawn chair, crumpled and shivering. With her knees to her chest, she lies on her side with her back against the door. But she still tears the tender skin around her eyes with her jagged fingernails.

I have never seen my mother bleed before. Not on purpose. Not like this, doing it to herself.

Lexie catches Mother's wrists and starts to hum.

"The snake," Mother says. "It took the baby."

I shake my head. She always says this.

"Shush, Tabitha. That's an old wives tale, and you know it," Lexie says in a voice that could get me to eat broccoli. She is a good babysitter. It's funny to me that she is my Daddy's baby sister. Baby sitter. Baby sister. I play with the words in my head, rearranging the letters.

I twist a piece of my hair around my finger as tight as I can. It breaks, and I pull out another and wrap it around my pointer finger.

"How 'bout a song?" Lexie says.

Lexie was supposed to go away to college, but they say she's blown her opportunity. Her friend, the musician, comes by on Sunday mornings and plays gospel music for her. He says Lexie misses going to church, but only for the music. Lexie says that isn't true. She misses the coffee cake, so once, the musician brought her a coffee cake. If my mother is sleeping, Lexie will have a cigarette with him on the porch and complain if he's ten minutes late and tell him he should really trim his beard. She always smokes for a long time after he's gone and tells me to stay inside.

Lexie sings for my mother, just like she did me that once. Lexie has a pretty singing voice. She does *Landslide* like the Dixie Chicks, but soft and shy, like she's not done it much, like it's her last choice.

"Well, I been afraid of changing cuz I built my life around you . . ."

After a few songs, it works. Mother doesn't claw at her face any more.

I unwind the hair and my finger slowly turns pink. I wiggle it to be sure it won't fall off.

"I hate this door," Mother says, stretching her ankles. "I hate this snake-ridden house."

"There was just the one snake, Tibby. When I first came. Sophie tells me you and her used to dance in the grass barefoot."

I want to fling open the door and point to the yard. I want to say, "That grass. You and me. Mimi steamed oysters, and we ate them with hot sauce and crackers." My mouth waters at the idea of something other than peanut butter, but my mother won't remember oysters.

When she looks at me, it's like she wonders how I got there.

"You should believe me," Mother cries. "I hate snakes. I hate this door." She cries until there are no hates left, and she is shuddering in sleep on the Oriental rug.

The baby was a boy. He was supposed to bring my daddy back, but his heart stopped beating. That's what they say.

So, it's up to me. But just like Lexie, I've blown my opportunity.

Lexie pulls a pillow from a chair and rests Mother's head on it. Lexie finds me hiding and guilty in the hall. She takes my hand and leads me to the front of the house.

"One cigarette won't kill The Adoptee," Lexie whispers, pointing to her stomach. She means her b-a-b-y, but she won't call it that and gets mad when the musician does. She says this whenever my mother is done freaking out. She holds up a finger, raises her fair, almost invisible eyebrows. "I'll pour you some Kool-Aid when I'm done. One cigarette. I promise. And I'll make spaghetti for dinner. You like it."

Lexie brings my mermaid book to the entryway. "Watch her, OK?"

I begin coloring again, but not really. I stare at my mother.

They talk about her in whispers, but I hear. They know that on bad days she spends most mornings raking her scalp with her overly-long nails that Lexie can't convince her to trim. From the crown of her head to the base of her neck. Lexie tells them all about it. She's really a double-agent.

I lean over my mother and whisper, "Go outside, the weather's nice." I say it as many times as I can until my sweat drips into her ear, but she doesn't move.

I creep to the kitchen door and search for Lexie. It is never one cigarette. I pull Mother's favorite chair to the kitchen sink and stand on it, searching the yard for Lexie. She is talking on the phone, walking back and forth, her ponytail snapping like banana licorice. Whip, stomp, whip, stomp, stomp. Maybe it's the musician again. Sometimes she calls him when my mother is asleep.

" . . . needs big drugs, Peter. I mean, big, big drugs. They're right. Sophie's blue eyes can't get any wider, staring at Tibby like this. You can't keep ignoring them. Something has to change. You have to . . . you have to come get her."

I press my ear against the screen and strain to hear more. My heart is booming faster than I can think.

"Now, Peter. You have to come now."

I glance at Mother—still sleeping—and run to the bathroom.

This is even better than I hoped for. This is what my mother wanted. This is what she's needed ever since she saw the snake in the yard. My mother made Lexie watch it while she called my daddy to come home from gambling in Biloxi to kill it. He never came, and the snake slithered under the house. We never saw it again.

So, I have done it. I have helped, but Mimi would say, "First things first."

I have to hide my contribution.

I open the cabinet door. Shifting lemon-scented soap, I snatch the drugstore snake with its cheap, half-painted tongue and carry it away with shaking hands. I creep down the hall and hide it under the loose vent in my bedroom. Hiss, hiss, hiss. Then I slide back to the entryway and flatten myself on the floor as if I'd never left Mother's side.

It's a page of mermaids. Coloring those tricky sirens of the sea, I press the crayons deeper into their green slimy tails as sweat trickles down my neck.

Lexie comes inside, tucking her hair behind her ear. "Hey, want to go to the pier for a while? We can see the dolphins. I've got money for ice cream."

So I'm not there when Daddy takes Mother away.

Nope.

In a lilac-scented nightgown with half-scabbed eyelids, that's how I remember her.

Lexie teaches me a new game called Uno. Sometimes, I win.

I decide to keep quiet about the snake. I think of taking it to the curb like Lexie does the trash every Tuesday. Getting rid of the snake might make me feel better, but I don't want to feel better. I don't want to be left alone, either.

At night, the whispers come. Never mention your crimes to anyone, they say. They prick at my ears like scraping pencils on that math test when I knew none of the answers.

We agree to keep my crime and the snake hidden. Then, the whispers go away.

But not for long.

I find Mother's pirate and queen book in the kitchen and read it at night, asking Lexie what every word means. I find Mother's lilac lotion and keep it on my nightstand.

School starts, and I don't bother to make friends. Teachers tell Lexie my vocabulary is "off-the-chart," but my math skills are stuck at "delayed." I decide to grow my bangs out, and Lexie takes me to CVS for the little hair clips. I ask her if they come in black. I want black jeans, black T-shirts just like her. But she says, "Age eight is too early to be Goth."

She buys pink and purple clips with flowers, and I feel like a baby.

For Halloween, the musician comes over, and we turn off all the lights and play Uno in the bathroom. He sings Lexie a song he wrote about whooping cranes and how they stay together forever. Her stomach moves. She smiles. We eat Fun Dip, play music loud to drown out the ding-dong of trick-or-treaters. Lexie falls asleep early, so he gets the TV remote. The musician and I watch a movie about a sea serpent. When he leaves, I tell him his song is stupid. I decide I am the sea monster, growing huge and sour like too much candy.

Thanksgiving isn't thankful, even though Daddy has given the house to Lexie and me, and he visits some weekends, like divorced dads. This is silly though, because it is Mother's family's house, and she will come back, right?

They make us go to church, and then to one of the aunt's houses for turkey and mashed potatoes. When we get back home, Lexie and Daddy argue because the only thing on me that has grown since school started is my bangs. They say my eyes look like a refugee's from Afghanistan or Russia or something. With Them it is always yap, yap, yap.

"She's too skinny," Daddy says. "Why don't you cook some meat or something?"

Lexie is not cooking meat. She says Mimi raised them on seafood, chicken and vegetables, and what is his obsession with meat anyway?

Daddy turns to me. "Want to go to the movies tomorrow, Baby Girl? There's popcorn. You love the warm butter. We can get cheeseburgers after." He smiles, but his teeth don't show.

"Movies give her nightmares," Lexie says. "She's still hasn't recovered from one Miles watched with her on Halloween, the idiot. And as for her weight, haven't you ever heard of post-traumatic stress?"

"I took away the stress," Daddy says. "We can talk about that later." He takes a framed picture of Mother and leaves, ducking under the door frame so he doesn't hit his head.

Lexie shouts, "You never talk about a damn thing."

They say that in that picture Mother looks like me. Sometimes I crawl in her bed when the musician comes over because he and Lexie argue forever. Lexie hasn't ever changed Mother's sheets, so they still smell like lilacs and unwashed hair. I think I'm the only one who cares if she comes back.

Five days after Christmas, one of Them rings the doorbell with our Christmas wreath in her hand. She has black and white hair and flushed cheeks as if she ran all the way.

The house smells like the pound cake Lexie burned. She woke up at daybreak with contractions and decided to get domestic by baking Mimi's famous Chocolate Wonder Pound Cake, but burned it. Then, she dropped it all over the floor when her water broke and called Daddy to come get her.

"Where does this belong, Peter?" Aunt Blanche says. "Christmas is over."

"Attic," Daddy says, tossing the wreath on the coat rack. "Take care of it later."

Lexie whispers, "Hide my lighters. That one cleans like a freakin' demon."

Daddy and Lexie go out the door, her doing that huffy-puffy breathing. Daddy hadn't even taken off his coat, just came to give Lexie a ride to the hospital to have The Adoptee. They leave, and I am abandoned with the third aunt, the holiest, Blanche. She was a nun once, so when I look at her, I try to imagine her really still and praying with that thing nuns wear on her head, but all she does is move and talk.

Aunt Blanche's hair is called salt and pepper. Her face flushes pink when she lifts the sofa and sweeps under it, behind it. She beats the cushions and vacuums them, too. She pinches when she tickles, but doesn't say she'd love to take me to her house, like the other aunts.

Nope.

She'll stay here.

"Bring me the other can of Pledge, Sugar," Aunt Blanche says. "And a new rag. And you can call me AB if you want. All the other cousins do. AB for Aunt Blanche."

With the cleaning supplies I find a pack of unopened Maverick playing cards, Mimi's favorite brand. I skip back to my room with the other stuff.

Aunt Blanche rips the sheets from my bed and dusts everything but the blinds. She has me emptying my toy box, adding old toys to a bag for the Goodwill. She tells stories about her and her sisters— "Mimi was the feistiest, God, rest her soul"—and how they used to be mean one minute and nice the next and how they'd get in trouble.

She frowns at my twelve stacks of finished coloring books that each come up to my hip and asks, "Aren't you lonely just living with Lexie? Isn't it awful quiet?"

I stop pulling things out of the toy box and think about who could live with us to make it louder. The purple Pegasus Daddy gave me for Christmas is sitting in the corner of my room. I haven't taken it out of the box. I think about putting it in the Goodwill bag.

"We have TV," I say. "But Lexie and I like to listen to the radio. We dance and sing. And play Uno."

"I never figured Lexie for the dancing sort."

"Lately, she kinda wobbles," I say and show her what I mean. I am glad Lexie had me change into my Christmas outfit, a green corduroy skirt and green tights with a green and purple sweater. Even if all we are doing is cleaning, I can twirl in my skirt.

Aunt Blanche starts talking about her son and how he lives far away, and she doesn't see her grandchildren very much, and I get the feeling that she's the one who's lonely, and Lexie and I have it covered. Except for the whispers that say Daddy doesn't come because I'm not as much fun as Biloxi. Or because he knows what I did.

"You could adopt Lexie's baby if the other lady backs out," I tell Aunt Blanche. "Lexie's worried she will."

Aunt Blanche laughs. "When that baby is a teenager, I'll be dead and gone. Besides, Lexie may change her mind once she sees it. Mother's instinct and all."

I get a twitchy feeling in my stomach. "I'm all Lexie can manage. They said that at Thanksgiving."

Aunt Blanche gets this half-smile and yanks the cord on the blinds, sending dust spiraling to the floor. "They? You mean, my sisters?"

I nod. "She'll be back in a few days, right?"

"If she doesn't keep the baby or move in with Miles. Lexie is known for zigging when she should zag." Aunt Blanche hands me the window cleaner. "Looks like your bag is full. Try your hand at this, and I'll start on the floors."

She takes the Hefty bag from my hands and walks out of the room. The floors? I bite my bottom lip.

It took Aunt Blanche five minutes to rip the ornaments and lights off our Christmas tree and another five to vacuum up the needles. She even found Lexie's lighters I had hidden in my bean bag.

The echoes of her steps reach the back door before I pop the vent loose. I reach down into my hiding place. I've been careful. I've pushed my snake back, out of sight, so no one would ever just see it. My heart beats like a hammer. I get down on my knees and reach in, up to my elbow this time.

"Where is it?" I whisper. "Where did it go?"

"Sophie?"

"Yes!" I jump, banging my head on the edge of the window frame. Tears of pain, then confession, drip from my eyes. I wipe them fast. She can't catch me.

"Oh, there you are. Wondered where you'd gotten."

"She's never coming back, is she?" I rip my hair clip from my scalp, pulling out a clump of hair.

"What are you . . . You mean your mother?"

"I left a plastic snake in the soap basket," I say, barely loud enough for her to hear. But I want her to know before she likes me too much. "It's my fault she's gone."

Aunt Blanche stands in the doorway, quiet, like there's more for me to say. She props the broom against the wall and leans against my dresser, which isn't really mine, it's some antique from grandma blah-blah-blah, which just means that most girls my age have white furniture, and I have this dark stained wood with drawers that don't open easily.

I can't look at Aunt Blanche. With the clip, I scrape a letter S into the back of my hand. S for Snake. Sophie. Or—maybe Aunt Blanche, the nun would understand this—Sin. I heard about it on TV once. It means shit we do wrong. The S is just a white mark, just dry skin. But at the bottom curve of the S, blood comes to the top of my skin.

I shove the clip back in my hair. "Yep. I'm the reason. You should know that."

Aunt Blanche walks over and looks at my hand. "Sophie, you've hurt yourself." She takes the clip out of my hair and inspects my scalp. "You put the snake in the soap, and you're sorry?"

I nod and bite my lip to keep from crying.

"Lexie found your snake a long time ago. It's okay, Sugar." She stares at my hand, clucking. "We can fix this right up."

It's just a scrape, nothing like my mother's eyes.

I look at Aunt Blanche and frown at the clump of hair springing from my purple flowery clip. "I think I want to lie down," I say.

Aunt Blanche gets up and makes a place for me on the bed, but I walk to my mother's bed and crawl under the covers. I want to sleep where she slept, but it's not right. The sheets don't smell like her at all. They smell like Tide.

Stupid, stupid silent tears roll into my nose and I am glad for my mother's box of Kleenex on her bedside table. I wipe the tears quietly and wonder where Lexie has put my snake, if she tossed him in the trash or hid him so I'd ask and have to confess.

He can't leave me. He is part of me. We have an agreement.

No matter what they say, we are the same. I have to find him.

Aunt Blanche creeps into my mother's room. She sits down in the rocker and closes her eyes, but doesn't say a word. She doesn't rock. She doesn't move.

My chin shakes, and I bite my lip to keep it still. I wipe hair out of my eyes and hold my bloody hand tightly.

We stay quiet so long I'm sure Aunt Blanche is asleep or worse, she's died on me like Mimi. And I think I can't miss her funeral because I've been sitting with her when she died.

"Aunt Blanche?"

She breathes, and I'm so glad she's not dead. "Yeah, Sugar?"

"I shouldn't have done it. I wanted her to be scared inside the house so she'd go outside like she used to." I swallow the knot in my throat and try to finish. "I thought Daddy was coming home to help her."

Aunt Blanche lets out a long sigh, like she's tired from all that cleaning.

"He did help Tibby. She's where she needs to be. You need a Band-Aid?"

I shake my head. I show her the Kleenex wrapped around my hand. "Lexie told the musician nobody goes crazy over losing a stupid baby."

"Humph. That's just inexperience talking," she says. "We can do better for your hand. Come on."

Someone pounds on the front door, but before Aunt Blanche can get there, the musician bursts in doing his own huffy-puffy breathing, running his fingers through his hair, grabbing it, doing a tiptoe-dance in his Converse. "Where's Lexie? Where's my baby?"

Aunt Blanche is only halfway out of the rocker, but she acts like he comes through our front door every day. "At the hospital, Miles."

I straighten the bed and try to pretend like I have not been crying, but he acts like I'm not even there.

The dryer beeps, and Aunt Blanche squeezes past him to the laundry room and presses buttons on the dryer.

"I can't let her give him up," he says, nearly running into Aunt Blanche. "What room is she in? Has she had him yet? She's not answering her phone or anything."

"Well, Miles." Aunt Blanche smiles out of the right side of her mouth. "I suppose she's busy." She opens the linen closet and pulls out the first aid kit.

"I gotta get down there," he says. "What would she want to hear? I mean, I know what I want to say, but so far authenticity hasn't worked. I wish I was more like Peter. You know, smooth."

I frown. If I tell him what I know, I'll lose Lexie forever.

"Really?" Aunt Blanche says, squirting ointment on my hand. "More like Peter?"

"He got Tabitha Barfield, I mean. Holy . . ." Miles glances at me. "Miss Alabama? Come on." Miles drops to his knees on the Oriental rug and rubs his eyes.

"What's he doing?" I ask.

Aunt Blanche says, "Young man, are you on something?"

"Just love. I was up all night. Writing a song. But it doesn't make any sense. Want me to sing it?"

"No," I say. "No more singing."

"Jesus," Aunt Blanche sighs. "Save this idiot."

"I was made to sing," the musician says. "I don't know what else to do."

Aunt Blanche slaps two Band-Aids on the back of my hand and gives my wrist a pat.

"Maybe you've done enough and should leave Lexie alone. She'll make her choice."

This sounds like a good idea to me, except his beard is trimmed and he still looks as gray as an oyster. The musician sits down and crosses his legs like it is story time. If he is giving up, I hope he isn't giving up here.

"I gave her my heart," he says, as if he cut it out and put it in a box. "I gave her everything. And she's giving our baby away. I don't know what she wants."

He sounds like I *feel* about Lexie's leaving. His eyes aren't wild like Mother's. I wouldn't want anyone to look that way, though. I am starting to think there are things about Mother that aren't right at all. But maybe, the way the musician feels about Lexie is just fine. Being a little sick over someone might be okay.

I pluck a hair from my scalp and start to wind it around my finger. "Lexie likes that whooping crane song," I say.

The musician lifts his chin.

The hair breaks. I look up at him. "She made it her ringtone."

"She did?"

"After you leave, she sits on the porch and plays it over and over. She cries. I hate that song. But maybe, if you played it for Lexie . . ."

He reaches forward and touches my sore hand. "Sophie. You're the most honest person I know." He takes off, leaves the front door wide open, cranks his car and tears down the street.

"Not at all like his family, the Whites," Aunt Blanche says. "Impetuous. A straight shooter. Sensitive."

"His songs stink," I say.

"If Lexie likes them, he's her man."

My stomach feels hollow, like I've eaten the last Oreo.

I get up and poke through Lexie's collection of old record albums, pull her desk chair over and reach high to the top of her bookcase. Nothing. I don't find anything.

"Nada," the musician would say.

"Oh, there you are," Aunt Blanche says, popping her head into Lexie's room. "Can you strip Lexie's sheets? We'll do her room next. I'm not sleeping on dirty sheets."

I walk beside Lexie's nightstand and pop open the vent. My snake lies coiled tightly with the same half-painted tongue. I close the vent, but keep my eyes on him, as if he might become real and slither up my arm at any moment.

There's a scraping sound in the hallway, and I peek to see Aunt Blanche lugging our dry Fraser fir out the front door.

"Sophie? Anything you need to throw out?" she calls. "I see the truck coming."

"No, ma'am."

The snake makes me feel kind of worried, but I take him to my room. The first thing that hits me is the smell of lemon Pledge. Aunt Blanche has left the blinds open. Sunlight pours through the windows across the white eyelet bedspread. The mirror gleams. She has even dusted my Madame Alexander "Around the World" dolls. Mother gave me those, every Christmas and birthday. My room has not been this clean since Mimi was here.

I sit on my bed, staring the snake down. The garbage truck comes and goes, but the snake stays the same. I turn him sideways, wondering how he could ever look real. I want to take him back to the bathroom and see how he looks, snuggled in the soap.

Aunt Blanche pushes open the door to my room, shuffling the deck of Mavericks.

I shove the snake under my pillow.

She winks at me. "If you're going to get good at hiding your secrets, Sugar, you need to learn a new game. Quit your pouting, and I'll teach you Poker."

I give her a quick nod.

When she isn't looking, I toss the snake into my toy box, alongside the Pegasus from Daddy. He doesn't Hiss, Hiss, Hiss, doesn't call to me like he used to.

I follow her into the kitchen. "Aunt Blanche, do you like oysters?"

"Only steamed," she says.

She cleans off the table with a wet paper towel, sits downs and starts shuffling the Mavericks.

"With hot sauce? How about crackers?"

"Garlic butter makes it better. Your Mimi and I disagreed on quite a lot."

It doesn't matter to me what the differences are. There's enough sameness to get me through. I nod and pull out Mother's favorite chair, watching as Aunt Blanche deals the cards. She starts to explain Poker.

I stare at the cards and can't make sense of anything. Not until I know one thing for certain. "Aunt Blanche?" I ask through a tight throat.

"Yes, Sugar?"

"Would you mind reading my tea leaves?"

With a smile, she lays down the Mavericks and puts the kettle on.

I hope we don't see snakes.

Never Promised You a Rose Garden

Kimberly Brock

The trouble with growing up rooted deep in a family, tucked safely in a pretty valley south of the Mason-Dixon, is how your future lies in front of you like a clean sheet just off the line. Ask me. You'll take it for granted.

All my life, I knew when the first crocus would come up by the back step of Mama and Daddy's house. I knew when the first hay would come in from the field, when the scent of a wood burning fire would curl out of the chimney, and when the sunflowers would stand taller than a man. And I knew that on the first fall weekend I'd clean out Mama's perennial beds so they could bloom again the following spring. There's something about that kind of security that will make you believe you have all the time in the world. Until you don't.

When my baby sister called, I'd just topped the hill overlooking the farm. "I'm already pulling in the drive, Bossy Mae," I said. She hated when I beat her to the punch.

"I hate how you answer the phone, Beth. And how do you know that's why I called you?"

Since she'd had her little girl, Leslie lived by a schedule that would have made the Marines proud, and for some reason, she'd seen that all the rest of us were put on schedules, too. She assigned our family responsibilities, and mostly we all went along just to avoid conflict.

"This is Wednesday. Aren't you supposed to be at work?" she snapped.

"I took a personal day."

"Well, Lord, that must be nice." Leslie worked as a bank teller and regularly complained about day care for her daughter. "It's like I drop her off, and they spend the next three hours rubbing her down with every germ on earth. I can't remember when we slept all night. I'm about to fall over head first."

"Oh, I'm sure," I said.

"What's that supposed to mean?" The way she sucked in her breath, it was a wonder my ear didn't snap off the side of my head.

"I understand, Les. It's got to be exhausting, keeping up with all you do."

"This is not about my Pampered Chef party, because I already told you I had to do that. I promised a friend. You think I'm not out at Mama and Daddy's every extra minute I have?"

"I didn't say that." In fact, there was a lot I wasn't saying. Like how I hated the damn Pampered Chef, for one thing. I could have let her have it between the eyes, told her everything about my fears, the appointment looming ahead of me, how sick I'd been. But all I wanted was to get down in the dirt and not think for a little while. "Maybe I can't blame a kid, but I had too much going on last week, Leslie."

"Oh, that's nice. Like you know anything about my life or what it's like to be a single mother."

"Pampered Chef doesn't have a gizmo to help you with that?"

"Just grow up, Beth, and go help Mama. Enjoy your personal day."

She hung up on me. Everything with Leslie had always been a fight. That was the Hyde in her, Mama's side. Leslie helped Mama set out bulbs. Leslie set tables and baked casseroles. If you needed a flower arrangement, Leslie was your girl. We could admire her contributions to no end. But the thankless job of pruning back Mama's garden always fell to me. What Leslie couldn't understand was that they were hallowed ground. They were the altars of Mama, and I couldn't get there fast enough today.

The farmhouse looked like a starched, white apron squatting on the green hillside, and I wanted to crawl underneath it and hide. But first, I went around to the shed out back to get Mama's pruning shears and a pair of her old gloves. I needed to work up the nerve to go inside. I'd never been any good at keeping things from Mama. If I meant to make it through this day, I was going to have to keep my head down. All I wanted was to clear those flower beds. In a few months, they'd spring back to life. Whatever else came and went, you could count on it, if you were willing to do the hard work. Today, I needed to believe that was still true.

I opened and shut the heavy shears. All I knew for sure anymore was that I was ready to lop something off.

The smell of coffee and bacon and cinnamon toast hit me when I walked in the kitchen. Mama wasn't a hugger in general, but whenever I walked in that house, I inhaled down to my toes, and it was the best kind of comfort.

"Why doesn't my house ever smell like this," I asked, "even when I make the same thing?" I went right to the cabinet for a mug and a dish.

"Cause it's your Mama's house," she said, the secret pleasure of it showing around the edges of her smile. She was already putting on a roast for supper. "I'm surprised you could find it through that snarling mess of a yard. Your daddy has lost his mind with those rose bushes."

She looked like a smaller version of herself to me, and I watched her, a little stunned I hadn't noticed before how she was aging. Her white hair swept back off her forehead, thick and wayward, like she'd just come through a stiff wind. She was wearing a god-awful red and blue cotton pants set, another one Leslie must have gotten her, wrinkled from a morning napping in the recliner.

The time was, she'd kept herself and everything in this house so neat we had trouble finding things. I looked at the place now and wondered if she'd just given up or if she didn't care anymore. Leslie said she was doing it to get a rise out of Daddy, but as far as I could tell, he didn't seem to notice, so long as he could find his paper and the remote.

"Where's Daddy?" I asked.

"Commissioner's meeting. You know he can't sit still."

I gnawed on my toast. I was anxious to get to work. "If there's not a job to be done, he'll make one."

We all knew Daddy wouldn't be good at retirement. He was a born mediator, and now that his kids were grown and his in-laws had passed away, he'd gone outside the family for his cheap thrills. But really, we were circling the wagons around Mama. He wanted to be home for her.

That's when he'd started with the knock out roses. There were a dozen or so the first year, but now they lined the drive and sprang from every formerly bare spot on the property so the place reminded me of Sleeping Beauty's castle where the thorny bushes were about to take over. He proudly made the rounds like a horticultural General, Sevin Dust in hand, and the roses were abundant.

Mama had nothing good to say about them. "He thinks he's the Atticus Finch of north Georgia, fighting for justice and city water for the poor county folk. Everybody knows he wants it for his roses."

I laughed. "Has to think he's in charge. Same as Leslie."

"Well, you don't have to listen to her," Mama said, even though we both knew Leslie was not so easily dismissed. "Why are you taking off work, just to come out here?"

I shrugged. "It's a teacher work day."

She was sneaky, cool as a cucumber, but I knew Mama was looking for signs I was lying. "It's Wednesday. Aren't those things usually at the first or the last of the week?"

"Yeah, well, I told Leslie I took a personal day, and that didn't fly, either. Call it what you want. I'm here to behead your gardens."

Mama looked at me sideways, but she was too glad to have me at the house to make a stink. "Fine, if that's what you say. But you ought to find something better to do with your time off than come babysit me. I can manage. Or your daddy can help me. It's still hot as Hades out there, anyway."

I sipped my coffee and considered the work ahead. "I need to dig today," I said. "That's all."

The morning heat was already pressing down when I pulled a chair around back for Mama and got down to business. She was still trying to talk me into waiting for a cooler weekend.

"It'll be cold soon enough," I said. "You'd better enjoy the heat while it lasts."

Mama's old garden gloves fit snug and stiff on my fingers. If you didn't look close, you might think the hands inside of them were hers. Mama sat barefooted in her chair in the shade with her *Guideposts.* Occasionally, she'd read me a line or two to get my response. Sometimes, I'd look at her and think she might be praying. The morning crept toward noon, and the heat bugs droned in the Johnson grass, but I had one bed nearly cleaned up and mulched for first frost.

"I guess Leslie thinks I'm one foot in the nursing home, lately," Mama said, watching me work on the second bed. "I told her she'd better keep a bedroom ready for the day me and Daddy decide to come move in with her."

We laughed because Mama was just messing with Leslie, but I worried. "You're going to give her an ulcer."

"She's good with the hard stuff," she said. "You remember that little guinea pig? She sat out here all day long, holding that thing 'til it died."

Mama was right, of course. And I did remember.

"She may drive us crazy, but Leslie's the one you want in a fight," Mama said.

"It's a good thing, because that's about the only way I get her."

I grunted, cutting through thick stalks and pulling out the dead leaves of the daylilies. While I taught school and kept a house with Cooper, I was jealous of the way Leslie had been making up for lost time with Mama, meeting needs, cooking dinners, carting her to town and back while they shared mothering tips.

"I don't know what you do to this stuff," I grumbled. "It's like a jungle out here. You'd think the deer would eat some of it up."

"Don't blame me. Talk to your daddy."

"Why? Is he peeing on the foxgloves?"

"Hell if I know. I wouldn't put it past him. That man is obsessed." Mama scowled at the bushes and shook her head. "He's put in a new bush every time I turn around. I told him, he's a politician. People are going to think he's burying bodies up here. But he's dug so many holes it's a wonder the entire hill doesn't just give way. We're living on a mountain of chicken shit."

"Aren't we all?"

"Granny would have lost her mind. She always said the smell of roses made her think of the funeral home."

Then, there it was. "It takes a lot of manure to have a garden worth growing," I muttered, Granny's favorite thing to say whenever we'd complained. I was thirty-two years old, a fifth grade teacher, and still I didn't know if she'd meant life was the manure, or if we were. Later, when Mama said it, I didn't know if she'd meant to encourage us or tell us to suck it up. Honestly, it worried me. If I couldn't figure out something as simple as a garden analogy, what else might I be missing?

I considered this Mama-mystery for the thousandth time while I attacked the last stalks in that bed, scalping them to the ground. The second bed was almost cleared. One more, and summer would be put to rest.

"Some days," Mama said, "when I sit out here, I swear I can just hear her talking to me."

"Mama, Granny's been dead three years. I doubt she's worried about Daddy's roses."

She shrugged and looked down the hillside to where my grandparent's house sat empty. "I guess she still whispers in my ear."

"Well, maybe you shouldn't listen to her."

Mama laughed out loud at this. "Honey," she said with a pleading kind of humor. "You are misunderstanding."

"Well then, make me understand." There were so many things I needed her to explain that I didn't know where to begin. "Life's just full of crap, and we're supposed to be glad about it?" I sat back on my heels, trying to clear my head. I must have been getting dehydrated. "Or is it that people are full of crap, and there's no use trying to change them? Just accept it. That's what Granny always did. She wanted us to act like everything was fine, all the time. Especially when it wasn't."

"I didn't mean to light your fire, Beth," Mama said.

"I just think sometimes you should be able to complain. You should be honest when something is hard. If you were, maybe Granny wouldn't be haunting you now."

"Maybe you know everything, Beth." Mama's tone said I had things left to learn, like maybe daughters invite their Mamas to haunt them, whisper in their dreams, come to them in the scent of their pot roasts and the sharp tongues of their children. One day my daughter would teach me.

All of a sudden, the heat on the back of my neck made me sick. I stood too quickly. The blood rushed to my head. It was too hot to be out there. But all I could think was if I had to pass down the gifts of my grandmother today, what would come back with the turn of the earth, and what would be consumed and forgotten? Did any of it matter, how we sweetened our tea or bounced our babies or planted our summer squash?

"What's got into you?" Mama asked. "Are you and Cooper fighting? Is this about moving off from here?"

"Me and Cooper don't fight. You know that. People have to talk to fight. And you're not supposed to know anything about moving yet. I told him I hadn't said anything about it. Besides, it might not happen."

Cooper wasn't afraid of a place where his accent would instantly lower his IQ, and shortening was a specialty item. This move was something we'd kept to ourselves, mostly because it was going to send my family into a tail spin. But Cooper and I dreamed of rugged mountains, picturesque towns with wineries and cold streams, and the Pacific Ocean.

Today, however, I was grateful he was gone so I wouldn't have to look him in the eye. In a blink, he'd know while he'd been out rustling up a living, something inside me had gone wrong with our dream. He'd hide his disappointment and fear and want to make everything better. If Cooper was right here, right now, he couldn't do a thing to help me.

Before I knew it, so much honesty brought up my breakfast, all over the nearest bunch of Daddy's rose bushes.

"Well, that's pretty," Mama said, smiling at the mess dripping from the bright pink blossoms as she came to where I stood and lifted the hot weight of my ponytail off my neck. "I told you it wasn't a good day to be out here. Now, let's cool you down." Calm down my hot head is what she meant.

Inside, Mama put mint tea in front of me like she'd done when I was a little girl and my temper would get the better of me. I wanted to bury my face against her chest and let her take the burden of my fear, but instead I drank my tea and tried not to cry. What she didn't know couldn't hurt her.

The aroma of the pot roast was thick and rich, and my stomach clenched and twitched again. She shuffled to the laundry room to bring a mountain of clean towels to the table. She was never still, only slower. I watched her begin to fold and stack them before I grabbed one. I knew the bones of her wrists, the curve of her neck, the familiar movement of her routines. I could remember sitting at this table as she taught me to fold laundry. Back then I'd been proud of my stack of washcloths. Now, watching our work pile up fast and predictable, I wanted Mama eternally here with her stack of towels. How ridiculous I was, a grown girl going through my life expecting to be doing this for always, learning her ways.

She seemed convinced I was feeling better when she said, "If I'd known you were coming, I'd have made plans to be home for the rest of the day," like she'd read my thoughts. "I'm leading a session in about an hour over at New Hope."

New Hope was the counseling center where she volunteered; Mama's new mission in life was working with these women who'd lost their kids to the court while they battled addictions and abuse and desperation.

"You have to do that today?"

"I'm not the one throwing up my Eggos," she said, lifting her eyebrows so she looked just like Granny when she'd drawn hers on too high. "If you could finish this up for me, that'd be a big help, Beth. That heat's not going to let up. You can come back early tomorrow," she said, solving all problems.

Just come home where you belong, she was saying. But I didn't belong here anymore. I belonged home with my husband, or at least I should be there when he got back. And it bothered me how this house had changed without my noticing. As bad as I hated it, I had to admit I wasn't a child anymore, and hiding out in my Mama's house couldn't be the answer to everything. All I could do was fold a few whites, finish the flower beds, and face my Jonah day alone.

"I can't come back tomorrow, just because it's hot today. I have an appointment in the morning," I said a little too sharply. "And Cooper's coming home Saturday. This is the only day I have to get those beds done."

I knew I sounded hateful. But she was leaving when I needed her, even if she didn't know it. She was going to strangers while I was left here with the way she'd made me.

"Well, you do what you're gonna do. But you can put some more water in the roast. Learn something so you can feed Cooper's offspring right."

Oh, shit fire. She thought I was pregnant. "Whose fault is it I only know three recipes?" I said. "Cooper won't starve so long as he can survive on biscuits, banana pudding and turkey dressing."

I wished she'd stay and open her cookbooks and spend days in the kitchen with me, telling me everything she'd never told me before. I wanted to look at baby pictures and hear the stories of how Leslie and I were born. I wanted to know why she'd married so young and what she'd dreamed about as a girl. I needed her to show me again how to lay out a pattern and how to find four-leaf clovers on the first try. But I was trying to throw her off the grandbaby scent, so I was being ugly. It was so hard to hide from Mama. I'd thought coming here would make me brave, clear my head, help me make sense of what I was about to do. Instead, everywhere I looked I saw more I stood to lose. And there was Mama, watching me, like I was an egg timer that should have gone off. I felt the disappointment for both of us.

Regardless what she thought, she didn't ask. Mama was smart enough to know that wasn't how you got the real answers. And then she noticed the clock. "My stars! I've got to get cleaned up or I'm going to be later than usual. Takes me ten minutes just to find where I've left my boob."

My heart shrank to a hard little pit in my chest. I swallowed the terrible memories of two years ago when the world had almost ended. "You should just keep it in the car," I said. I made a joke, Lord help me. "Hang it from the rearview."

I rinsed my glass at the sink and didn't look at her. We'd talked about Leslie, roses and ghosts, but we'd never talked about the cancer. It was the poison Mama swallowed with a quiet smile while the rest of us watched in horror. She gave us her legacy; she gave those girls her pain.

She left me there a few minutes later. There were two flower beds left to clear. They'd take me the rest of the afternoon. But I didn't think that would be long enough.

During the heat of the day, I decided to eat a sandwich and wait for the sun to drop lower. The house was empty, and I ended up on the living room floor, surrounded by a hundred little slips of paper and wrappings and box tops, all the handwritten and collected recipes that Mama had saved over the years so she could make cookbooks for us girls. Some of them had been handed down for generations, food that had graced the tables of our family through Civil War and World War, Great Depression and Baby Booms. Talking to Leslie had made me remember them.

I was supposed to have divided them and made three books, one for me, Leslie, and her little girl, Kayla, who wanted to give them out on Mother's Day. But I'd forgotten. Now every recipe seemed precious. I read each one and stacked them on my lap until they covered me with Mama's secrets, and I fell asleep under their sweet weight.

When I woke up, the sun was already dropping into late afternoon, and the recipes were only a small stack of scribbled notes that would have to go back in a box.

By the time Daddy came home, the roast was done, and I was back outside, the second garden finished. I had the hose out, rinsing my breakfast off the roses, and I'd had time to really study those bushes.

"Daddy, if you keep on planting these things, nobody's going to be able to get up the drive."

He wasn't worried. His Buick could plough a hole through the wall of China. He chuckled as he walked toward me like Humpty Dumpty in slacks and loafers, a southern gentleman. The freckled dome of his head was pink in the evening light.

"When you get to be an old, retired man you'll do crazy things, too," he said. He led me over to the swing in the side yard. We looked across the rolling hills, down to my grandparents' house and over the blue, hazy ridge. Daddy pushed the swing with a steady rhythm I adapted to easily. "Your sister called."

"I'm on family probation, I know. I can never do the right thing by her."

Daddy laughed. "Ah, I wouldn't worry too much about it. She gets past things fast." He was a genius at choosing his battles, the mark of a great politician. He slipped me a peppermint from his shirt pocket and folded his arms across his belly.

"I put those first bushes in when your mama was sick," he said. "I did pretty good with them. They don't ask for much, just what they need, and then you've got to leave them alone. Like a woman." He squinted at me in the sun. "I couldn't keep up with gardens such as your Mama's, going every which way."

"She can't either, now."

"Well, you know she's always liked to be in the yard. Now I think she does it more to get you out here."

"Here I am," I said. "Where's she?"

"Where she's always been. Up in somebody's face, telling them to wipe their nose and get on with it. Wouldn't change her for the world." Daddy put his arm around me and squeezed my shoulder.

"Everything's changing. I wish I knew why sometimes this family seems like the twilight zone."

"This house is built on an old Indian burial ground," he teased, another of Granny's famous claims, being half Cherokee, and therefore a survivor of great suffering. "We can't be held responsible for a single thing that goes on here, or didn't anybody ever tell you?"

"Be careful what you wish for. Mama says Granny's complaining about you."

"Still her favorite son-in-law, even from the happy hunting grounds. Meanest old squaw I ever knew," Daddy exclaimed. No love lost there. "Cooper getting home soon?"

"A few days."

Daddy stood and snapped a bloom from one of his bushes and handed it to me, another little token of affection. He lived in a house of women, and we puzzled him. He kissed the top of my head and told me he loved me. "You ought to stay and eat. Your mama's got a roast," he said, and left me to my work.

When Mama got back, we sat down to dinner. The roast tasted as much like hers as if she'd made it. Daddy complimented her, and she accepted. It didn't matter who'd put the water in the pot all afternoon. Some things would always be hers, I realized.

It was dusky dark and time to go when I wandered out back to survey my work. I'd done what I'd come for, and now I stood back to assess my mark on the world. It didn't amount to much.

Mama came out to stand beside me. "You did a good job of it," she said. "I never told anybody, but it depresses me, watching everything

78

fade off. That's why your daddy put in those roses."

"You knew why he was planting them?"

"Because, honey." Mama reached for my hand, then twined her fingers with mine. "That's what I told him to do. Because he was about to drive me crazy, hovering and looking worried, bringing me every little Confederate button or arrowhead he found, trying to come up with something to say to me when there was so much we couldn't talk about. Sometimes you've got to give the people you love a little help when they need to take care of you."

I'd been looking at those roses for years, and all I'd seen was Daddy's growing fear of losing Mama. Now I saw through Mama's eyes and realized that all along I'd been looking at love, the kind he just couldn't stop.

We stood there a moment, looking at the quiet earth. "Mama," I said, drawing a shaky breath, "it feels late."

She let go of me and bent down, heavy and cumbersome, but she reached her fingers to gently touch the soil like she might touch a dreaming child. "Well, right now we've got time," she said. "Sit down here with me." Instead of pushing herself back up, she sat on the ground in the dying light. I sat next to her. The crickets and cicadas burred softly on the warm air. The sweltering heat had hardly cooled down at all.

"I'm not pregnant," I said. Every month I'd been saying those words for two years, but they didn't get any easier. But tonight there were harder things that needed saying. "I'll tell you everything, but first can you tell me something?"

"Like what?"

"Do you believe what you say about the garden? I know what you mean, I think. That hard times make you stronger. But do you believe it?"

"No," Mama said simply. I looked at the outline of her face, confused.

"Then why do you say it?"

Mama just watched me with those Granny eyebrows. I wondered if she was hearing her mama now. "I heard what you said before about Granny and about being honest," Mama said. "So here it is. I'm giving you the secret to life. Will that make you feel better?"

I nodded, my head aching from a long awful day of holding back.

"Beth," Mama said. "We're all afraid we're full of shit. And the only lucky folks are the ones who realize that's a good thing."

"Mama."

"Now listen, that's the truth. We have inside us everything we need to grow, to survive, to be what we were intended. I had this same talk with Granny when your daddy and I moved into this place. Who do you think put these perennial beds in with me? She told me if I was going to amount to any kind of woman, or be a good wife or a mama, I'd have to love the manure as much as the blooms. And if I was smart, I'd put on my hip boots and start shoveling."

"And you've been digging ever since."

"Leslie's the one you want in a fight. But baby, you're the one that gets in with me and digs my beds."

Tears filled my eyes. I'd had it wrong in every way. Granny had been saying it just the way I thought. We were the manure. But we were the garden, too. Mama's love could embrace both. Her sacrifices protected and nurtured us, but she had faith that something of ourselves was completely innate and stronger than what she'd given us. She believed it of herself, or she'd never have survived to see this fall. And I realized that's what she was asking of me and Leslie now that we were grown. To find faith in ourselves.

I shook my head, exhausted and heartsick, annoyed I'd spent so much energy avoiding this moment, terrified to believe I could have half the strength she'd shown me.

Mama leaned back and closed her eyes, swatting at a mosquito. She bumped her shoulder against mine.

"I don't know how to tell Cooper what I need," I admitted.

"Well, God in heaven, don't tell him roses."

We both laughed until I began to cry, and the tension in the evening air broke into a thousand little pieces, flitting around us like fireflies.

I dug my hands into the soft, cool dirt and held on. "Yesterday morning," I admitted, "I found a lump."

Cooper couldn't plant rose bushes for me, but Mama was right. Given the opportunity, he knew the words I needed, even over the phone. "You are your mama's daughter. Whatever it is, it doesn't stand a chance."

I loved him for reminding me I was meaner than the average woman.

The doctor's office was beautifully decorated in tranquil colors with a pitcher of cool, cucumber water like we were waiting on a spa treatment. Mama and I settled on one of the sofas. To my surprise,

Leslie was already there with a pinched look about her mouth. She'd filled out most of my paperwork. Now we sat together in the quiet moments waiting for the nurse to take me back.

"I cleared the beds," I said to Leslie. "But Mama made me leave the manure for you."

She sniffed, but didn't put up a fight. It meant the world to me that she was there.

I looked around the room at the others, their faces blank and eyes worried. But I saw rose bushes. I saw the perennial beds, resting for a new season, preparing for spring. Whatever had grown in us, it could not compare with what would grow from us. I wished I could say that to each of them. I hoped their mothers came to whisper faith in their ears.

When the nurse called my name, Leslie picked up my purse. "Before we go back there, I want something clear," she announced. I thought she might slap the nurse, and I stepped between them. "I hate the damn Pampered Chef."

We stared at one another for a brief moment before the rest of the women began to snicker. We were in it together, me and so many mothers and daughters, armed with patchwork quilts, Sunday hymns and strings of pearls.

I took her hand. It was that simple. "I love you, too," I said. We stepped through the door together.

Whatever waited for us beyond this point, I knew now what I'd really been looking for in that dirt: the secret to life, what survives. I would let the people who loved me care for me, and I would measure my life by the love I felt for Cooper and Mama, Leslie and Daddy, the children I taught and the flowers I planted. I understood the legacy of my mother was finally my own. We were the stories about babies that lived through the night, crops that came through droughts, mason jars full of moonshine and the secret to sawmill gravy. We were the garden that came back every spring. Women who knew the value of a good pair of hip boots.

Bedeviled Eggs

Jane Forest

Lately, when I go to a covered dish supper or the church potlucks, I bring the same thing. Potato salad. It's easy. Even someone like me, who can't cook, can do an unexciting, basic potato salad. Mine has lots of hard boiled egg and real bacon crumbles, a spoon or two of pickle relish and mustard, along with finely diced potatoes. It usually disappears, all but a few yellow smears in my bowl, which, as you'll all agree, is much better than bringing home a dish that's hardly been touched.

If they only knew how ashamed I feel inside when I bring out yet another bowl of potato salad. It means I've miserably failed again. But that was my secret. Nobody knew but me. And now, because of one little lie I told, I'm in an awful fix.

It all started with my grandmother, and her sterling silver deviled egg tray. It's a thing of pure beauty, that egg platter. Twenty-four precisely etched hollow scoop-shapes, arranged in a petal pattern, radiating out from a filigreed circle that's meant to be the center of a sunflower. Swooping handles on either side, made to look like silvery sunflower leaves. Best of all, the gleaming silver cover, with attached little hooks that cunningly rotate around two silver ladybugs poking up from the bottom of the tray to hold the lid down.

Even as a little girl, I remembered loving the sound the family would make when it was ceremonially presented at holidays. Grandma made a yearly production of it. She'd wait till the table was loaded with every dish imaginable, from every other woman there, then as we were about to join hands and say the blessing, she'd gasp, as if she'd forgotten.

"Oh! The deviled eggs are still in the refrigerator. Wait. Don't start without me."

Then she'd fluster and flap the front of her apron, and scurry to the kitchen while the rest of the family smiled knowingly, as pleased as she was to take part in this little family ritual. The toddlers would be stuffed into their highchairs and bibs attached, the middlin' ones went back to arguing about who had to sit next to who at the kiddie card tables, then suddenly Grandma'd be back, standing in the door frame between the kitchen and dining room, with the gleaming sunflower egg tray.

For a second, we'd all get quiet. Then that sound . . . not a gasp, quite, but a thick ooooooh, as we all inhaled in unison, so we'd have enough breath to awww, and compliment Grandma on how stunning and lovely it was.

Next, the hustle and bustle as dishes got shifted to the right and left to make room on the table for the egg tray. We had every side dish you could think of at these family gatherings: baked beans, green bean casserole, and three bean salads. Carrots swimming in brown-sugar glaze. Corn on the cob. Corn off the cob. Sweet potatoes with mini-marshmallow topping. Pasta salads. Jelled salads. Potato salads with and without mustard or celery or onion, depending on which Aunt had brought them. Cornbread. Biscuits.

Uncle Rick would always grab for his wife's rolls, and claim that they could just sit on HIS plate, since he was planning on eating them all anyway. Uncle Mike would snatch a roll from the basket, determined to get one before Rick ate them all. Aunt Betty would rescue her rolls from her husband, and Aunt Carol would bop her husband Mike on the head for his lack of manners, and everyone would laugh.

When order was restored and space was cleared, the covered platter would be ensconced in a position of honor. Grandma would select two of us middle-sized girls to untwist the hooks from around the ladybugs, then the oldest boy would be asked to lift the lid. More ooohs and ahhhs as we all peered at the twenty-four perfect deviled eggs, to see how Grandma had decorated them this year. Finally, after more ooohs and ahhhs, we'd all join hands to pray, then us kids would bring our plates to the 'big' table for our folks to serve us, and the meal could begin.

Growing up, I watched carefully. Grandma'd told me that someday, the egg tray would belong to my mother, and eventually, it'd be mine, to pass on to my oldest daughter. So at the Fourth of July picnic, when the eggs were uncovered to reveal red paprika and tiny red pimento stars on top of the fluffy egg-filling, I studied and remembered. Christmas, when each egg had a round of green olive, and the sunflower center sported a wreath of holly and a red bow, I memorized the layout. Then Easter Sunday each half-egg was decorated with a miniature cross made of slivers of green onion, I watched and absorbed it all. And as I helped Grandma polish her silver before each holiday, I took extra effort with a Q-tip to get into the veins and crevices on the handle-leaves and the intricate filigree. It was beautiful, and it was going to be mine someday.

I didn't understand at the time, of course, that for Mom to get the egg platter, it meant Grandma would be gone. That took some of the joy out of it. And I certainly wasn't expecting the breast cancer that would steal Mom away from me early, and put the egg plate in my hands well before I turned thirty. For several years, I couldn't even bear to look at it. Maybe if I hadn't craved that silly platter so much, Grandma and Mom would still be here.

Even after I finished college, married my husband, Tom, and grew a couple of rugrats of my own, the egg tray stayed hidden in my attic. None of the family mentioned it at our gatherings, and nobody brought deviled eggs, either. I think they knew how I felt.

Then, one late spring day, as I wondered and fussed over what to bring to my son Jimmy's kindergarten picnic, my daughter Amy, who'd just turned eight, suggested we take deviled eggs.

"Brownies again?" I pretended I hadn't heard her as I looked in the cabinet. "Brownies are simple." I don't cook much, but I can mix up some brownies, like I usually do.

"C'mon, Mom," she wheedled. "Everybody likes eggs, even little kids. And they're easy. I helped Kim and her mom make them last time I spent the night there."

"I'll think about it," I replied.

She knew what that meant. There was room for her to keep arguing. There was hope. She ran to the refrigerator, skidding the last yard in her sock feet on the slick tile.

"One of these days, you're going to fall down and . . ." I started, but she finished the sentence with me, ". . . bust my head open, sliding on the tile."

She rolled her eyes at me and opened the fridge. "Look, we already have eggs, a whole dozen, plus three in this old carton. And a jar of pickle relish too. We put pickles in, when we mashed up the yellow stuff at Kim's house."

I joined her at the refrigerator, resisting the urge to do a little sock-foot skidding of my own. I really WOULD fall and bust my head open. Hmm. We always had a jar of mayonnaise. And for an audience of picky-eater five-year-olds, it'd probably be better not to worry with fancy toppings. What else went in deviled eggs? I realized then it'd always been Grandma and Mom who had made the eggs, never me. The only thing I ever did with eggs was add them to brownies, or scramble them for breakfast. I really didn't cook much. But how difficult could it be? Simply boil 'em, peel 'em, cut them in half, mash up the yolks with other stuff . . . spoon it back in.

I raised my eyebrows at Amy, who was hopping up and down in excitement beside me. "If we make deviled eggs, you're going to help? Even if I give you a really tough job to do?"

"Yes, yes, yes, YES!" she squealed, as she spun and slithered in a sock-enhanced dance move and pumped her fist.

Then her eight-year-old brain started getting suspicious, despite being ecstatic to get her way. The dance slowed, as she tilted her head to look at me. I grinned. It was fun to watch her grow mentally—even a year ago, she wouldn't have caught on to the "really tough" part of my sentence so quickly.

"Wait. Wait a minute, Mom. What's the tough part? What do I have to do? Is it something gross?"

"Nope, not gross. First, you'll have to do a little treasure hunting in the attic. I need a blue box, about this big." I showed her with my hands. "Can you find it and carry it down here to me?"

She nodded and skipped off down the hall toward the narrow attic staircase. I pulled open the fridge again and got out the eggs, then a big saucepan from under the stove. I'd better start hard-boiling the eggs. I twisted the left tap on the faucet full force. If I started with the water hot, I'd learned when making tea, it'd boil faster. Pretty soon, all twelve eggs were in the water, the burner on high, and little bubbles forming on the bottom of the pan.

I also got out the bag of potatoes, selecting a few to put in the oven to bake for supper. Baked potatoes, with some frozen chicken strips, and maybe some canned green beans . . . that was my kind of cooking.

Amy called from the top of the attic steps. "Mommmm—come look. This one, Mom?"

"Yep, that's it." I answered, sticking my head around the corner to check. "Bring it to the kitchen table."

I got a damp paper towel and wiped a thick layer of dust off, suddenly blinking back tears as I saw my grandmother's familiar handwriting on the box. How could I have not shared this part of my heritage with my daughter? I resolved right then and there to bring back the family tradition of the deviled egg platter. Slowly, I untied the string that held the box closed and lifted the lid.

"Ewww, what's that?" Ever fastidious, Amy backed up a step. The egg tray was nestled safely in tissue paper, but the years of neglect had tarnished the once gleaming silver.

"That's the tough part, my sock-footed friend," I teased Amy. "This is a tray to hold twenty-four deviled eggs. It belonged to my mother, and before that, to her mother, your great grandmother, and someday, it will belong to you."

"We're going to put the eggs in that? But it's all black and nasty."

I got the plastic tub of silver polish and a soft cloth from under the sink, noticing, as I passed the stove, that the eggs had started boiling merrily. How long did it take eggs to hard boil, anyway? Three minutes? No, that was too short. Five? That was soft boiled, wasn't it? Ten, maybe? Well, they weren't done, yet, for sure. I moved back to the table.

"Watch this." Dabbing up a smear of the fragrant polish, I took a swipe and a couple of hard rubs in one tarnished egg-shaped hollow.

"Ohhhhhh," exclaimed Amy. "Underneath, it's shiny, like your jewelry, the bracelet with the turquoise."

"Exactly." I replied. "See, when you rub off the black, it's real silver, shaped like a sunflower, with little ladybugs on the . . ."

A loud cracking noise came from the boiling water on the stove behind us. We both turned to look. Another loud pop. Amy pulled the stepstool over to the stove so she could see.

"Gross, some of the white stuff in the eggs is coming out in the water!" She curled her top lip. "I don't think it's supposed to do that. When Kim's mom made HER eggs, it didn't."

I resolved right then and there that I wouldn't be calling Kim's mom for advice. Another two eggs snapped loudly, one right after the other. I hurriedly turned the burner off under the pan, grabbed my hot mitts and removed it from the heat, then looked at Amy. "Maybe we'd better not plan deviled eggs for the picnic. It'll take a long time to polish the egg tray up, first. You might not get done."

She settled down at the table with the silver polish, busily rubbing away. I looked at the mess in my saucepan. Well, some of them looked okay. But even if eight eggs were good, and I cut them in half, there'd only be sixteen out of the twenty-four egg spaces filled in the tray. I couldn't take the platter with that many empty egg-shaped hollows. And I only had three more eggs in the fridge. Oh, well, I wouldn't really take a silver egg tray to a kindergarten event anyway, right?

Thinking furiously, I ran cold water in the pan. All these hard boiled eggs, but not enough. What could I make? Egg salad sandwiches? No, that sounded more like a luncheon, not something for a pack of kindergartners. Looking at the stuff sitting out for the eggs, I nibbled at the problem like a dog with a flea on his butt. Pickle relish. Mayo. Eggs. Potatoes. No, the potatoes were for supper. Ah, but that's it. Potato salad. It looked like picnic food, and if I didn't put onion and celery in it, five year olds would probably eat it. MY five year old would, anyway.

That's how it all started. Me and potato salad, I mean. Amy never did finish polishing the egg platter—like most kids, she had a short attention span when the work stopped being fun. But after both kids were in bed that night, I stayed up and shined every nook and cranny in the egg tray. I was bound and determined to learn how to make twenty-four perfect deviled eggs and bring back the family ritual of the silver egg platter. And I was going to do it before Amy got too old to think of it as a long-established family tradition.

That was almost two months ago. I still haven't been able to make a full set of twenty-four deviled eggs, though it's not for lack of trying. Something always goes wrong.

Now I keep trying to sidle up to the folks who've brought deviled eggs to various functions and unobtrusively ferret out some hints, but what they suggest never works for me.

Of course, I went to the library first, for some research. Do you know there's not a book on how to boil eggs? There are books with recipes for soups, breads, vegetables, pastries, and desserts, but nothing for a beginning cook on eggs. But while I was at the library, I bumped into Aunt Carol. I didn't want all of the family to know that I can't boil an egg, but I thought it'd be safe to ask her. She said she starts with a pan of cold water, adds an ice cube, then her eggs, and brings them to a slow boil, on medium heat, to avoid cracked eggs. But her nosy friend Laura overheard us talking eggs, and claims the long slow boil is what makes the greenish tint to the yolks. She says *she* puts a good sprinkle of salt in the water, and *that* keeps them from cracking.

I went immediately to the grocery store after leaving the library, bought another dozen eggs, and went right home and tried it. Both of those hints, together. Cold water, ice cube, good sprinkle of salt. Slow to boil, instead of putting the burner on high. Ten were fine, two popped. I made tuna with lots of egg in it for *my* lunch, using the two that popped.

When I tried to peel the rest of the eggs, four of them stuck to the shell so bad, they looked like a lunar landscape, pocked with craters. Those sad little nibbled-at eggs got chopped and made into potato salad. Luckily my husband Tom loves potato salad. I took the last six eggs, the ones that peeled nicely, and made twelve deviled eggs, just for practice, just for family.

The next day, I gave the kids each two leftover deviled egg-halves in their school lunches, and that's where I made my big mistake. And that's what made me tell the lie that got me in trouble.

It started because I ran into the school that afternoon to pick up the kids, instead of just driving around the loop, because I needed to chat with Ellen Keyes, who teaches sixth grade. She's in charge of the silver anniversary supper, at the church we attend. Jimmy and Amy were dashing around, in their usual set-free-from-school exuberance, thrilled to be in the "big kids" room. Ellen pulled out her list of committees to show me where she needed last-minute volunteers. I was aiming for the decorations committee, but it was full. Ellen dug in her tote for more sign-up sheets.

Jimmy was engrossed in watching the activity in the huge fish tank, but Amy brought her busybody, sociable little self over to lean on my shoulder. "What'cha doing, Mrs. Ellen?"

"Your Sunday School class is planning a skit for the celebration Sunday at church, right?" answered Ellen. "Your mom is helping me plan the other stuff for that day. A silver anniversary is a big event."

"Silver?" asked Amy. "Silver, like my mom's egg tray? Jimmy 'n' I had two deviled egg halves in our lunches today, and I traded one to Britney for some of her barbeque chips. They were good. Mom, can we go home now?"

"Go watch the fish tank with Jimmy," I responded. "Mrs. Ellen and I will finish quicker if we don't get interrupted, okay?" I turned her around and swatted her bottom to send her on her way faster.

"Ah, I do remember that sunflower tray," reminisced Ellen. "Your mom used to bring it to big functions at the church, and it was lovely. You know, that would make an attractive centerpiece for the appetizer table, and it fits right in with the silver theme the decoration committee's trying to do. Let me put you down to bring some deviled eggs, is that okay? We've still got a space left on the food committee. The eggs and maybe some cookies or brownies would be perfect, we need a few more desserts."

What else could I do but agree? I flat out lied and told her that I'd *love* to make some eggs and bring them in the silver tray. Now, I'm desperate. I'm on the food committee, they're planning on my eggs as a centerpiece, and I can't hard boil twenty-four pretty eggs to save my life! I had one place left to turn to. I knew it was the source for the best gossip, and the women who went there were like an extended family to me, but could I find the secret to deviled eggs there? Before Sunday's Silver Anniversary Dinner?

Friday morning, I called and made a totally unnecessary hair appointment at GoodCuts salon. Highlights and a trim might make me feel better about myself even if the eggs didn't turn out right. Deftly and somewhat nonchalantly I thought, I turned the conversation to eggs while I was getting shampooed. Ann Carter claimed, while she was combing me out, that it's all in the enamel pan she uses. Wendy Richards was listening as she rolled up Julia's perm, and she said she uses a Teflon non-stick pan to boil her eggs, and they turned out just fine. Nary a one would crack

Leaving the salon, I bumped into my Aunt Betty, who was coming in for her usual color touch-up, and asked her. She should know, she'd been cooking forever. She said I could use anything BUT an aluminum pan. But after twelve minutes at a simmer, she said, move them from the boiling water to ice water, to cool them quick, so they'd peel nicely . . . and not have that green tinge to the yolks.

Then Jennifer Baxter approached me as I unlocked my minivan.

"Old eggs." She whispered in my ear. "Use old eggs, not fresh. They'll peel better if the eggs aren't straight from the hen, I've heard." Then she nodded at me, got into her own car and drove off.

How had Jennifer heard about my egg difficulties so quickly? Did the whole town know by now? Mentally, I made a list of the people I'd talked to. Aunt Carol and Laura, Ann Carter and Wendy, Julia and Aunt Betty. Yup, word was out, and now it was probably going to be in the help wanted section of the newspaper, too. I beat my head on the steering wheel.

That afternoon, I picked up the kids at school, took them home, got them changed into their soccer uniforms, then dropped them off at practice. The assistant soccer coach, Valerie, slipped me a note as she passed me, jogging around the field with the kids:

Add a cup of vinegar to the cold water. Bring the eggs to a boil, then turn off heat. Cover the pan, and let the eggs sit in the hot water for 15

minutes. Eggs will be perfectly cooked.

On the way back home, I stopped at the grocery and picked up a bottle of vinegar and another dozen eggs, checking the expiration date carefully, getting the oldest ones available. The boy stocking the shelves gave me a funny look, but at this point, I didn't care one whit. As I waited in the checkout line, my husband's sister Rosemary drove her cart up behind me.

"Shake the eggs," she said, looking around to see if anyone was within earshot.

"What?" I replied, looking around a bit surreptitiously myself. I felt like I had been cast in a bad spy movie. I wanted to cover up the carton of eggs in my hand.

Rosemary moved closer and lowered her voice. "Before you put the eggs in the water to cook them, shake them real hard first, each egg. It'll help the yolk cook in the middle of the white, instead of close to the side."

"Thanks, Rosemary, I'll try that." I checked out and hurried to my van before I was approached by anyone else with egg advice.

When I got home, I shook all twelve eggs. I only dropped one. It shattered with such a satisfying sound on the tile floor that I was tempted to throw another one. And I absolutely hated to try to clean up slippery, slimy raw eggs on the tile. I ignored the splatter and stepped around it. Instead, I put four eggs in my little blue speckled enamel pan, and three more in the deep non-stick skillet I use when I make spaghetti. The last four, I put in my stainless steel soup pot. I put salt, cold water, and an ice cube in all three pans and started them to heating. On medium.

I sighed gustily and started picking up the eggshell from the mess on the floor. Ohhh, the nasty slipperiness of egg whites. Then I had an awful idea. But hey, nobody was home but me, who'd know? I tiptoed to the back door, put my fingers to my lips and whistled. Before I could even get my fingers out of my mouth, Rowdy was there, so full of tail-wagging enthusiasm that his butt was wagging too. I let him in and pointed to the egg on the tile. But from behind me, I heard first one, then another egg crack in the boiling water.

That's where Tom found me when he came in with Amy and Jimmy, sweaty from soccer practice. One wife, about to crack, surrounded by three pans of water, each with good eggs and one cracked egg, now soaking in ice water. One dog with a guilty grin, still gleefully licking the tile floor where the egg had smashed. Like Humpty Dumpty, I'd hit bottom. Only the family dog was happy.

Tom saw my red, tear-streaked face, and turned and herded the kids right back into the living room. I could hear him telling them to head upstairs, change out of their dirty uniforms, put the clothes in the hamper, take a shower, put their soccer gear away, start homework, feed the hamster—the same routine they followed every day. Then he joined me in the kitchen. I told him everything. The reason for all the egg salad sandwiches and bowl after bowl of potato salad he'd eaten the last month. The reasons he'd never seen the silver egg platter.

Together we peeled the eight good eggs and the three broken ones. Tom ran out to get pizza for supper . . . and another dozen eggs. After we fed ourselves and the kids, we settled in for a night of family egg-cooking.

I shook all of the eggs first, as Rosemary had suggested. This time, I hung on to them. The dog was disappointed. Tom showed me a trick that his mother had taught him . . . before he put the eggs in the water to boil, he took a pin and poked a small hole in the "fat" end of the egg. Amy filled the stainless steel pot at the sink, and Tom moved it to the stove. Jimmy added the ice cube to the water, after I told him Aunt Carol's suggestion. I carefully added all twelve eggs. Amy measured out a cup of vinegar. Jimmy poured the vinegar into the cold water in the pot as Coach Valerie had suggested. I added a shake of salt. Tom turned on the heat.

The eggs came to a boil. Amy set the timer, and we covered them and let the pan sit for fifteen minutes. Tom poured out the hot water and replaced it with cold. Jimmy was happy to add lots more ice cubes to cool the eggs down quickly.

When they were cool, Jimmy rolled the eggs on the table to crack the shells, then we all peeled them. Every single egg came out perfectly. After that, it was simple to cut them in half, remove the yolk, and make the stuffing. Amy measured the pickle relish. Jimmy mashed the yolks. Tom stirred in a little mayo. I spooned the filling into a baggie, then clipped a corner open, and squeezed it back in the eggs.

Together we packed the twenty-four prettiest egg halves you've ever seen into the silver egg tray. I guess it took a family, a village (and a darned good egg of a husband) to take the devil out of those eggs.

Not through My Window

Willis Baker

In my youth, serious crime didn't exist in the world as we knew it, at least not in our small, southern town. While bank robberies, rapes, and murders dominated the headlines of large cities, our small town paper focused on benign headlines such as, "Train Trestle Collapses," "Mayor Walks out of Budget Meetings," and "County Bank Celebrates 100th Anniversary."

Our most notorious criminals were a group of five to seven local drunks. While they couldn't afford the price of their booze, neither did they turn to crime, but rather bummed their nickels here and there, which was the price of a can of Sterno, or "canned heat," from which they strained the alcohol. Thus, they were known in the vernacular as "The Canned Heat Gang." They kept their sin out of the eyes of the public, with one exception—the trail of empty cans strewn along the bank beneath the river bridge.

The town's people went about their business, occupation, and personal lives feeling secure and safe. Therefore, whether it was early morning, afternoon, a balmy evening, or even late at night, Mother, a waitress at a downtown drugstore/restaurant, walked unescorted to our home located exactly one mile from the center of town.

An incident the summer I transitioned from elementary school to high school almost changed that, and it involved one of the "Canned Heat Gang." To use Mother's words, "The way he looks at me, I feel like my clothes are being peeled away, leaving me naked and invaded." The night the incident occurred was the first to challenge our family security.

Mom ran the home, Dad scheduled and organized the chores and maintenance. Liza, my paternal grandmother, served as the spiritual elder. She assured that our lives were governed by Christian morals and benevolence.

That particular summer included the mammoth chore of painting the exterior of the house. The west slope of the property added an additional four feet to the height of the wall, necessitating extension ladders to reach the soffit. Trepidation had already been introduced as a factor early in the project because Dad had determined that at age fourteen, I was old enough to do my part, including some moderately high ladder work. Mom disagreed, insisting that I had no business working on a twelve-foot ladder.

This type of disagreement was not uncommon in the household since Mom and Dad had given up three children to death at early ages, one at birth. Naturally, being the only survivor of four children, anything they saw as prospective danger to me raised the level of anxiety. But given more to reason than emotion, Dad saw to it that my life maintained at least some semblance of normalcy compared to that of the average fourteen-year-old boy. This event was such an occasion.

Dad and I had journeyed to the hardware store to purchase the several gallons of white, exterior house paint required for the job. As it was with small southern towns in those days, Main Street was busy with people tending to their daily lives, patronizing the local businesses that drove the town's economy. Leaving the hardware, we ran into Police Chief Joe Wilson. Joe was a homegrown boy Dad had known all his life. The two had no more than started their conversation than out of the store came one of the "Canned Heat Gang." Well known for what seemed to be the sole purpose of their lives, it was assumed the brown bag he carried bore the gang's alcohol 'fix' for the day.

That particular day, the lot of purchasing the 'heat' apparently had fallen on Burley Davis, who lived with his wife and three children in what was literally a two-room shack beside the tracks several blocks south of us. His son, Jerry, and I had played together since we were children. Still, merely the fact Burley lived in the neighborhood concerned Mother. On multiple occasions, she'd said, "On one of his drunken binges, he could walk up that railroad track and right in my back door." She had expressed a similar concern relative to her late evening walk home from work. "You mark it down that someday during that walk I'll encounter Burley Davis," she had said.

Although no woman had ever reported such an incident, Mother was concerned simply with being in his presence. "It's certainly not appreciation in his eyes that dresses down a woman."

Observing the sizable brown bag that Burley carried, Joe said, "He's hit up a lot of people to get enough together to buy that size bag of 'heat.'"

"And that's not even considering how many others they hit up for the cash to buy the 'light bread' to strain the stuff," Dad added.

"Never did understand that process," Joe replied as we watched Burley straggle up the sidewalk in the direction of the river bridge.

At the house, Dad decided we should start on opposite ends of the west wall and converge at the chimney. Unique to the house were two small windows high on the wall at each side of the chimney. They were so high that only a taller man could see out the windows from inside the living room.

By the time we had lunch, scraped away peeling paint, and puttied windowpanes, it was approaching mid-afternoon. By late afternoon, we had painted only to the bottoms of the two small windows high on the wall. Dad worked nights at the theater, and since it was getting late and we planned to start early the next morning, he decided to leave the ladders leaning against the exterior walls.

Typically in the summer, the post-supper evening activities entailed Granny studying her bible, Mother calling her sisters and my practicing piano. To close the evening I would watch TV or listen to records.

Shortly after 11:00 p.m. that evening, Mother was in the typical 'close down' mode, preparing the light snack for Dad's arrival home around 11:30 p.m. Her voice came from the kitchen. "Time to turn off the record player and get ready for bed."

I had all but fallen asleep on the living room sofa while listening to the 45-rpm record player that sat on a table against the west wall of the living room. I turned it off and again collapsed on the sofa. In the absence of the music, the loud rumble outside the window next to the chimney was unmistakable. Still half asleep, I really didn't think much about it until Mom hurried into the living room.

"What was that noise?" she asked.

I looked up to find a dishtowel firmly gripped in her hand and watched her upgrade the expression on her face from concern to alarm. Something was wrong.

Granny looked up from her Bible. "That rumble came from outside the window next to the fireplace."

Mom instantly left the room, returning quickly with the hand-hewn wooden stepper Grandpa had made for her. Being only five feet tall, even in her shoes, the stepper enabled her to reach the higher shelves of the cabinets that extended almost to the ceiling. Her sudden pull opening the window curtain validated her earlier fears. Staring at her through the windowpane was a face.

"My God, it's Burley Davis! Get the gun, Liza," mother ordered.

"Now Kathryn, you know how I feel about guns," Granny replied.

"I'll get it, Mom," I said, now wide awake, indeed shocked at seeing the face of Burley Davis glaring through the window.

"Son, don't be silly," Granny said. "The doors and windows are locked, so no one's going to get in this house."

Granny's words didn't seem to console Mom, who was now in full panic mode. "I knew this was going to happen. I knew it! I knew it! I knew it! What are we going to do?" She suddenly stopped her tirade and shouted, "Someone get the gun."

The words had hardly left her mouth when I heard the rumble of another sound, even above the pandemonium of the moment. While it was the simple sound of Dad's car pulling onto the gravel drive, it turned the feelings of a fearfully cold chill into a warm sense of assurance and deliverance. Rather than running to the bedroom for the gun, I ran to the front door to greet Dad.

"Don't you dare go out there," Mom commanded.

But I'd already unlocked the door and was running onto the porch. With my Dad's arrival, my bravery swelled, and I jumped off the porch to view the window. Burley Davis was still on the ladder, but not like I'd expected to find him. Apparently scared by Mom seeing him, he'd panicked and nearly fell. His overalls had caught on the ladder, all but ripping out the butt end. He tried to hold onto the ladder with one hand, while trying to recover his overalls with the other.

I laughed as I ran toward Dad. "You're never gonna believe what happened," I said, completely out of breath both from running and laughing.

Dad had exited the '51 Chevy truck, his green metal lunch box in his hand. "Hey. Slow down, Son. What's all the excitement about?"

"It's Burley Davis. On the ladder."

To Dad, the rapid rat-a-tat-tat, machinegun fire of my sentence, while intelligible, made no sense because every beat of my heart only infused my body with more adrenalin. "What about Burley Davis?"

I attempted to answer, but my lungs had been depleted of air sufficient to operate my vocal chords.

"Son, you're hyperventilating." He placed his lunch box on the hood of the truck, opened it, unfolded a brown paper bag, placed it over my nose and mouth and said, "Breathe into the bag until I tell you to stop."

While the human brain can act on adrenalin, it cannot 'think' on adrenalin, thus I didn't understand but did as I was told. After several seconds, Dad continued, "Now, calmly tell me about Burley Davis."

When my voice came to me, the volume was not from my lungs, but from the tension in my diaphragm. Even so, I'm sure the harried look in my eyes signaled the urgency of the situation even more than my voice.

Dad straightened his back and laughed as he calmly placed the bag back in the lunch box and closed it. He walked around the truck, opened the passenger door and the glove compartment, and pulled out the shiny, aluminum flashlight kept there for emergencies. After gracefully hopping over the three-foot brick retainer wall to the lower level of the yard, he turned on the flashlight, its revealing light gradually finding its way up the ladder at the left side of the chimney. Nearing the bottom of the window, sure enough, the light found Burley Davis, drunk out of his mind.

"Hello there," Burley stuttered, weaving back from the ladder, again almost losing his grip. "Not a bad evenin' at all outside is it?"

"Burley, I may be wrong, but for some reason, at this particular moment the weather somehow doesn't appear to be an appropriate topic of discussion. What do you think?" Dad asked.

By this time, although heavy with irony, the calm in Dad's voice had eased even my nerves, and I was anxious to learn where this conversation would go next.

Meanwhile, Granny had made her way onto the porch, but Mom hadn't followed.

"If my recollections are accurate, this is the second time that we've had an unsolicited visit from you. I recall that at the last visit, I let you walk down the steps of the back porch, but only after receiving a promise that this would never happen again. Am I right?"

"Well, seems like that would be correct," Burley said, leaning back, attempting to step down the ladder. But his foot slipped, and so did one hand, leaving him holding on with a single hand.

"Whoa, watch it there, Burley. You stay where you are. Failure to keep your promise from your other visit means that this time, though it's a ladder and not steps, you're not coming down the same way you went up."

As Dad leaned over, placing his hands on the foot of the ladder, Mom arrived on the porch. "No, Bill. Don't," she said, panic lacing her words. "Don't make him fall. He could die or worse."

I was unaware of the previous incident Dad had spoken of, which made me wonder what kind, and how many other criminal activities had gone on that I hadn't known about.

Momentarily, Dad abandoned his original intent, straightening his back, giving his full attention to Mom's request. "Myrtle, a breach of principle's involved here." He laughed before he continued. "Besides, you know you can't hurt a drunk, only damage his ego. And even that's doubtful because drunks have no shame."

Burley chimed in, almost belching his words. "She's right. A fall like this could hurt a fella."

One of Burley's feet slipped yet again, bringing a gasp from Mom, destroying any calm that might have begun to settle on the situation.

"Burley Davis, when it comes to my home, you've peeped in the wrong window, and for your last time. I'm jerking you off this ladder, and if that doesn't kill you, I might just shoot you." Dad again reached for the foot of the ladder.

Granny rejoined the conversation, her comment calm but poignant. "Son, this is not the Christian way to resolve this."

"Mom, I understand, but this is more than tom foolery. Even Jesus wouldn't stand for this. I should've put a stop to it the very first time it happened."

"Please, Bill, wait," Mom said, interrupting. "I called Helen, and she said Joe was on his way even as we spoke."

Now I knew why Mom had been delayed in following Granny onto the porch.

"Please," Mom pleaded, the tension in her voice drained like a deflated balloon.

Dad braced himself, giving a gutty growl as he picked up the foot of the ladder with Burly still swaying at its top. Dad had always been a reasonable man, leaving me surprised he'd ignored Mom's plea. More surprising was his having ignored Granny, whose wisdom he'd always recognized and heeded. By the same token, when Dad was convinced he was right about something, he rarely changed his mind.

"Whoa . . ." Burley called from the top of the ladder, trying to control its precarious sway.

Suddenly the ladder shifted, the scene resembling that of a circus act: a man on the ground supporting a ladder, another, whose comedic gyrations on the ladder tempted the dual threats of the unforgiving forces of both gravity and motion. To me, comedy became terror when Dad unexpectedly took two quick steps backward.

Mother turned her head, locking herself in Granny's arms. Granny's words were caught in her gasp, "God have mercy on him."

At that point everything seemed to go into slow motion: the creaking voice of the twisting, falling ladder, and Burley's vocalized fear synchronized with the wild flail of his arms as his body yielded to the gravity pulling him toward earth. While I couldn't see his eyes, I'm sure they were in the grips of a far greater fear than mine, witnessing what was to be the epic event in my young life. The ladder slapped the ground, followed by the splintering crackle of the wood, but most disconcerting was the slam of Burley's body.

While the sound could be described as a thud, it bore no resemblance to the sound of an inanimate object striking the earth. It was that unmistakable, sickening dull thump, when a human body with life and feelings encounters a cold, inanimate earth with no life and no feelings. The desperate, dry, grunting sound to regain the breath slammed from Burley's lungs was beyond frightful. But even more amazing was that he was obviously still alive.

"You've broken my back; I'm ruined forever," he said.

"I don't think so." Dad laughed. "Stand up Burley, or I'll jerk you to your feet with nothing but the hair of your head."

"I can't get up. It's my back. I think it's broke."

"Well, there's only one way to find out, Burley." Dad stepped across the ladder, grabbing the other man by the collar of his dirty, tattered shirt. "You're so filthy I hate to even touch you." Dad looked at me. "Son, this is no man. This is a coward, a sluggard, a drunk, a common peeping tom. His kind is the reason we know there's a hell to shun and a heaven to gain."

With his strong arms, Dad hauled Burley up and shook him as if he was no heavier than a fifty-pound sack of potatoes. "I ought to snap your neck, you weasel. I'm not a man to question God, but when I know a low-life like you exists and the demands required of the righteousness of God, I sometimes wonder about his reasoning in the creation of something like you."

With that, Dad turned Burley around and let him stand. Looking toward the porch, Dad said. "See, Myrtle? There's no broken back, no broken bones, just a drunken embarrassment to the human race."

I identified with the pain and agony of Burley's body, but even more, the ultimate insult to what little integrity the man had left. After all, he was a husband and father of three children, one of them a playmate and friend I'd known all my life.

Like mother, I too cried, but on the inside.

Dad began shoving Burley toward the ditch that marked our property line, kicking him in the seat of his ripped pants as he went, Burley barking like a dog with every kick.

Granny again entered the conversation, but as was her way, with limited words and in complete calm. "Son, don't be cruel to the man."

Dad hesitated, looking back over his shoulder. When moms spoke, or for that matter dads as well, we Southerners listened. She had stood through the entire commotion with her arms crossed, almost emotionless.

"That's enough," Mom said curtly. "The man's suffered the consequences of his deeds."

Dad let go of Burley's collar, and he collapsed in the ditch. "I should let Will get my gun and just shoot you right here. That would put you out of your misery and save the community any further embarrassment."

I finally garnered the courage to move close to the two men, looking down into Burley's face. It was at that moment the question rushed into my mind that, knowing Granny's absolute devotion to faith, mercy, and benevolence, why she hadn't objected to Dad's suggestion that he should just shoot him? That could only be for one reason. Just as Dad respected Granny's rebuke, she knew her son could never shoot anyone for anything other than self-defense.

Suddenly Dad again jerked Burley up by his arm.

"My arm . . . my arm . . ." Burley cried.

Dad kicked Burley in the seat of the pants one more time, turned him around and pointed a finger in his face. "It's a sad case when people like you exist who aren't worth killing, and worse, require the sympathy of a woman to save their sorry lives. I will make you a promise, Burley Davis, if you ever step foot on my property again, you'll be taking your life into your own hands. Understood?"

The approach of Chief Joe's police cruiser, without sirens or flashing lights, interrupted the scene. Only a slight skid of the tires in the graveled drive suggested any urgency. Fortunately, none of the neighbors had been awakened or noted anything out of order, which explained Chief Joe's restraint. He obviously did not want to raise any unnecessary alarm.

Once out of his car, Chief Joe passed the porch and tipped his hat, saying, "Miss Liza, Myrtle." He greeted me as well with a slap on the back. "Will."

"Evenin', Joe," Dad greeted.

"Evenin', Bill. My guess is what's gone on here tonight needs little explanation beyond what is visible?"

"That's right. Mr. Davis' unannounced visit scared the daylights out of my family. Will and I worked late this afternoon, and I didn't have time to put the ladders up. Don't ask me why our 'visitor' here would have chosen to climb a ladder when he could've just peeped in the windows on the porch."

Joe scooted his police cap back off his forehead as if that somehow helped him in resolving the dilemma of Burley's choice. "Well, when you have people determined to numb their mind and body with booze, and who have no concern for the pain and suffering it inflicts on their families and the community, don't go tryin' to reason their other decision-making processes. Sometimes my brain literally hurts just from trying to reason the mind of such people; it's a crazy world, Bill."

"Amen to that."

Joe looked around, his eyes examining the area. "Is there any other property damage?" His visual search stopped with the splintered ladder, and he laughed. "Other than the obvious, that is?"

"Not that I'm aware of," Dad replied.

Joe turned his attention to Granny and Mom, who had remained on the porch. "Any pain and suffering anyone can't recover from?"

Mom gave a non-verbal reply with a negative shake of her head. Granny simply said, "Sin's been committed and the sin recompensed."

Then Joe looked to Dad, who shook his head as well.

Lastly Joe addressed Burley. "Burley Davis, despite any crime you committed here, because of your own stupidity you're lucky to be alive. You would have probably not survived the fall had you been sober. At least that appears to be what happened. And, since Bill is apparently not pressing charges, luck has fallen on your side in both instances. Therefore, I would go gentle-like into what is left of the good night. Be thankful you can return to your family, and seal it with a personal promise to yourself to never repeat this kind of thing again."

"Yeah, yeah," Burley murmured as he staggered off.

We walked back to the porch in quiet. Joe said, "Well, I guess that concludes this ridiculous situation. Sorry you folks had to suffer this kind of thing, but then that's the reason we need people like me. You folks go to bed and get some rest. Tomorrow's a new day."

He bid us a good evening, again tipping his hat in respect to the two ladies present. Before he stepped into his cruiser and drove off, he paused, as if speaking to himself, and said, "Tomorrow will indeed be another day."

Inside the house the atmosphere was at the least, let us say, tense, not to mention the remaining unspent emotions. Silence reigned. Mom leaned back against the kitchen counter, a handkerchief in her hand, occasionally touching it to her face. The coffee pot broke the silence, percolating its dark brew into the clear glass dome that sat atop the shiny stainless steel pot. The sting in the tension abated like the coffee after spiking the cap of the percolator, then slowly draining down the glass dome.

Granny poured two cups of the hot coffee, handing one to Mom, the other to Dad. "A good cup of hot coffee can often serve for more than just drinkin' liquid."

For the first time since we'd entered the house, Mom and Dad's gaze locked on one another, obviously trying to read each other's thoughts. Mom broke the standoff, blotting her cheek with the handkerchief and looking away. Dad plopped down into a chair at the dining room table with a heavy sigh. Still, his eyes never left Mom whose head remained bowed.

"Bill, you know you don't have any sense when you're mad," Mom said.

The Great Depression had left Dad's memory scarred. Grandpa had been ill and unable to work the farm, thus Dad had worked doubly hard for what had left the family with little more than survival. The worst side of poverty is not the poverty, but the broken spirit it can leave its victim.

"Kathryn, don't be that way," Dad said, pulling me to his side, rustling my hair with his large hand. "I'm sorry you had to witness what you did tonight, son, but I'm also glad you did. Because sooner or later you will have to deal with the fact everything about this world is neither right nor good all the time."

He seemed to go inside himself for a moment, a forlorn expression gripping his face. Unexpectedly, he smiled, turned up his cup and swallowed the last of his coffee. "Whether we like it or not, there are bad people in this world, and things we can't afford to leave undone. Sometimes, we have to address reckless and irresponsible behavior such as that of Burley Davis."

"Joe could have jailed him for a while. That would have taught him a lesson," Mom countered.

A clawing sound came from the back door. Granny opened it, and Chubb, my champagne, miniature sheep dog entered.

"Where were you when we needed that bark of yours," I asked, rustling his coat that was so furry sometimes you couldn't tell the difference between his head and tail. That's when Dad came forth with one of his sayings that often gave real definition to things.

He laughed heartily. "Locking Burley Davis up in jail would be about as effective as makin' old Chubb here sleep in the bathroom on a cold winter night."

I laughed until Mom glared at me, but when I couldn't stop laughing, she could no longer remain stern and laughed as well. That seemed to put out the last spark of contention. We all met in the middle of the kitchen, and Dad folded us into his arms in a group hug. Even Chubb stood on his hind legs, trying to paw his way into the family huddle.

The final words of the evening were those of Granny as she did her duck-like waddle toward the hallway. "Lord, do help us to be Christian in these days of trial, tribulation, and turmoil."

Moments later the house was dark, and everyone was in bed. But sleep evaded me, my mind trying to digest all the things my eyes had witnessed, my heart had felt, and my ears had heard that evening. One thing was certain. For apparent and sensible reasons, Dad had told Burley Davis, "Not through my window, you don't."

I realized I had, indeed, been privileged to see through several windows that evening: one revealing a sinner needing forgiveness, another a criminal deserving both judgment and sentence, another a victim needing compassion, and last but not least, a misguided parent who had totally abandoned his responsibilities to his family, his community, and most importantly, the indulgence of self completely absent any regard for others.

I was sure there were a multitude of other windows through which the events of that evening could have been viewed, but my last thought before closing my eyes was that of being thankful. Through the window of family it is clear that no matter what the challenges, none are beyond the powers of love and forgiveness.

The Circle of Life

Clara Wimberly

When I walked into Mom's room, my sister Janice was sitting on the other side of the bed. She had a notebook and a pencil and was gazing down at it intently. She looked up as I came in. "Oh, you're here. Where was Mama born?"

"Sherwood," I said.

I went to Mom's bed.

"Happy Birthday," I whispered. She was 94 years old today, and I had no doubt that if she hadn't developed Alzheimer's, she'd still be working in her flower garden, raking pine needles and picking stray limbs out of her yard. She was a hard worker and a meticulous gardener.

She rarely opened her eyes any more, rarely spoke, and if she did it was just ramblings that couldn't be understood. She was a mere shadow of the active woman she used to be. Having Alzheimer's was bad enough; being in a nursing home for seven years was horrible. But I think what I hated most was that the vital, interesting, proud, well-kept woman who was our mother disappeared years ago and was never coming back.

I don't know when I began thinking of the woman in this bed as someone else entirely. But I had long ago separated her from the woman I knew as my mother.

"Sherwood, Tennessee?" Janice asked.

"Yep," I said, sighing heavily. I turned away from the bed and sat in a chair across from Janice.

"What's wrong?" she asked.

"Nothing," I said. "I just never get used to seeing her this way. I'll never understand why this happened to her or why she's had to endure it so long. It makes me sad."

"You can't let yourself be sad. You have to think positive," Janice said, forcing a cheerfulness I sometimes wondered if she really felt.

"You can't think bad things and be sad when you come in here. It's not good for either of you."

"Okay," I said, knowing better than to argue with her. We had long ago passed the point where I was the big sister or she was the baby sister. We became equals many years ago and now we were both growing older with grown children and grandchildren.

"Can you believe she's ninety-four? A few months ago no one thought she'd make it to this one."

"I know," Janice said. "She's amazing."

"What are they saying about her this morning?"

"She's having problems swallowing." Janice put her notebook aside and moved closer to the bed, brushing Mom's hair away from her face. "And she's very congested."

"Her skin is so soft," Janice said. "She has hardly any wrinkles. The nurses are amazed. I have more wrinkles than she does."

"She always had nice skin," I said, smiling. "It's her Dutch ancestry, I guess."

A vision popped into my head of one of our many trips. Mom always bought refrigerator magnets as a memento of where we'd been. I could see the one in my mind's eye now—it was a Delft blue tulip with the words "I've Dutch Roots." Mom loved it.

"I didn't get any of that fair, flawless skin," Janice said.

"I got the fair skin, but I don't know about flawless," I said, thinking of my own problems with sun-damaged skin. "Personally I always wanted to be tan." Mom and I had fair skin, blonde hair and hazel eyes, while Janice was dark with brown eyes and brown hair. Her skin tanned easily, and as a girl she'd loved nothing better than lying in the sun while Mom and I had to find a shady spot.

"Her breathing seems more labored today," I said.

"That's from the congestion. Every time she eats she gets congested," Janice said. "I told them this morning not to feed her any lunch. They need to give her a chance to get over this first. You know what they told me?" She looked over at me, her eyes wide with disbelief, lips compressed as she shook her head. "They said they have her birthday cake waiting for her in the refrigerator—they keep reminding me as if I'm somehow depriving her."

"Good grief," I said, nodding my agreement. "How do they think she can eat something like birthday cake?" I muttered, mostly to myself.

"I told them she can't." Janice took a deep breath and sighed. "They say they have it soaking in milk."

"That sounds appetizing," I said.

"What are you working on?" I asked, nodding toward her notebook.

"The obituary. The one you did last year when we thought she was dying. I still had it in my computer where you'd sent it to me. I'm just adding a few things." She picked up the notebook. "How should I say this about where she was born?"

"She was born in the small mountain community of Sherwood," I said.

"Oh, so it is in the mountains," she said, writing. "I've never been to Sherwood."

"Up the holler, Mom used to say. Don't put that in," I added, laughing. "She used to talk about when she was a baby and when she cried, the foxes would come near the house and yelp."

"You sure it wasn't coyotes?" Janice asked wryly.

"I'm sure she said foxes. And I like the idea of foxes," I said.

"You're a romantic."

"That's true. It's the writer in me," I said, smiling. "I make a story out of everything, always did. If there's an abandoned car parked on the side of the road, I begin to imagine what happened to the people inside. I'll have a chapter written about it by the time I get home. But I'm sure it was foxes," I added, glancing sideways at her.

We both laughed.

"Well, I definitely didn't get any writing talent," Janice said.

"Be glad . . . it's a burden," I said, purposely teasing her.

She just shook her head.

"No wonder you and Mom butted heads so often. She didn't do drama. She was the most practical woman I ever knew," Janice said.

"Tell me about it," I said. "She always hated my flair for the dramatic even when I was a little girl. To her, emotions and feelings didn't equate with anything she knew or liked. Made her uncomfortable."

We both nodded in agreement.

During the past few weeks, when the nurses had begun telling us that Mom was at the end stages of her disease, my sister and I sat beside her bed for hours. Sometimes my daughter Suzanne joined us. We talked about everything. And even now we never seemed at a loss for conversation.

"You have a visitor."

I turned and saw my daughter in the doorway. She had her arm around one of the residents. I wasn't acquainted with this patient, though I'd seen her around and knew her name. It was my habit to come in, wave to the nurses at the front desk and go back to see Mom. After my visit I would leave, wave goodbye and see you later. I am basically shy, though no one believes it. Janice, on the other hand, is very outgoing. She knew every patient's name on the Alzheimer's Unit and also knew the names of the nurses and nurses assistants and anyone else who worked there.

"Hey there, Maizie," Janice said. "What have you got?"

Maizie, a small thin, gray-haired woman with big eyes, stepped toward me and handed me a teddy bear.

"For me?" I asked. "You're giving your teddy bear to me?"

"Yes," Maizie said. "You need it because your mama's sick."

"Oh, that's so sweet of you," I said. "But I think you should keep him. He likes you better."

Maizie stepped back, and her eyes grew even larger. "Why, you are so full of it," she said.

I'm sure my mouth flew open as I stared at her. "Why do you say that?"

"Because you're telling a story," she said. "It don't like me better. Why, he can't even talk, he ain't even a real bear. Are you just crazy?"

She seemed so normal that I wondered if she really had Alzheimer's. I shrugged my shoulders and looked toward Janice for help, but she was laughing so hard she couldn't say a word. Thankfully one of the nurses came at that moment and took Maizie and the bear back down the hallway.

Suzanne came in and pulled another chair across the room to sit with us.

"Well, that was awkward," I said, feeling rather sheepish.

"It's okay, Mom," Suzanne said. My beautiful thirty-eight-year-old daughter, so protective, is always on my side. She has a career she loves, works hard, is a great mother and wife, a good sister to her two brothers, and a wonderful daughter. Besides all that we're best friends. Sometimes when I look at her I can hardly believe how lucky I am.

"Maizie is a pistol," Janice said. "She's in the early to moderate stage of Alzheimer's, about like Mom was when she was in the assisted living place. Remember some of the stuff she said?"

"Oh, I do remember," I said. "She seemed so normal but would say outrageous things."

"Oh, yeah."

"You know what the last thing was that Mom said to me that made sense?" I asked.

"What?"

"It really wasn't that long ago. Just a few months actually. I was here one day, and she was mumbling, completely incoherent. I talked back to her though, and suddenly she said, 'I think I'll just go to the house.' She was clear as day. I was so shocked that I repeated her words. 'You think you'll go to the house?'

'Yep,' she said. So I told her that I'd go with her. She said, 'Well, get Frank, and let's go.'"

"Really?" Suzanne looked over at Mom.

It seemed impossible looking at her now that she had said such a thing. That she'd said anything.

"Wonder which Frank she meant, Daddy or Frank our brother," Janice said.

"I don't know. Probably our brother. She probably thought she was working in the fields, and so she would be talking about getting her little boy and going to the house."

We all fell silent for awhile.

"I'm always amazed that sometimes out of the blue she just comes up with something like that," Janice said.

"As if for a moment something clicks inside her brain, and she's lucid," I said. "I think one thing that troubles me most about Alzheimer's is that you never really know if they're in there—if they think and can't speak, or if they hear you but can't respond. If I think about that too long it really bothers me."

"Then just don't think about it," Janice said.

"Granny used to say that." Suzanne laughed. "On one of our trips to Shakertown when I was about thirteen. The house we stayed in was big—can't remember which one, but you could hear pretty clearly through the walls. One night we woke up, and we could actually hear a man snoring somewhere in the house. Do you all remember that?"

"I do," I said, laughing. "It was about three in the morning and pitch black outside. Shaker Village is so quiet. The snoring woke me up, and I couldn't go back to sleep. I read and turned over in bed about a dozen times. Mom was snoozing away in the other bed. I think I finally woke her up without meaning to. She turned and looked at me and asked what was wrong. I told her I couldn't sleep because of the man's snoring. She gave me such a look and muttered 'just don't think about it.' Then she turned over and went right back to sleep."

"Yeah," Janice said. "Must be where I get it."

"I wanted to shout—how can you not think about it? Oh, that was funny. Mom was always so practical and nonsensical. I swear she could lie down in a patch of cactus and go right to sleep, and she expected you to be able to do it too."

"And her hair," Janice said. "You know how particular she was about her hair."

"I remember she used to wrap toilet paper around her head before going to bed," Suzanne said.

"I always thought that was funny. And we never went anywhere that she didn't ask how her hair looked or declare that her hair looked awful," I said. "You all would tell her that we were a long way away from home, and we'd never see any of those people again."

"Didn't make a bit of difference to her," Janice said.

"Nope," I said.

"You know what I remember most about those trips?" Suzanne asked.

"Lord, do we want to know?" Janice laughed.

"You probably remember being bored to death," I said. "We dragged you all over the country looking at old houses, historical villages, Presidential homes, not to mention various inns and stagecoach stops. Not exactly what a teenaged girl is looking for."

"I loved it," Suzanne replied. "But you know, even as young as I was, I remember thinking how fearless you all were."

"Fearless?" Janice hooted. "Us?"

"You all didn't seem afraid of anything," Suzanne said. "You never expressed any fear at driving anywhere. Interstates, back roads, mountain roads—rain, snow, tornado watches—it didn't matter. I don't remember ever hearing any of you say maybe you shouldn't go here or there, or that we should cancel a trip. I never heard you express any fear or any doubt about where we were going or that we were four females, alone. You'd just pick out a place and go. Anywhere you wanted."

"Maybe we just didn't have enough sense to be afraid of anything," I said.

"No, you're free birds," Suzanne said. "Just like me. Where do you think I got it?"

"Lord," Janice said. "You are a free bird." She nodded at Suzanne. "You spent that summer at Cape Cod all by yourself. Now I could never have done that."

"Me either." I leaned over to pat Suzanne's knee.

I remembered that trip well. I was terrified of her driving there, of her living with people she didn't know, working for an organization I wasn't familiar with, soliciting for them door to door in an unfamiliar place. I was just terrified, but I tried my best not to show it because really I did want her to be free and indeed to be fearless.

"That trip was the reason I finally gave in and bought a computer and got online so we could talk every day," I said. "I think I bought you your first cell phone for that trip too. If a day had gone by that I didn't talk to you, I'd have been on my way to Cape Cod."

"I don't doubt that," Suzanne said.

"Yes, and Mom and I would probably have been in the car with you," Janice said.

"Seriously, you all taught me a lot about being a strong woman," she said. "Without even trying."

Mom continued to grow worse. She was agitated and would grimace and shake her head. Sometimes she seemed scared, and that just killed me inside. I couldn't stand to think of her being afraid. Maybe she was in pain, but we just couldn't tell. She'd been on comfort meds for quite a while, and now the doctor decided it was time to add pain and anxiety medication to relieve her fears or whatever suffering she was having.

Janice and I both felt we should be there with her when she died. But it soon became clear that we couldn't be there night and day. It was exhausting, and we both had family obligations.

I lived ten miles away from the nursing home, and so when I was home, I felt like I was a thousand miles away. I went home one afternoon feeling completely worn out. But after a while I was agitated and sad. I couldn't stop thinking that I needed to be back at the nursing home.

It was long after dark when I told my husband, "You're going to think I'm crazy, but I just have to go back."

He was concerned and offered to go with me, but I said no. It was something I needed to do alone.

When I got there around nine, Janice had gone home. I was surprised; she had more energy than me and seemed able to stay for hours at a time. But it was good that I had some time alone with Mom to say what I wanted to say.

I sat by her; she was resting well. The medications were helping her. There was no more grimacing or moving about restlessly.

She wasn't one to express her emotions, even when we were children. I never heard her tell anyone she loved them, although she could express it in a card or letter. I am completely opposite and needed to tell her how I felt. I needed to put to rest the worry that I might not be with her when she died. I knew my restlessness at home was because I felt I would be letting her down if I went home, and she died during my absence. So I sat and held her hand and told her all the things I needed to say. I told her it was okay if she needed to go, and we weren't there.

Outside, as I was leaving, I looked up at a huge old live oak near the parking lot. I could see the light of the moon shining through the branches. The wind rustled the leaves softly, and the stars blinked silently in the dark sky. Suddenly I felt as if a huge burden had been lifted from me. I went home and slept peacefully for the first time in days.

A week after Mom's birthday, one of the nurses came and told us what we could look for physically as the end grew near. Janice told me that she had already begun to experience some of those physical markers.

I called Suzanne and told her; she said she wanted to be there. Suzanne is a grown woman, but she's still my baby girl. I would not have asked her to be there if she didn't want to be. I knew how hard it was for me, and I didn't want to put that burden on her. But I was so glad she made the decision to come.

I've always been afraid of death, and even when my dad died, whom I adored, I could not touch him. Ironically only two weeks before, Mom's last sibling, her sister Rose, passed away. She was my favorite aunt. I'd spent summers with her, and she'd always been so good and kind to me. Rose knew how much I loved her, and I knew that she dearly loved me. When I got to the funeral home and saw her in her casket, I hugged her without thinking and placed a little angel pin on the lapel of her pink suit.

When Suzanne got to the nursing home that Saturday afternoon, we all sat talking about our families, our trips and about mom's funeral.

"I thought just graveside services," Janice said. "A couple of hours visitation beforehand and then to the cemetery for services. What about music? I know you made a list of songs you liked when we planned this before."

"No sad songs," I said.

We all agreed to that.

"I'd love to have a violin or a flute," I said. "And that's all. Something simple."

"Which one?" Janice asked. "I have a friend who plays a flute. I'm sure she'd be happy to do it."

"Remember the time we were at Shaker Village and saw the outdoor wedding?" I asked.

"I remember that," Suzanne said. "It was so pretty. The wedding was in a clearing between the houses, beneath some locust trees. It was very foggy and we stood back, watching from a distance."

"And we heard the clear beautiful sounds of a flute floating on the air, coming out of the fog," I recalled.

"Mom loved that," Janice said. "It was something she talked about often."

"A flute it will be then," I said.

"But the casket will not be opened," Janice said adamantly.

I didn't say anything, but I thought of our brother who had not seen Mom in years. Wouldn't he want to see her one last time?

"She would absolutely hate for anyone to see her like this," Janice said. "Her hair is awful; she long ago hid her partials, and they've never been found. You know she would hate it. I'm going to get her a nice soft nightgown and some house slippers, and that's going to be it."

"Okay." I shrugged. "Whatever you want."

It was late in the day when we saw a beautiful hummingbird come to the tall pink phlox just outside the window. It lingered there for several minutes, and we remarked on how Mom loved flowers and hummingbirds.

None of us said anything. But there was an acute sense of what we were waiting for and a definite sense of resignation and dread.

Suzanne and I decided to get a drink and walk outside for a break. We sat on a bench close to the doors of the nursing home. In a few minutes, the hummingbird appeared again, right in front of us, flitting over the shrubs and flowers. Suzanne and I, both believers in signs, looked at one another, got up and hurried back into the nursing home and down the hallway.

Janice was standing on one side of the bed, and I came to stand on the other. Janice held Mom's hand. I took her other hand, and within moments she sighed heavily, different than anything we'd heard before. I held my breath and leaned toward her, watching for her next breath. It didn't come.

I turned and asked Suzanne if she would go get the nurse. When she came, Suzanne and I stepped to the foot of the bed with our arms around each other. Janice was still beside Mom.

The nurses listened for a heartbeat, and as we waited, I thought of what my Aunt Rose's pastor had said at her funeral only two weeks ago. "When a baby is born, we laugh, and when a person dies, we cry. It should be the other way around." I tried to think hard about those words as the nurse told us Mom was gone. Janice had been telling me for days that this would be a happy day, but somehow, even though I understood what she meant, I couldn't seem to get it through my mind.

I had never seen a person die before. Had never heard their last breath leave their body or felt their hand grow cold in mine. Surprisingly, I didn't find it scary—it was truly a profoundly moving moment much like when a child is born. It was part of the miracle of life, and grieving though I was, I felt lucky to have shared such a deep emotional moment with my mother and sister and my sweet daughter.

The next morning Suzanne, Janice and I met at the funeral home. Our director was a man a guy Fats, someone I'd gone to high school with. In our small town, everyone knows everyone. He was a kind, down to earth man whose only purpose seemed to be to help us through this in any way he could.

We sat around a table, arranging pictures of Mom throughout her life. We described what we wanted for her service. When Janice said she wanted a closed casket, Fats protested.

He picked up one of the pictures of mom when she was younger. "Your mother was a beautiful woman. We can make her beautiful again."

"No, that's not necessary," Janice insisted. "She wouldn't want anyone seeing her this way, and I'm not going to have it."

"Okay," he said. "But let's do this. Let us fix her hair and her teeth, give her a little makeup, and then if you still want a closed casket, that's what we'll do. But I think you'll be pleasantly surprised."

Neither Suzanne nor I offered an opinion one way or another. Janice had been the main caregiver for Mom. They were extremely close, and whatever she wanted was okay with me. Janice seemed lost in thought and perhaps for the first time a little doubtful.

"I'm going to go right now and buy her a soft nightgown," Janice told Fats.

"And hose," he said. "I can't bury a self-respecting southern lady with no hose. It wouldn't be proper."

"I was just going to get house slippers," Janice said.

"House slippers are okay. But hose too," he insisted, looking at her over his glasses.

"Okay, hose." She rolled her eyes.

For the first time we all laughed.

Janice went to buy the gown while Suzanne and I went shopping to buy my husband a new white shirt. Suzie and I were happy to be out, away from funeral homes and nursing homes, away from the ever-present reality that my mom and her grandmother was gone.

"You know," she said, "I wish we could find something that the four of us could wear—kind of a commemorative."

"The four of us? You mean Mom too?"

"Yes."

"That's so sweet," I said. "What do you have in mind?"

"Oh, I don't know. A pin or bracelet . . . I'll know it when I see it."

We looked in several stores, walked though the mall and treated ourselves to a cookie, trying to pretend a little normalcy. Then we continued looking.

As soon as we approached the jewelry counter of the next store we saw some bracelets on a table. Suzanne went straight to them. "Oh, I think this is it."

There were some black knotted cord bracelets with sterling silver pendants. There were several different sentiments expressed, but the one Suzanne reached for had a beautiful Family Tree in a silver oval. It looked a lot like the Shaker Tree of Life symbol that we all knew so well. The writing in the box said Family, and beneath that a short verse: *Family is a link to our past and a bridge to our future.*

"It's perfect," we both said.

Suzanne began looking through the bracelets. "Let there be four, please let there be four," she said. Then she lifted her hand, holding up four bracelets with a triumphant smile.

"Four!"

"Yay," I said, laughing.

After leaving the mall, our first stop was the funeral home where we asked them to put one of the bracelets on Mom's wrist. We were about to text Janice when she called and asked where we were.

"The funeral home," I said.

"Good. Wait for me. I have something to show you. I'll be right there."

I assumed she was bringing the nightgown for us to see. But when she got out of her car she was carrying a long flowing dress of pale yellows, pinks and greens.

"Mom made this for me when I was in high school," she said. "It's always been one of my favorite dresses, and I've had it hanging in the closet all these years. I'd kind of like Mom to wear it." She held it out in her arms for us to see. "What do you think?" She seemed a little hesitant.

I was surprised. Janice had become a little matter of fact over the years. This was the sentimental side of my sister I hadn't seen in a while. She was quiet and subdued and very sweet.

"I think it's just perfect," Suzanne said. "Granny made this? Wow, it's really beautiful."

We stood there in the middle of the parking lot, the three of us touching the dress. The full skirt had several rows of decorative hemming around the bottom and on the bell sleeves. The material looked like fine muslin and was very soft and feminine. It wasn't a dress Mom would have chosen to wear, but it had her in it. She had created it for her daughter with love and care, and the quality of the work showed that. She never did anything halfway.

"It is perfect," I said. "I can't believe you've had it all these years."

"It was always one of my favorite dresses. But I have mixed feelings about it," Janice said. "I hate to part with it, but then I think—what better way to use it, you know? So you think it will be all right?"

"I really do," I said.

"I vote yes," Suzanne said. "Definitely."

"What were you all doing here?" Janice asked.

We explained about the bracelet, and Suzanne handed her a box. "This one is yours. Wear it to the funeral."

"You've already given them one for Mom?" she asked.

We nodded as Janice took the bracelet out of its box and placed it on her wrist. Tears filled her eyes, and she reached out to us. We all hugged there in the parking lot with the beautiful dress between us and the bracelets on our arms.

"People will think we're nuts," she said, wiping her eyes.

"Oh, they'll just say—it's those crazy Rogers girls—wonder what they're up to now," I said.

When we arrived the next afternoon for the funeral I felt a little anxious. Fats had already told us that Mom looked beautiful, and we were going to be pleased. Still I felt a little apprehensive at seeing her, remembering how she looked before.

When I saw her in the beautiful dress, her hair curled around her face, makeup perfect, lips and mouth perfect, I cried. She looked young and lovely. Janice, Suzanne and I just stood there, unable to speak, unable to stop looking at her. It was a truly amazing moment. In fact we said later she looked as if she could come back and would be perfectly normal. There was no sign of the frail, withered little woman with Alzheimer's.

When my brother and his family came in, I turned to Janice. "She looks so pretty. Do you think it would be all right if they see her?"

"Sure," she said, without hesitation. "Any of the family who wants to see her can come in. But we're still having a closed casket during visitation. She still wouldn't want people looking at her, or making remarks about how she looks."

Later the funeral procession made its way through town down the main street lined with huge old trees and beautiful antebellum homes. Cars pulled over and stopped as we passed; even joggers and walkers along the street stopped and stood silent. Policemen stood on each corner with their hats over their hearts. That showing of respect is one of the southern traditions I love most and I was touched and proud.

It was nearing sunset when we stood on the hill at the cemetery where my mother would be laid to rest beside our dad. After a few words by the pastor, the sweet sound of the flute drifted over the quiet crowd, playing the old Shaker tune "'Tis a Gift to Be Simple." I had been the only one who didn't want the dove release, feeling it was a little corny. But when the white birds flew, and one lone dove flew up to join them in the air I could not hold back the tears.

I'd heard my sons talking earlier, and one of them made the remark that his grandmother's death had given him an odd feeling—as if he were stepping forward, as if he were moving up in the chain somehow. The other one agreed, and I knew exactly what they meant. I had felt it when Dad died.

After the service, Janice, Suzanne and I stood together, arms entwined, the family bracelets on our wrists. As the three of us stood there in the waning light, saying goodbye to the fourth, I felt that sense of moving forward that my sons had spoken of, and I wanted to hold my family close. We were three women of different ages and life experiences, taking that next step forward, and our being together somehow made it easier.

Life has its happy moments and its sad. It has a rhythm and a time that we can't change. This was our own Circle of Life, our family's affirmation that life and generations move on.

We did so having seen our mom and grandmother restored to her true beauty and dignity. We had come together as a family to do our best for her.

And I knew she would be pleased.

Lessons On A Paper Napkin

Kathleen Watson

Prologue

Mama says there are things that have always been a part of your life and there are things that just feel like they have always been a part of your life.
For those things, there are beginnings.

I traced the delicate lace on my dress while I stared at the photos grouped beneath the "Bride and Groom" banner, lost in so many thoughts I wanted to swat them away like mosquitoes buzzing around my head. The picture of Mama and Daddy caught my eye first, and I tried to find Daddy's face in the blurred images of my memories. It had been so long since he'd died, but I could still feel his fingers on my cheek when he'd wiped away a tear and smell the lingering scent of his cologne when he'd kiss me before going off to work.

My hand was almost to the picture when Mama walked over and snaked her arm around my waist, pulling me in close to her body. The heady fragrance of her orchid corsage swirled around us both and mingled with the softer scents of jasmine and roses clutched in my own hand.

"Your daddy sure was a handsome man," she said with a sigh, but no trace of sadness darkened her words. She turned to look at me, her heels putting us nearly eye to eye. "I see so much of him every time I look at you."

The lump was already half way up my throat, but I swallowed it back and smiled anyway. "I wish he could be here today."

Mama kissed me lightly on the cheek then thumbed the pad of her finger across the spot. "He is, honey. I've heard half a dozen stories about him today. People remember him." She hugged me tighter. "*We* remember him."

We stood there in the wake of our memories for a moment looking at the other pictures, when Mama pointed to one and asked, "Remember this?"

The grainy black and white photo showed me and my three best friends—Cami, Alice and Marie—sitting on the welcome sign at the Audubon Zoo in New Orleans. They were all standing in the wedding today, as much a part of my life now as they had been that hot May day. It had been our sixth grade class trip, a yearly tradition at Sisters of the Sacred Heart as the kids graduated from the private school. We were clustered shoulder to shoulder, hardly a whisper's breath of space between us. Huge grins showed off the braces we'd all gotten that summer. But it wasn't my friends' smiling faces that captured my attention. It was the girl in the photo with us, standing so far to the right she was just a step away from being out of the picture. A tight-lipped smile barely cracked her face as she peeked out from beneath layers of unruly dark hair.

"Yeah," I finally croaked in answer to Mama's question. "That was some day."

I slammed the car door as Mama called my name. She used the full Mary Margaret for emphasis as I retreated to the schoolyard, but I knew she would not carry our fight out into the open. She'd never make a scene. I could hear my own frustration echo in her voice, and even that tiny bit of similarity was enough to drive me crazy. We were different, that's just all there was to it. I would not be like her. I wouldn't. The rebellion in me at purposefully ignoring her was new, and it still tasted sour on my tongue and felt heavy deeper down inside. The nuns at Sacred Heart were good at making us feel guilty, and I'm sure later when we had to go to weekly confession I would have to say a rosary for my actions. Lately I said a lot of rosaries.

The other kids in my sixth grade class ran around like leaves scattered on the playground, swirling from their own excitement and pent up energy. From the looks of it we were the last to arrive. It was Friday in the final week of school and the entire sixth grade class was going on its traditional trip to the zoo in New Orleans to celebrate graduation. It was a big deal in our little school. A day away from school and the nuns. A day away from uniforms and plaid skirts that the boys liked to flip up or peek under. A day to be free. But my freedom had been stepped on, and I was not happy.

The principal, Sister Rose Claude, called Mama yesterday to see if she could join the group at the last minute. Unlike most of the other mothers, Mama worked, so she never went on daytime school trips. That was fine with me. It was the only benefit I could find out of her working as a teacher at the junior high. Next year she'd be teaching my friends. That was a nightmare I didn't want to think about yet.

I spied my friends waiting near the idling school bus and stomped intently through the hedge to the closed circle of three girls. They were my best friends and my sole source of comfort the last few weeks, ever since Daddy died driving home from Baton Rouge, leaving me and Mama alone to deal with each other. Neither of us was really good at it, and there didn't seem to be any hope that things would change. Hot tears stung the corners of my eyes, but I swiped them away with a slash of my hand. Daddy had been the link between what he called our 'mirror-image souls.' We'd studied atoms in science, and it seemed me and Mama were more like atoms in space: we collide on occasion but mostly just circle one another from a distance.

"Well is she, or isn't she?" Camille prodded, twirling a long ribbon of red hair between her fingers. I'd called Cami last night as soon as I knew about Mama. Cami and I had known each other as far back as I could remember, the sister I'd always wanted. She'd gotten a little brother last year, and I think she would have agreed with the trade in a heartbeat.

"She is," I answered with a huff, tossing my blue jean purse over my shoulder and crossing my arms across my chest. Every girl I knew was eager for her breasts to grow. Mine had, and already I wished they'd go away.

As confirmation of my revelation, we all turned to watch Mama get out of her car. The shiny silver paint of the car reflected the morning sun, and it circled around her like a halo. She checked her reflection in the side view mirror then picked her way through the parking lot, a large purse draped over the crook of one arm and a picnic basket held in front of her like a shield, reminding me of a picture I'd seen of Joan of Arc going off to battle. The ends of the white scarf tied around her head flapped in the warm May breeze, announcing her approach like the terns when you got too close to their nests. She waved at the four of us, her fake smile causing her eyes to close tightly, then turned to join the teachers and other parents standing by the front door of the school.

"That's just uncool." Alice's sentiment pretty much summed it up for us. She smacked her gum and planted a hand on her left hip, her fingers running along the glitter belt she wore with her shorts. "Why do parents always have to ruin everything?"

"And why does it always have to be *my* mother," I whined. It was bad enough Mama was a school teacher, always calling or writing my teachers when I did poorly on a test. But next year there was a good chance that those of us going to the public junior high school would have her for English. Could there be anything worse? I was already nervous about switching from private school to public. Having my own mother as a teacher in the same school was just mortifying. I hoped there was a rule about kids being in a parent's classroom, although that wouldn't help my friends. And would they blame me?

Marie patted my arm. "Maybe they won't put us in her group, Meg." Marie could find something nice to say about anything. Normally we liked that about her. Today it was just annoying.

I rolled my eyes. "Oh, come on, Marie. You know they always put kids with the parent."

"Yeah," Alice chimed in. "It's s'pposed to build *good bonds*." She exaggerated the last two words to mimic Sister Rose Claude. We'd all gotten a lecture from her yesterday on the things we should get out of the trip. We were told to be on our best behavior, otherwise future classes may not get to go. Like I said, the nuns used guilt whenever they could. Sister Rose Claude said it wasn't just a day of fun, either, but a day to build bonds that would last a lifetime. Belle Terre was a small town at the edge of the parish, and most of us had known each other our entire lives or were related in some way. How much more bonded could we get?

That thought dragged my attention to the one person in our class we'd not known since kindergarten, who'd come into our world as different as she could just a few months ago.

Evangeline Rayne.

Even her name sounded different. I'd gone to the same school with the same people for the last seven years. Same teachers. Same friends. I'd known most of them even before that. I knew enough at twelve to know different was not good.

"I didn't think Evangeline was able to go on the trip," I whispered to the others, and their heads swiveled in unison.

"I heard Mama tell Daddy last night the nuns had called. Maybe they were looking for donations so she could go," Marie added, running the gold cross back and forth on the chain around her neck. "It wouldn't be right to leave her out."

"The trip isn't that expensive," Cami snipped. "She gets free tuition. You'd think her folks could at least pay for this."

Every year Sacred Heart gave scholarships, finding families that couldn't afford the private tuition. We all wore uniforms, so in theory we all looked alike, but everything about Evangeline made her stand out. Although she was our age, her dark skin and oddly up-tilted eyes gave her the grown up look of a movie star. Her long hair looked limp and barely combed, not put up in a ponytail or pulled back with barrettes like the rest of us. She sat at the bottom of the front steps by herself, a greasy brown grocery bag crumpled up beside her.

"Don't be that way, Cami," Marie scolded softly, and we all refocused our attention on our own little circle. "Father Gabe said we're not supposed to judge."

Cami stiffened at Marie's words. "Thank you, Sister Marie," she said angrily. But at Marie's hurt look she quickly added, "Sorry. I'm not judging. Just wondering."

Our talk turned to other things, but the image of Evangeline stayed with me, and my gaze wandered back to her several times over the next few minutes. We were all wearing sundresses or shorts to fight the Louisiana heat and humidity, but Evangeline dressed in long sleeves and long pants that rode up near her ankles. She didn't have on socks or tennis shoes either, but these big clunky black shoes that a kid might wear when trying to play grown up. The worse thing about her outfit, however, was the blazing black and green plaid pattern zigzagging across the top and bottom of her clothes. It was enough to make your eyes hurt.

Kids and teachers mostly ignored her. She sat in the back of class or at the end of the table at lunch. Her parents didn't come to any of the open houses or parent-teacher conferences, hadn't attended the Christmas assembly where we sang stupid songs and acted like we were happy about it. Like the thought of junior high, she made me nervous, but I wasn't sure why.

Sister Rose Claude interrupted my thoughts, calling us together so we could line up to board the bus. Like every other day, she had us close our eyes and bow our heads for a prayer. I hadn't been closing my eyes for prayers lately, wanting to watch for any sign that God was watching or listening. I hadn't seen anything to convince me and didn't see the need to thank Him for anything. Daddy had died in spite of everything I'd been told would keep us safe. Be good. Go to church. Pray. Along with the sadness, I'd been filled with a powerful anger over the last few weeks. Sometimes I couldn't breathe it hurt so much. He was gone, and I didn't see the need to keep on praying to someone who didn't listen.

Before the prayer ended, I looked around at the group and found Mama standing next to Evangeline. When they raised their heads, Evangeline said something to Mama, and Mama laughed, her eyes wide as she tilted her head down to Evangeline's level to respond. Her eyes didn't crinkle when it was a real smile, and a spark of jealousy caught in my stomach, but I shook it out. Why did I care if Mama smiled at Evangeline?

Alice, Cami, Marie and I hurried to the front of the line so we could get seats near the back of the bus. Although barely seven o'clock, the bus radiated heat like a humid tin can in the morning sun. We quickly lowered the windows, sat down and added to the rising level of chatter bouncing around the inside. As usual, boys paired off on one side of the bus and girls on the other. It's not that we weren't allowed to sit together, it's just that no one really wanted to sit together.

I could see Mama and Evangeline over the heads of my friends walk onto the bus together and take a seat at the front of the bus. Like Mama's smile, though, I wasn't going to let it bother me. I didn't want to be with Mama. Why should I care if Evangeline did?

I pushed the thoughts of Mama and Evangeline out of my head, wrapped up in my own world with Cami, Alice and Marie. Did I need any more?

By the time the yellow bus squealed to a stop at the gates of the Audubon Zoo, we were all sweaty and ready to explode with energy. Cami, Alice, Marie and I spilled onto the pavement in a samba chain, our voices a rising chorus of the Latin rhythm we'd learned in dance class last Saturday. The parents formed a semi-circle around the bus, our own personal fence line to keep everyone close.

I pulled my new Instamatic camera out of my purse and waved it at my friends.

"Let's take a picture near the sign!" I yelled to Cami, Alice and Marie, and they tromped over to the "Welcome" sign without question.

I ran to Mama and slapped the camera in her hand. "Take our picture!" I demanded then joined my friends, pushing and squeezing between them with giggles and flying elbows.

Mama sat down her purse and picnic basket and then to my shock, turned to Evangeline. "Why don't you get in the picture too?"

Evangeline's face flashed this mixed look of joy and horror like she was afraid to get so close. Her face went from Mama to me, then back to Mama. Mama put an arm around Evangeline's shoulder and walked her part way to the sign, once again leaning down to whisper in Evangeline's ear like she'd done after the morning prayer. She took the paper bag clutched in Evangeline's hand and shooed her forward.

Cami, Marie and Alice went quiet as Evangeline took up a seat at the end of the cement base, as far from us as she could get without falling to the sidewalk. I sat there in silent anger, shooting Mama eyefuls of contempt as she framed the picture. I felt this little burn start in my chest and spread to my fingers and toes, heat filling up beneath my skin. This was a picture for my friends, not hers. Marie started to elbow Cami, and within seconds we were giggling again, Evangeline's intrusion in our group momentarily forgotten.

Mama looked over the edge of the camera and shouted, "Everyone say 'Elephants can dance!'"

In unison we yelled back at her, and Mama snapped the picture. Evangeline bounced off the seat like it was on fire and quickly put some space between us. She hovered a small distance from Mama, plucking nervously at the edge of the greasy paper bag she'd retrieved and glancing in Mama's direction. I was struck still for a moment, watching Evangeline stand as quiet as a statue while she waited to see what Mama would do.

The look on her face made my chest hurt. With her chin tucked in close to her chest, she watched Mama from beneath the fall of her bangs. Her knuckles were white clutching the edge of that paper bag. Dozens of people moved around Evangeline, but her eyes were only for Mama. Had I ever wanted for attention that badly or looked so ... alone? I was an only child, but my world was filled with people. Grandparents. Uncles. Aunts. Cousins. And that was just family. I looked at Cami, Marie and Alice. They were as much a part of my family as my blood relatives. Did Evangeline have brothers or sisters? Did she have friends outside of school? Everybody had somebody. Didn't they?

Mama bent to gather her things from the sidewalk, stopping to stare at a family walking past pushing a stroller. She watched the mother and father until they disappeared behind the zoo gates, and I couldn't take my eyes off her. Her shoulders lifted then fell heavily with a sigh, and her face changed with the small motion, like she was releasing whatever thoughts filled her eyes with sadness. Mama turned and beamed another smile at Evangeline and handed the picnic basket to her. Mama pointed to Mrs. Leonard standing near the bus. Evangeline nodded her head, pushing her fly-away hair behind her ear and taking off like a shot.

When Mama looked to me, she whispered seriously, "I need to talk to you, Meg."

"Not now." I snatched the camera from Mama's hand and turned towards my friends. Besides, she had Evangeline to keep her company. She didn't need me. That thought didn't sit easy as I wandered back to Cami, Marie and Alice.

"We're trying to figure out which group everyone will be in," Cami said as I rejoined the circle. She pulled her long hair up and fanned the back of her neck.

Alice sighed, scanning the crowd. "I hope we all get to stay together. It won't be any fun otherwise."

"Marie?" said a voice from behind, and we all turned to see Evangeline standing behind us, her hand stretched out towards us. A delicate gold chain and cross winked in the sunlight. Her hand shook like she was too cold to stand still. "I think this is yours. I found it on the ground near the bus."

Marie gasped, her hand clutching her neck. "Oh my goodness! That was my Nana's." She delicately took the chain from Evangeline's hand.

Cami and I each had a hand on Marie's shoulders during our little samba number. "It must have broken as we got off the bus," Cami offered.

Evangeline stood still again, her eyes wide, hands in tight fists at her side, while Marie studied the chain. "I—I just found it," she stammered, and her voice cracked. "I think the clasp broke."

I read more meaning in the words and tone, like she was afraid we'd think she'd stolen it.

Marie threw herself at Evangeline and wrapped her arms around the girl's neck. "Thank you so much, Evangeline. I'd have died if I lost this."

Mama walked over to see what the commotion was about and hugged Evangeline's shoulders as we told her the story. "What a great pair of eyes you have, Evangeline," she exclaimed loudly. "How many people walked by that exact spot and didn't see a thing?"

Evangeline blushed, but her shoulders drew up around her ears as if waiting for more than thanks to come her way. "It was nothing, Mrs. Adams. I just got lucky."

"Then I'm glad I'm with you today because I can always use a little luck," Mama gushed.

Mama told Marie she would hold the necklace in her purse until they got home, that way it wouldn't get lost. Marie, Evangeline and Mama walked off towards the others while Cami, Alice and I waited behind. Marie chatted with Evangeline as they walked.

"That sure was nice," Alice observed. "That necklace means a lot to Marie. Remember when she got it at her birthday?"

Cami and I nodded. I ran my fingers over the Instamatic camera in my hand. My birthday was in another week, but Mama had given me the camera last night. It was a gift from my dad, she said. He'd gotten it early so I could have it for this trip, and she'd nearly forgotten about it after his accident. Knowing he'd been thinking of me made me want to smile and cry at the same time.

"Her nana died right after Marie's birthday, didn't she?" Cami asked, looking at me and the camera. "I think it belonged to her grandmother's grandmother too."

Marie and Evangeline came running up behind us, but Evangeline stopped further away, letting Marie approach alone. "Hey guys," Marie said a little breathlessly. "We're all in the same group!"

"Are we with my mom?" I knew the answer before I asked.

"Yeah." Marie took me and Cami by the hands, pulling us towards Evangeline. Alice pushed us from behind. "But it'll be OK. We're *together!*"

The parents and kids all split off into their groups, taking different routes once we were inside the zoo gates. It was a Friday morning during school, so the zoo wasn't that busy. A few moms with babies in strollers and a few old folks my grandparents' age. Hand in hand, Cami and I ran straight for the Bengal tigers exhibit. When we started planning the zoo trip in February, Daddy showed me the news article about a new Bengal cub that had been born. He'd gotten the school to schedule the trip for today since it was the first day the cub was to be on display. I still had the article on my bulletin board at home.

Cami and I were at the fence already when the others caught up. The mama tiger lay sprawled out on a big rock, her giant body shading the cub. The cub rolled playfully against her belly as it batted at the air with its big paws. Mama tiger's eyes were closed to slits, but her head swiveled whatever direction the cub moved.

"Why don't they have all the tigers in there with the mom?" Alice wondered aloud, pointing out the rest of the tigers behind a big fence at the back of the exhibit.

"Because the other tigers could hurt the baby," I informed her, feeling wise with the information I'd read in the paper. I hopped up on the bottom rail, leaning as far over the fence as I could to snap a picture.

"That's right, Meg," Mama agreed, grabbing the back of my shorts and pulling back slightly. "Sometimes you have to introduce new members of the family slowly, so everyone can get to know one another."

"Sure wish my mom and dad had thought about that before bringing home my baby brother last year," Cami said, somewhat jokingly.

"A baby brother wouldn't be too bad," Evangeline said out of the blue. She watched the mother and cub intently, almost like she was seeing something else. Her chin rested in the palm of her upturned hands, her fingers drumming along her cheekbone.

"I guess an older brother could be worse." Cami matched Evangeline's pose with her chin in her palms.

"It is, trust me," Alice chimed in, the youngest in her family and the only girl with three older brothers. "Older brothers are really bossy."

"Older sisters aren't much better," Marie added. "And they're *always* in the bathroom or on the phone."

"A sister would be cool," Evangeline added the same time I said, "I wouldn't mind a sister."

We laughed at that, but I'd never thought about how different our families were from one another. Marie was a middle child. I was an only child. Cami, the oldest of two. Alice, the youngest of four. Was Evangeline an only child like me? Or the only girl? She didn't say more, and I didn't ask.

"Who wants to go see the elephants?" Marie yelled, already pushing away from the fence and leading the charge to the next exhibit. Evangeline ran close on her heels. Cami and Alice followed suit but Mama pointed at my untied shoe lace and pulled me to a nearby bench. She sat down and patted a spot next to her so I lifted my foot.

Mama reached for the shoe but I pushed her hand aside. "I can do it," I argued, and went to work on the laces. I bite my nails so I wasn't having much luck.

She brushed my hands aside. "I know you can do it. Doesn't mean I can't help."

The attention felt good, but I'd never admit that to her. Being with Mama lately was a lot like being on a roller coaster. There'd be a slow climb but when we hit the top and pushed over the peak, we usually screamed a lot. Kinda like this morning. So we were on the slow climb again.

Mama kept her attention focused on my shoe but asked, "Why don't you like Evangeline?"

The question caught me off guard. Evangeline had always been on the outside, but did she choose to be, or had everyone just kept her there because she was new? It never occurred to me to let her in. "It's not that I don't like her," I explained, but it felt weak. "I just never thought about it. It's just always been me, Cami, Alice and Marie." When you said it out loud, it didn't sound very nice.

"There's no room for Evangeline in there?" She finished tying my shoe, and I removed my foot from the bench. Mama stood, and we started a slow walk towards the others. "You've never had to be the new kid. It's hard. I was a new kid once."

I knew this story. She and Granny and Papa Ted had moved to Belle Terre when she was my age, after they'd lost everything in Hurricane David. Her older sister, who I was named after, had been killed coming home from work after the boss wouldn't let the workers leave early enough to avoid the storm surge. Papa Ted said that so much loss made family and friends more special because they could both be gone so quickly. Since Daddy died, I'd understood that more. I couldn't remember thinking about Daddy during the day when he was alive. Now, I thought about him all the time.

"Do you know anything about Evangeline?" Mama prodded.

"Everyone knows she's a scholarship kid." I jumped in little circles, suddenly anxious to be away from these thoughts. "Someone said she lives near the school 'cause they've seen her walking in the morning." Sacred Heart didn't have buses because it was private, so parents either had to bring their kids or, if they lived close enough, they walked.

"She doesn't live near the school, Meg," Mama corrected. "But she does walk. She lives with her grandfather, and he can't see well enough to drive."

I didn't want to know why she lived with her grandfather. It couldn't be good. I bounced further away from Mama. "Look, next year. I promise. We'll make sure Evangeline gets included more." And I took off to join the others. Mama called out my name as I ran away, but I pretended not to hear.

We made our way quickly through the elephants and lions but skipped the petting zoo, all agreeing it was for babies. Mama kept moving us forward by promising we could ride the train over towards the monkeys and visit the gift shop. The train was always my favorite part. Back in October school closed for a day so the teachers could attend some meeting. Daddy took the day off work, and we'd come to the zoo, just the two of us.

The train's whistle screeched loudly, setting off the birds in the aviary. We ran the final distance just as the train was pulling to a stop. Mama went to buy tickets, first giving us instructions not to board without her. We all piled on moments later, Evangeline and I falling into the same row from opposite ends. I studied her from the corner of my eye as the train started to move. Words crowded in my brain but got lost on my tongue. Why was she walking to school if she didn't live nearby? Mama would never let me walk alone in the mornings. Belle Terre was a small town, but not that small.

I almost asked about her parents then remembered what Mama had told me about Evangeline living with her grandfather. "Have you ever been to the zoo before today?"

Evangeline perked up a little bit, a half-smile tilting up the corners of her mouth. She pushed back a sweep of hair. "My daddy used to take me when I was little. We'd spend the day looking for pennies then go make wishes in the fountain near the sea lions."

"I know where that is! Daddy and I . . ." But I stopped, a pain in my heart stealing my voice. I looked away from Evangeline, suddenly scared I would start to cry. For the first time since his death, I wanted Mama to hold me.

Evangeline scooted closer and reached out to hold my hand. Her fingers curled around mine, and as the tears stung my eyes and clouded the world, I couldn't tell where her hand ended and mine began. The train whistle screeched, and the train started to slow. As we pulled to a stop in front of the gift shop, Evangeline squeezed my hand once and let go. She hopped off the train without looking back.

Mama rounded us up and pointed us towards the gift shop. Cami, Alice and Marie dashed off. I was about to join them when Mama grabbed my hand and told me to wait. I saw her slip some money to Evangeline real secretive, and when Evangeline shook her head and tried to give it back, Mama told her it was a reward for finding Marie's necklace. Evangeline hesitated, staring into Mama's face before giving her a big hug and a kiss on the cheek. Had I ever seen Evangeline smile so big? Had I ever noticed whether or not Evangeline smiled before today?

I opened my mouth to protest about being held back, but Mama raised her hand to shush me. "I know. You'll get to go to the gift shop in a second. But I need to talk to you first."

Not happy, I whined, "What did I do?"

"You feeling guilty about something?" Mama laughed. "I just need to talk to you, and since you ignored me this morning, this is our best chance."

The memory of this morning flashed back. I'd still been angry about Mama forcing Evangeline into my picture. Curious, I let her lead me to a bench beneath a large tree.

"I'm about to tell you a secret, and I need your word you will not tell anyone." She cupped my chin in her palm and looked hard into my eyes. "This is very important, Meg. More important than anything you've ever done."

I nodded my head, scared and feeling like the night Mama came to tell me about Daddy's accident. Whatever she was going to say would change things. Still, it felt kinda grown up that she would trust me with something so big. The thought of not sharing with Cami, Alice or Marie was a little strange, but the look on Mama's face made me sit up a straighter. "OK. I won't tell anyone."

"I'm telling you this because I think you have a right to know, and I want you to be part of the decision." She let go of my chin but kept her body angled towards me. "Months ago Sister Rose Claude came to me and your daddy about needing a foster family. Do you know what that means?"

"A foster family takes in kids that have nowhere else to go." I swallowed hard, my mind filling in pieces of the puzzle before Mama showed me the whole picture.

"Yes. Kids that have lost their parents or who've been taken away from their parents because they're not safe at home."

The thought of not being safe in your own home was as odd to me as having no family at all. I followed the path that Evangeline had taken into the gift shop, thinking about her parents that hadn't shown up to parent-teacher day or the Christmas pageant.

"Your daddy and I wanted very much to do this, and we'd filled out all the paperwork so we could be the family this child needs." Mama leaned back against the bench, taking my hand in hers. I didn't pull away, knowing what came next. "After your daddy died, I wasn't sure I could handle it on my own. Then I realized I'm not alone. I have you."

I twirled her wedding ring around her finger, focusing on that while lost again in the sadness and anger that filled me when I thought of Daddy. "You're talking about Evangeline, aren't you?"

"Yes, I am."

Things in my stomach fluttered. "But she has her grandfather."

"Her grandfather is very sick. Evangeline has no one." She tilted my chin up again with the tip of her finger. "I'm not asking you to give me an answer now. I just want you to think about it. One more question, then I'll let it go for now. What did you pack for lunch today?"

Confused, I shook my head. "I don't know. You packed our lunch."

"Yes, I did." She kissed me then walked off.

I didn't want to think about anything so important right now. I didn't really know Evangeline beyond today but knew how she was treated at school. What would people do if she came to live with us? Would they treat me the same way? I didn't like worrying about that, either. Daddy always said to treat everyone with respect. Would I have treated her different if someone had told me about her family? Probably, but that didn't say much about me, and I knew Daddy would be disappointed. Shame flooded and warmed my face. But it wasn't fair of Mama to expect me to do this. Hadn't we been through enough this year?

Alice and Evangeline ran out of the gift shop and plunked down on my side of the bench, interrupting my thoughts. I was relieved, actually. They were busy painting their nails with some glitter polish Evangeline had bought, and I watched the two of them huddle together like they'd been friends forever. I didn't see Cami until she dropped down next to me on the bench.

She lifted her hair off her neck and fanned her neck. "I don't care what Mama says, I'm getting my hair cut this summer."

"I can French braid it if you like," Evangeline offered as she put her nail polish back in her bag. Cami squealed her delight and within minutes, Evangeline had her hair neatly plaited. She tied it off with the ribbon around a packet of stationery she'd bought.

"That's awesome, Evangeline," Alice said, waving her fingers through the air to dry her nails. "Can you teach me to do that?"

Evangeline shrugged, and she seemed uncomfortable with the attention. "Sure thing. If I can learn it, anyone can."

Mama and Marie finally came out of the gift shop, and we continued on through the zoo. I fell back a bit as Evangeline ran ahead with Cami, Marie and Alice. I thought back to this morning when Evangeline wouldn't sit near us, and now . . . it was like she was one of us.

We were all getting pretty tired when Mama announced it was time to meet up with the rest of the class for lunch at the picnic pavilion near the front gates. Mrs. Leonard met us there with our lunches. Mama took our picnic basket, reaching in to grab something.

"Go get us a table, girls," she directed, and before I turned away I saw her pull the Baggie with our bread slices from the basket and toss it in the nearest garbage can. What was she doing? She silenced my question with a look, so I joined the others.

Cami, Alice, Marie and I paired off across the table. While the others tore into their own sack lunches, neatly packed in plastic lunch boxes with carefully trimmed sandwiches, tin-foil wrapped drinks, and Baggies of potato chips and Little Debbies for dessert, I waited for Mama to set ours out. Evangeline unwrapped her own bag slowly.

"Oh no!" Mama exclaimed, and we all stopped to see what was wrong. "I forgot to bring the bread for our sandwiches."

But I'd seen it. She'd packed the bread but had thrown it away.

"I have some bread, Mrs. Adams." Evangeline reached into the greasy paper bag and withdrew a can of Vienna sausages and a full loaf of bread.

That was her lunch for today. Bread and Vienna sausages. I thought back to what Mama had said about her grandfather and how he couldn't take care of himself. And even when we were fighting Mama always took care of me. I'd never thought about what to pack for lunch today. I knew Mama would take care of it. But Evangeline didn't have anyone to think about her lunch this morning. Maybe Evangeline didn't have anyone to think about her *ever*.

Mama spread a large white napkin across the table between the three of us, connecting us like the three points of a triangle. She chatted about the day and about all the neat things we'd seen, especially the baby Bengal tiger and how the entire pride would help raise the baby as he got older. Everyone in the family had something to share with the baby, she said. Then I thought back to today and all that Evangeline had shared with people who'd never shared a single thing with her.

Mama laid out her homemade chicken salad, chips, sweet pickles and cold drinks, carefully putting it all within reach of both Evangeline and myself. Some homemade pound cake sat off to the side, waiting for us at the end. Evangeline looked like she'd never seen so much food before, and maybe she hadn't. I didn't think about what we'd have for lunch today, or any day, come think about it. I knew it would be here. Then again, I thought Daddy would always be here too. I looked at Evangeline and saw a little of myself. Only I still had Mama.

Mama made up sandwiches and passed them around. We ate between the laughter, and it filled me up as much as the food. The tightness in my belly disappeared a little. I still had Mama, and for the first time since Daddy's death, I was glad.

After we ate, the others ran off, but I stayed to help Mama pack up the basket and throw away trash. There was so much I wanted to say but like before, the words got crowded and tangled in my throat.

Mama hugged me and kissed the top of my head. "It's OK," she whispered, and I leaned against her for a minute, relief and happiness pushing away some of the sadness that still filled me.

I found Evangeline a bit later at the water fountain. Twin streams of water shot from the pitchers on the statue's shoulders, the glittery reflection of all the coins in the water twinkling on the little waves.

"Look what I found." I held out my hand, showing her the two pennies clutched in my palm. "Want one?"

Breathless, Evangeline took a penny and held it tightly between her hands. "On the count of three?"

We counted off together and tossed in our coins. I watched the coin twirl slowly to the bottom and made a wish.

"Come on you two!" Cami corralled us from our spot in front of the picture collage and herded us towards the church baptistery. "A wedding waits for no one."

I lined up with Cami, Alice, and Marie, and waited while Mama adjusted the bow at the back of my gown. The organ music swelled in the chapel, and the familiar strains of Mozart's *Ave Verum Corpus* echoed around us.

"Thank you," I whispered in Mama's ear, fighting back more tears.

"Whatever for?"

A door opened behind us, and we both turned to watch the bride enter from the vestibule. Dressed in Mama's wedding gown, I'd never seen Evangeline look more beautiful or happy, not since the day she first came to live with us. Her relaxed smile beamed out from behind the veil as she took her place beside Mama.

The tears fell, and I let them, for I couldn't think of anything that made me happier today than seeing that smile on Evangeline's face. "For giving me a sister."

A Roasted Pig

Tom Honea

Cut Bank

Early Spring 1910

"Mr. Francis," Earl Dupree broke the silence, "them wild hogs is been gittin' worse through the winter. Comin' out from the woods, rootin' in the corn fields and such."

They had made the rounds of the fields adjacent to the house, the trading post, the barns. The horses sensed their day was nearly over, quickened their pace toward the compound.

"Hup," Francis Jennings sounded. "Boar? We never had wild boar in Ashe County that I know of."

The house itself was on the highest point of the slight rise. It faced the south and was ringed from north and west by mature oaks. Only the roof tops and chimneys, and the two ancient pin oaks between the trading post and the roadway, showed from Francis' and Earl's vantage point.

"I been hunting that bottom land nigh on forty years now, Earl. Don't remember seein' no wild boar."

"These ain't actual wild boar, Mr. Francis. These is hogs got out from the pens. Some from here on the place, some down on the Row, some at farms all around. Been down in that swamp, breedin', ain't no tellin' how long. More of 'em ever year, gone wild.

"They ain't comin' outta the bottom land. Been up toward White House, toward East Fork. 'Cept now they gittin' closer, comin' up in the fields. Be rootin' up new corn soon's we plant, it comes up . . . Preacher feller over on East Fork road seen 'im, big boar hog. Big as a short-legged horse, the man said."

They both laughed, neither of them believing the preacher.

"And what is it you're suggestin', Earl?" Francis Jennings was ready to end the day, get on to home and family.

"We don't deal with these hogs now, Mr. Francis, it ain't gonna be a pretty sight. Corn fields . . . vegetable gardens. Come May, won't be nothin' left. Might be we could git some dogs, go down in them woods, root 'em out, so to speak."

"Git some dogs? . . . Go lookin' fer 'em?"

"Yes sir. I hear 'ed a man down in Louis'ana's got some hog dogs. Gentleman named Mr. LeCocq."

"LeCocq, huh? French fellow . . . Isaac, if I remember right. Isaac LeCocq. I'll have a word with 'im, see can we borrow them dogs for a while."

They rode into the yard outside the horse barn. Fat Back rose, laboriously, from his perch at the double doors, took the reins of the two horses. Francis walked off toward the house, to Torie, the children. "Wild hogs," he muttered under his breath.

So it was arranged. Francis and Papa Thomas made the trip down into the edge of Louisiana, to the LeCocq farm.

"Look like curs, LeCocq. How is it these dogs is hog dogs and them over yonder ain't? How come mine ain't?"

"Ha." It was more a burst of air than a laugh. "These dogs is trained. Them dogs yonder, yore dogs, most likely'll go off chasin' deer or possums or bobcats. These dogs is trained to stick to hogs, ain't gonna git distracted."

"They's four dogs there, Mr. Jennin's," Issac LeCocq said. "You welcome to 'em. They don't come back, however, it'll cost a Jersey yearling apiece."

"A yearling a piece? That's a mite steep, LeCocq. I never heard of no dog was worth a Jersey cow." Francis slapped his felt hat against his leg, wiped the sweat from his forehead.

The debate, the bargaining went back and forth; it was spirited, but amicable, without animosity.

LeCocq reminded Francis, "You got Jersey cows, I got hog dogs."

"You a hard man, LeCocq."

They shook hands.

Francis loaded the dogs into a make-shift crate on the back of a farm wagon. They crossed the state line back into Mississippi, ran up the logging road parallel to the rivers back to Cut Bank.

"Now, JJ," Francis told his son, "we got to feed these dogs, might even play with 'em a little. We let 'em loose lookin' for them hogs, we don't want 'em heading back to Louisiana, want 'em thinkin' this is home."

"Yes, sir."

So JJ fed the dogs, morning and night. For the first several days he kept them in the pen reserved for bitch dogs in heat. Gradually he let them out for short periods, first one at a time, then two together, and finally the whole four of them.

"I think we can take 'em in the woods now, Papa," he said at supper that night.

"You can call 'em in, can you? Git 'em back home?"

"Yes, sir," the boy answered. There was pride in his voice, a smile.

On the following Tuesday, Francis told Earl Dupree, "Tell Fat Back saddle us up some mules come mornin'. Leave at good daylight."

"Mules, Mr. Francis?"

He laughed. "You too proud to be ridin' a mule, Earl?"

"Naw, sir. It's jus' you don't ride mules much."

"Better'n a horse down in that swampy land. Don't mind gittin' their feet in the mud and muck, don't mind pushin' through all that tangle of briars and brambles."

"How many'll we be needin'?"

"Five. Me an' you an' JJ, and Papa wants to go."

"Mr. Thomas wants to go?"

"It'll do him good. You know how much he enjoys the woods. An' we need one pack mule. Luke Denton an' most likely his boy'll be joinin' us up past the school house. 'Course they got their own mules. And, Earl, bring that long-barrel twelve-gauge we keep in the horse barn. An' a box a double-aughts."

Supper that night was strained, quiet. The sound of tin utensils clacking against dishes was louder than usual. JJ kept his elbows close to his sides, crossed his ankles, squeezed his knees together. He stirred his food, ate quickly, excused himself at the first possible opportunity.

"I don't like it a bit," Torie said as soon as the boy was out of the room. "Tomorrow's a school day."

"Books ain't all a boy needs to know," Francis answered. "Besides, we need to manage the dogs. He's the one been feedin' 'em, mindin' 'em."

"It's a bad precedent, Francis. He has enough trouble at school anyway. He'll be thinking anything is an excuse not to go."

There was a long silence, then: "Well, it's decided. I already told him he could go."

They rode from the barns east, toward the rivers. Five mules, three men, two white, one black, a twelve-year-old boy. They carried a canvas water bag each, a sack containing three syrup cans with corn bread, fried pork ribs, a jar of honey and a small arsenal of guns.

For the better part of three days they scoured the woodlands, first east and then north of the farm. The Denton's, father and son, joined them the first two days. Otis Butterbaugh on the third day. The first three days there had been some signs, but no hogs. Then, on a Thursday, the dogs found hogs, bayed. By the time the men and boys and mules fought their way through wet underbrush, the quarry was gone.

At the end of a week they slogged through a cold spring rain, mud and muck. But luck was with them. They found a sow and a litter of half-grown piglets. Francis shot and killed the sow with the Mauser. JJ and Paul Denton caught six of the piglets, carried them home in croaker sacks.

The dogs came home, tongues lolling. The sow was field dressed, thrown across the pack mule's broad back, carried to The Row and roasted through the long cool spring night.

Saturday all of Cut Bank community gathered around the trading post. Friday's rain had given way to a warm spring sun. Torie and Mama Jennings sold an abundance of Prince Albert tobacco and the new cola that had come on the market. Shotgun shells had sold out by mid-morning, unusual in the spring of the year. A rousing game of horseshoes drew a ring of spectators.

"Goin' out today, Mr. Francis?" someone asked. He was asked, "Goin' lookin' for them pigs? That boar? . . . It's got to be a big ole boar in them woods somewhere."

Francis stuck his thumbs under his belt, leaned his shoulders back. "Them dogs are plum worn out," he said. "Rest 'em a day or two. Give it another go on Monday. Might be needin' some rest myself. I ain't as young as I used to be."

"Some of us was thinkin' we might go with you. Git in on the fun, you might say." There was a general restiveness among the gathered neighbors.

Francis ran his thumb and fingers of his left hand over his mustache, his chin and down his neck. He didn't really want the woods full of gun totin' farmers. Any self-respecting swine would be in the next county before the sun was up in the treetops.

"We roastin' a couple a-them shoats," he told them. "Oughta be ready by mid-day ... You fellers find some horseshoes, break out a couple 'a checker boards and some dominoes. Have a tournament, sort of, something to eat later on."

"You should a seen them two boys chasin' them pigs," Otis told the gathered crowd. "You'd a-thought it was the county fair. Chasin' a greased pig. Why, they'd jump on one, git they arms aroun' it, wrap it up and it 'ud jus' squirt out the other end. Chase starts all over again." He tamped down the tobacco in his pipe.

"Didn't know you was there, Mr. Otis," somebody offered. "Best we could tell them pigs was caught couple days ago. You was up in White House lookin' to buy a pair a mules."

"Well," he answered, hurruped, "was there the next day. Right there with 'em, wet, it rainin' the whole day. Heard it first hand, practical did anyway. How they chased them pigs down, runnin' through them vines and limbs, divin' on the ground for 'em."

"Startin' to sound like yore granddaddy, Mr. Otis, tellin' all them stories." The crowd hooted. "To hear him tell it, he near lost the war all by hisself. Didn't need no help from General Lee ... all them other fellers."

Otis Butterbaugh blew out a cloud of smoke, grabbed a horseshoe and flung it. "I don't know why I bother tellin' you fellers nothin'. Don't none of you listen." The thrown projectile hooked the iron pipe just along one edge, spun half around and clanked off to the left side.

The afternoon grew warm, the first such of the season. Some kid from East Fork, he had stumbled onto the goings on inadvertently, won out at horseshoes.

"We oughta kick his ass," the oldest Hinds boy groused. "Send 'im up the road. Damn foreigner."

Nobody offered to help. The threat died in the cooling afternoon.

Papa Thomas was declared dominoes champion. Checkers went on into the evening without a clear winner.

"What you diggin' there, Uncle Fats," Francis asked the big black man on Monday morning.

"Gittin' ready for that boar hog, Mr. Francis." He leaned on the shovel, wiped the sweat away with a bandana. "Diggin' a pit, gonna cook 'im."

Francis laughed. "We ain't got 'im yet."

"You 'a git 'im. I know you gone git 'im."

By sundown Tuesday Fat Back had the pit dug, big enough to hold a full grown steer. He lined the sides of the pit with old tin roofing, built a ten-inch earthen berm around the perimeter. Field hands with post hole diggers burrowed into the packed earth at each end of the pit. Forked tree trunks, the size of a man's thigh were dropped into the holes, tamped down.

"You got some vinegar down to the store, Miss Torie?" Sadie asked.

Torie looked up sharply from wiping the remains of a mid-day meal off two-year-old Mavis' face. "Vinegar?"

"Yes, ma'am. Earl and Fat Back gonna roast that pig. They ever git 'im."

"And you need vinegar?"

"Yes, ma'am. Fat Back say vinegar, garlic. But I ain't never seen no garlic, no lemon."

Torie laughed. "That's getting a bit fancy, Sadie."

"Fat Back, he learn that kinda stuff down in Louis'ana, he was young. That time he run away from home, was down that way."

"And just what is Uncle Fats gonna do with this vinegar and garlic and lemon?"

"Oh, it's lot more stuff, Miss Torie. Onions and herbs and pepper. A whole lotta salt, he say."

"Hup," Torie sounded. "Cider, maybe, not vinegar," she said. "We got plenty good hard cider left."

It was Sadie's turn to say, "Hup . . . " Then she said, "Fat Back, he cleanin' a old water trough, gonna put that pig in there. Mix all this stuff in a water barrel, pour it on top a that pig. Soak it all night, he say."

"Hot red peppers, Sadie. Forget the garlic. Use a lot of red peppers."

The dogs picked up a fresh trail that ran parallel to a slough. The tone of their clamor was different.

"They found that boar hog, Mr. Francis," Earl said, almost shouted. "They found 'em."

"You think, Earl? How do you know?"

"Them dogs know. Jus' listen at 'em. They knowin' that ain't no sow they trailin', no buncha little pigs. Them dogs has smelt boar hog before."

"Is this gonna cost me a Jersey calf?" Francis asked.

"Might be, Mr. Francis, might be."

They kicked the mules up, urged them, pushed them through the underbrush. There was no open trail. Even at the end of winter the vines and limbs presented a physical barrier. Muck from the recent rains sucked at the mules' feet.

"Hurry, Papa, hurry," JJ called. "Them dogs'll be needin' help."

Earl swung the machete with a vengeance, cutting through the tangle. The baying of the dogs grew more frantic.

They found the den dug into the bank of a slough, underneath the roots of an ancient water oak. Floods, for decades, had swelled the slough, making it a rushing torrent and washed away the dirt on the lower side. The exposed roots reached like extended, clawing fingers down into the slough, through the standing water and muck, into the dirt below. On the upper side, the roots were firmly anchored in terra firma. The tree itself grew straight up from the break between dry ground and the always wet, the difference in elevation a mere sixteen, maybe eighteen inches. The swine had gone in between the roots, burrowing underneath, ultimately dooming the ancient oak.

The boar hog, when the dogs got there, was backed up against the den, his hind quarters and flanks wedged in between the protecting roots. The front of his body swayed side to side, feet planted just wider apart than the width of his shoulders. His head, hung low to the ground, swung with the front part of his body, left to right and back again, the curved tusk jutting up and out from the lower jaw.

The dogs ran in hard against the animal, and like water breaking around a boulder in the shallow part of a stream, parted and went by on each side of the boar.

"Lord, they got him cornered, Earl," Francis shouted, slapped his mule on the rump, urging it on through the tangle. "He might be big as a short-legged horse. Jus' listen at them dogs." He surged forward, past

Earl and his efforts to hack a path, mindless of the vines and limbs pulling at and cutting across his body. He lay low across the mule's neck, forging his way forward.

The dogs, coming in from the boar's back and sides, fell down between the roots. They found no footing to come at him away from the head and tusk. Even climbing onto his back, his hide like armor against their bites, they were powerless to do him any damage. In frustration the youngest dog came at him head on.

"No!" Francis yelled. Not that the young male dog would hear, or heed the warning if he did hear. The boar swung its head, caught the animal just behind the left shoulder as he tried at the last second to dodge out of the boar's reach. The tusk ripped open the dog's skin, down to the ribs, from the shoulder across the side and up into the middle of the dog's back, laid it open. The animal seemed to hang in mid-air, then fell into the two inches of standing water.

JJ, riding into the mix, sat on his mule paralyzed.

"Git that dog outta that water," Earl said.

Suddenly both Earl and JJ were in the slough; JJ falling face down in to the muck, then up on hands and knees, cradling the wounded animal, moving him away from the fray; Earl pulling, beating back the other dogs from harm's way. The mules pushed out sideways, backwards, away from the madness of the barrel-sized hog, the clambering dogs, the black man and boy sometimes standing, sometimes on hands and knees in the muck and water.

"You awful close, Earl," Francis called out. "Stay clear a them tusk. We ain't wantin' you ripped open. Stand back some. I need a clean shot at 'im."

Francis dismounted, pulled the Mauser from the saddle scabbard, worked his left arm through the sling and racked the bolt back, forward, sliding a cartridge into the chamber.

The bullet struck the animal just above the right eye. In his excitement, Francis had pulled the line of fire up and to the right ever so slightly. The steel projectile rode up the front of the skull, between the bone and the skin, came out the top of the head ripping the hide open from the inside. The boar went to its knees, shook its head side to side, slinging blood. The dogs fought free from their tenuous constraint, rushed, in mass, the blooded prey. The wounded dog on the sidelines struggled to its feet, back into the maelstrom. The humans, expecting the shot to be fatal, stood frozen, transfixed for long seconds.

"Shoot 'im again, Mr. Francis, shoot 'im again," Earl said. He's gonna kill all these dogs."

The dogs had rushed directly into the boar's head and shoulders, unable to get through the oak roots to his rear and flanks. A second dog flew, ripped and blooded, out into the murky water. The two remaining dogs clamped down on the hog's right ear and jowl.

"Shoot it, Francis . . . 'Fore he hurts another 'en," Thomas Jennings shouted as JJ crossed between his father and the primal struggle, between hunter and hunted.

"Move, boy, move. I ain't got no clear shot."

JJ grabbed up the second wounded dog and moved farther out into the slough.

The boar turned his head to the right, toward the two dogs tormenting it from that side. Francis shot. The bullet passed just along the left jaw bone and entered the animal between the top of his shoulder blade and the bottom of his neck, into the animals vitals. It dropped straight down into the muck between the roots of the ancient oak.

They rounded up the mules, which was no small feat. Then they built a travois for the two wounded dogs.

"Papa," Francis told the older Jennings, "head on back with these dogs. See can Mama clean 'em up, sew 'em up, maybe. And, tell Fat Back to send a couple a hands and another mule. Tell 'im send a singletree and some trace chain, tell 'em. We gotta drag this hog outta here."

"Can I go with 'im?" JJ asked. "Maybe ride on ahead? Tell Mama, tell folks at the store we got 'im . . . Got that boar?"

"No," his father answered. "It ain't seemly to go braggin' about things. Folks 'll know soon enough. Anyway, me and Earl be needin' help to pull 'im out from between them roots, clean and dress 'im. We gonna cook this devil and eat him."

"And a wagon, Papa? Somehow we gotta git im in a wagon. He's way too heavy to load on a mule."

Fat Back had dry hickory wood burning in the bottom of the pit before the hunters emerged from the woods.

"Thought you was gonna soak 'im overnight," Francis said as the hunting party arrived in the mule yard and dismounted.

"Yes, sur, Mr. Francis. Gone soak 'im all night. Gone keep this here fire goin' the same, all night. Want a good bed a coals."

"Take a lot of cookin'. That's a tough ole hog." Francis eyed the big black man, a grin in his voice.

"We got a lotta time," Fat Back said.

"We be needin' a hickory pole, a straight one, big as my arm," he told the field hands. "Take a big pole to hold that boar hog up off the ground, offa that fire."

They scrubbed the carcass, rubbed it down with salt, lowered it into the empty and cleaned horse trough. They heated water in a ten-gallon black wash pot, added what herbs were available: four oranges from the shelves of the trading post store, hard apple cider and onions—there were plenty of onions. Torie had scrounged up a whole mess of hot peppers. The cooks chopped up everything really fine, to make the flavors go further. Then they poured the mix into the horse trough. They added cool water to cover the barrel chest and shoulders of the animal. Francis sent to Churchill for two kegs of beer.

Fat Back didn't leave the mule barn for the next thirty-six hours or more, supervising the marinating, a word he had never heard, would never in his life in south Mississippi hear. Supervised the cooking.

"Rake them coals out from the middle," he might say. "Gittin' too hot."

Or, to a field hand, or JJ, or even Francis or Mr. Otis, if they happened to be there. "Need to add some more firewood, some a that water soaked hickory."

They turned the pig hourly, rotating the thigh sized spit resting on the Y shaped poles at either ends of the fire pit.

In the first light of day Francis asked, "How much longer?"

"He 'bout ready, Mr. Francis. Grease ain't drippin' no more. We gon' build up the fire a bit, crackle up that skin. Then we ready."

Francis left the mule barn, the pit and glowing bed of coals, walked off toward the trading post.

Otis Butterbaugh brought peanuts.

"Thought I might set up a pot and boil 'em," he told Torie.

Torie stopped what she was doing, eyed him down the bridge of her nose. "You're gonna sell peanuts at my store?"

Otis laughed. "Give 'em away. For the fellows that come by for checkers or pitchin' horseshoes. A thing Francis might do if he was to think about it."

He pulled his wagon into the shade of three pin oaks just to the east of the store, unloaded a black cast iron pot and a croaker sack of peanuts. JJ fetched stove wood and fat pine splinters from the pile stacked against the horse barn. By seven-thirty, they had water boiling, poured in some rock salt. They added the sack of peanuts sometime before eight o'clock. Then Otis pulled the burning wood away from the pot, pushed the coals up snug.

"We wanta keep that water simmerin'," he said to nobody in particular. "Don't want it boiling away. Cook 'em slow." He laid a shaped oak plank across the top of the pot, holding in most of the steam.

By ten the word had gotten out in the community.

Big doings down at the trading post. Food and stuff. Mr. Francis even got some beer brought in!

By sometime shortly after mid-morning the first of the horseshoe pitchers arrived. It wasn't until some minutes later that anyone paid attention to the goings-on in the side yard.

"Hey, Mister Otis," somebody called across the way, "you smokin' out the local crop a mosquitoes? That pig has done been cooked."

"Boilin' peanuts." He pushed the straw hat up from the brow of his head, wiped away the sweat. "You fellows might want some later on."

"They ready?" another horseshoe pitcher asked. "Ain't had none yet this year."

"Not yet, boys," Otis told them. "Gotta cook 'em slow."

From time to time he added half a bucket of water, checked the goobers, tasted them for saltiness, added a little when needed.

At a little after eleven, late morning, Otis told JJ, "Git us a ax handle, somethin' to lift this pot, carry it around front."

The boy came back with a single-tree. They ran it through the handle of the pot, lifted, dumped out the excess water and moved it to the corner of the veranda in the shade. Otis ladled out a small pile of the streaming peanuts onto the plank table.

"Alright, lads," he called out, "fresh goobers here. Fresh outta the pot." A plume of steam rose from the mound.

"It's too damn hot to be eatin' them things, Mr. Otis," one of the younger players said from across the narrow dirt road.

The clank of iron horseshoes on iron pins resumed. Also, the sound of pitched iron onto the packed sand of the pits. No *ching* of iron against iron. "Go home," the shouts of derision came, the horse-laughs.

Cletus McWilliams, newly arrived on the scene, lumbered down off his buggy seat, squinted from his vantage point out in the open sun toward the shaded veranda. "Is them peanuts, Otis? Smells like peanuts."

"Fresh boiled, an' we ain't had no takers yet. Boys say it's too hot."

Cletus gathered up a handful, shook them back and forth across his palm, scattering the heat of the freshly boiled nuts against the calloused skin, cooling them to some degree in the warm mid-day air. He thumbed open a shell, popped the three exposed legumes into his mouth.

"Boys ain't old enough to know about simple pleasure," he told Otis. "Think it's all about girls or winnin' some kind of a game." He shelled open up another mouthful, moved across the veranda toward the open door into the little general store.

"Now, don't let them young bucks git into that beer 'till late in the day," Francis told Earl and Fat Back.

"I done put the fear a-God in 'em, Mr. Francis," Fat Back said, brandished an oak and wrought iron single-tree.

They all, the two black men and Francis Jennings, laughed.

"I see what you mean," Francis said. Then he added, "We'll cut you off a hind-quarter and a shoulder. Send it down later."

"Shorely would like to have some a them ribs, Mr. Francis," Earl said.

Francis laughed. "I'll see you git some." He turned, walked up the gentle rise from the barns toward the house and the trading post.

By noon there was a crowd. All of Cut Bank had come out. They moved the cooked hog to just off the veranda, set on a hastily built plank table, with the keg of beer on the shaded end of the veranda.

"Has this food been blessed?" the young preacher asked.

"No," Papa Thomas said. "Would you do the honors, reverend."

"Let's read some verses from the gospel of St. Matthew," the preacher said, opened his bible.

There was an uneasy silence.

"When Jesus heard it, He departed from there by boat to a deserted place by Himself. But when the multitudes heard it, they followed Him on foot from the cities.

"And when Jesus went out He saw a great multitude; and He was moved with compassion for them, and healed their sick. When it was evening, His disciples came to Him, saying, 'This is a deserted place, and the hour is already late. Send the multitudes away, that they may go into the villages and buy themselves food.'

"But Jesus said to them, 'They do not need to go away. You give them something to eat.'

"And they said to Him, 'We have here only five loaves and two fish.'

"He said, 'Bring them here to Me.' Then He commanded the multitudes to sit down on the grass. And He took the five loaves and the two fish, and looking up to heaven, He blessed and broke and gave the loaves to the disciples; and the disciples gave to the multitudes.

"So they all ate and were filled, and they took up twelve baskets full of the fragments that remained. Now those who had eaten were about five thousand men, besides women and children."

After the prayer, Francis carved the roasted pig, slicing off slabs of ham and shoulder. A ring of people three deep circled the table. Food seemed to materialize from wagons and buggies, from canvas sacks hooked over saddle horns. Roasted potatoes, pots of cooked greens, corn bread, whole baked yams, and a cauldron of baked beans.

"I've had beef jerky was easier to chew," Otis Butterbaugh announced to the gathered crowd. He held a carrot sized chunk of pork shoulder in his left hand and filled his mug from the keg. He glanced to be sure the young preacher wasn't watching too closely.

There were pies, a pound cake with the requisite pound each of butter and sugar, and a dozen fresh eggs. The four cups of flour seemed almost superfluous.

"We better cook us up another batcha these peanuts," Mr. Otis told JJ in the deepening afternoon. There was a steady line of takers for boiled peanuts.

When the second round was dumped onto the plank floor, Torie, standing in the doorway, straw broom in hand, asked, "All right, now, who's gonna sweep up these hulls?"

There was no shortage of volunteers.

Earl's seventy-seven-year-old mama, from down on The Row, said, "Toughest meat I ever et." She stripped another thumb sized piece off the hanging hind quarter, worked it into her nearly toothless mouth.

They would eat pit roasted pork for the better part of a week.

The citizens of Cut Bank drifted away. There were cows to milk, animals to feed, babies and small children to put to bed. Some few stayed deep into the afternoon, the coming evening.

Around several bonfires, flasks of whiskey turned up, warmth against the night chill. There was only one fight that needed breaking up. And, it not over a woman, but quail hunting. Torie and Francis sat on the veranda some hundred and a half yards from the trading post, the bonfires, the last hangers-on. Him smoking a last pipe of the day, her wrapped in a wool knit shawl.

"Should you maybe go down and send 'em home?" she asked. "The children will never sleep with this noise. And tomorrow's Sunday . . . Church."

"Day like today, they don't wanta let go. Didn't nobody plan it. It just happened," he said, not really addressing his wife's comment. "Jus' happened. Fellers wanta hold onto it long as they can. Kinda like a kid at Christmas, watchin' the sun go down. Wanta reach out with their fingers, catch the sunset. Don't wanta let go."

He drew deep on the pipe, savoring the strong, sweet taste of the Prince Albert tobacco. "Still, I'll go walk among 'em."

Torie watched him across the dark expanse between the house and the fires burning in the wagon road opposite the entrance to the trading post. Across the dark she watched him go to each group, each bonfire, watched him clasp someone's shoulder, reach out and touch an elbow. There was the occasional sound of laughter across the distance. She knew he did not say to them, *Go home, it's late.* She heard, at least imagined she heard, him say, *See you boys in church tomorrow.*

She stood, waited for him at the top step. Watching him come back across the darkness toward her, toward the house, seeing him silhouetted against the distant firelight. She knew that he would want her tonight, that they would make love.

Torie went down the four steps, met him a dozen feet out on the walkway. She saw him reach for her, felt him reach his hand under the shawl, trace his fingers from the back of her shoulder down to her hip.

Bringing Lula Home

Martina Boone

A shingle flew off the decrepit roof in the last gasps of hot, wet post-hurricane wind and grazed my temple before landing on the debris-strewn lawn. Wasn't enough the damned house and its smothering Spanish moss was sucking the life out of my body and slowly leaving me a wrinkled husk like every other resident in Watson's Creek, South Carolina. Now it was going to go ahead and kill me outright.

Rubbing the scrape on my head, I edged around a fallen branch from an ancient oak. Then I turned back to survey Watson's Landing for other damage. On the bright side, the house's two-story columns with their peeling white paint didn't seem to sag any more than usual, and the wide front steps hadn't completely collapsed. On the other hand, it was early yet. The river could still rise in the wake of the hurricane. It was too much to hope it would rise high enough to wash the house straight down the creek and out to sea. No, if my luck held, the water would come just high enough to bring half the town's well-meaning citizens out here to sandbag and eat through two months of grocery money in cucumber and cream cheese sandwiches.

Watson's Landing had survived malaria, yellow fever, British tariffs, the decline of Carolina indigo, Union shelling, and nine generations of spendthrift Watsons. It was long overdue for someone to put it out of its misery. That might as well be me as anyone—I didn't have a clue what else to sell to keep it standing. What I really wanted was to pack up my easel and brushes, run down the long, oak-lined drive, and keep on running. Which might at least have the added benefit of finally overshadowing the thirty-year-old Scandal. The night Mama's twin sister Lula had crept out in the dead hours with a suitcase full of antique silver and a driving itch to get out of town was still the talk of Watson's Creek.

More power to Lula. I couldn't run.

All I could do was scowl at the decaying landscape through a haze of humidity that left the air almost as blue as the indigo wash I worked into my paintings. Behind me, the front door opened with a groan of protest.

"You make sure there aren't any branches down in Great-Granny Brantley's roses, now," Mama called, peering out at me from the top of the steps before she opened the door even wider and let herself slump against the jamb. "After that you come right back inside here and call Joe Beaufort to check the roof."

"I can look for myself," I said.

"Don't you so much as think of climbing up on that roof, Ginnie Mae Watson Pinckney. It isn't seemly, and the last thing this family needs is another tragedy, and me with palpitations already from the stress and the storm. You stay right here where I can see you."

Squelching around the house in my battered old waxed jacket, sundress, and polka dotted Wellington boots, I ignored her, that being the only way I could cling to sanity. I was twenty-five and trapped in a time warp.

I rounded the corner, and my feet tripped to a stop. The shock and humidity stole all the remaining air from my lungs. While the storm had done relatively little to the front of the house, along the side here it had knocked the gazebo down. Splintered white slats of wood lay scattered all over the lawn along with the tattered shrouds of Spanish moss.

The gazebo we could live without. I couldn't say the same for the fifty-odd shingles that also dotted the ground instead of the roof where they might have done some good keeping out the rain.

Frowning at the roofline, I heaved a sigh of mingled outrage and relief. At least this took away my reason for climbing up there. I could calculate the cost from right down here: way too much. I'd be better off expending my energy carrying buckets and plastic sheeting up to the attics. Unless I could figure out a way to pay Chandler Construction's extortionary prices, the roof would have to keep on leaking.

Kicking a cypress branch aside a little harder than perhaps absolutely necessary, I turned and went back inside. There I discovered the phone lines were still down, the electricity was still out, and Mama was standing helpless in the pantry with a lighted candle and a whole-new-roof's worth of Watson pearls around her neck trying to figure out what to make for dinner.

"How are you doing, Mama?" I studied her face for signs of an imminent breakdown. "You holding up?"

She looked up at me with a vague frown and drew her sweater

tighter around thin shoulders. "I'd be better if this wind would stop knocking branches against the windows and making my heart jump. Lord, I'll never get used to storms."

"Why don't you let me fix you a sandwich," I said, drawing her back out of the pantry and taking the candle from her. "There's leftover chicken in the fridge we need to eat since we don't know when they'll get the electricity back."

Here in Freedom County, everything moved at a glacial pace. It had taken the Devil Oak in the center of Watson's Creek 1500 years to grow 65 feet high, and it took about that long to get through the Way-Things-Have-Always-Been-Bureaucracy to get anything done. That was just one more reason why I needed to get out.

In New York City, they had the Museum of Modern Art, countless art schools and galleries, and if I got nostalgic for mummies or ancient relics, I could find those at the Metropolitan Museum. I was certain they would have the lights back on in New York City a day or two after a storm at worst. In Watson's Creek, we had the Resurrection Tavern and the Betting Board, and all the old relics would be laying odds whether it would be two days or a week from Tuesday before electricity flowed again.

I fixed Mama a chicken sandwich and poured her a glass of sweet tea. After that, I settled her in the parlor with a fire, enough lighted candles to fill the pricket stand at the Episcopal Church, and an Agatha Christie mystery she had already read at least twenty times.

"I'm going up to the attics for a few minutes," I said, hoping she'd be asleep before she reached the end of Chapter Three. Reading always made her tired.

Two dusty hours later, I had covered about fifteen miles of moth-eaten sofas with sheeting from the box we kept next to Grandma Dupree's Easter china. I'd also checked stacks of molding, battered chests and bureaus for anything remotely valuable. Rocking back on my heels in front of a trunk of yellowing letters and old, stained petticoats, I contemplated the small haul of antique linens and silver-backed hairbrushes I had set aside to sell. I'd also found a horseshoe-shaped ladies writing desk that might bring a couple thousand dollars if I refinished it and drove it up to Charleston.

What I really needed was something more portable and quick to turn around, but there was nothing left. About the only thing I hadn't already raided—hadn't been able to bring myself to raid in the three years since my daddy had drunk himself into a stupor down at the

Resurrection and tragically insisted on driving home—was Grandpa Watson's collection of first editions. I hated even to think about selling those. Trouble was, Mama refused to believe things were dire. Our setbacks, as she called them, were bound to turn around just as soon as the economy righted itself.

"Interest rates will go back up, Ginnie Mae. Always do. You wait and see," she would tell me. And no matter how many times I explained that it didn't matter whether you were getting a quarter-percent or twenty-five percent, the interest on zero was still going to be the same.

The only way anything got sold to pay the bills was if Mama didn't know. Even searching the library was going to have to wait until after she went to bed.

Back downstairs, I prepared her heart medicine and a pot of tea, hot this time and liberally soaked with brandy. The knocker on the front door sounded before I could take it in. Blowing out a breath of frustration, I answered to find Joe Beaufort standing on the step, muscled forearm braced above him on the jamb.

Rain dripped off his new unfamiliar lawyer haircut and the same old Barbour jacket he'd worn since high school. "Came over to make sure you and your Mama are both all right," he said. "Trees down all over the road, and the phone lines may be out a while yet. Cell towers are out, too." He lowered his voice. "Is she driving you crazy?"

"She's just worried," I answered quietly. "It isn't too bad." I stepped back to invite him in. "We have some limbs down, but it's mostly shingles off the roof," I said more loudly. "How's everything in town? Your house? Your folks?"

His teeth flashed white and strong in the candlelight. Wiping his feet on the mat, he said, "They're both fine, and you know it would take more than a Category Two to do much damage to that old house. We have a few limbs down, but I'll take care of those in the morning. Then I'll come help you clean up, if you don't need anything tonight."

My lips tightened, but I stretched them into a painful smile. His help was the last thing I wanted. The more I let Joe help, the more he would tie me up with invisible strings. The next thing I knew, I'd be bound so tight, I'd be walking down the church aisle and sending our children to school in the same building where Emmy Jenkins had made me pinky swear we were both getting out of Freedom County to see the world.

Emmy had made it out. She had gone away to NYU and never came back. Even now she was living in New York eating real bagels for breakfast and pizza for dinner, and she had a spare room she was keeping warm for me. As long as I didn't let myself get sucked into staying in Watson's Creek forever.

"I don't need you," I said to Joe, softening it as much as I could with a smile, "but it's sweet of you to check on us. Can I get you a glass of tea or a cup of coffee? Something to eat? I made a roast chicken salad for Mama earlier. There's plenty left."

"Does that mean you finally got that generator like I suggested?" Joe asked, his eyes warming up.

"Not yet." I leaned back against the wall and crossed my arms. "It just means I've got an old camp stove in the back of the pantry, and I'm not afraid to use it."

He looked at me long and hard. Nothing had really changed between us. He'd come back, but I was still set on leaving. I didn't know why he expected a little hurricane would have made a difference.

"Well, all right then," he said. "I'll be back sometime after noon, I guess."

I watched him slide his long legs into the Mercedes he'd gotten as a high school graduation present before he went off to college and law school. He could have gone anywhere after that. Anywhere in the whole, wide world. Except maybe the Mercedes was another one of those invisible strings, tying him back to his daddy's law practice and Beaufort Ridge, his family's huge old albatross of a house. In its own way, that responsibility hung as heavily around Joe's neck as Watson's Landing did on mine.

The headlights on the Mercedes bounced off the ruts in the drive and paused before turning left down the highway back toward town. I waved even though I knew Joe couldn't see me. And then I shut the door.

"Was that Joe Beaufort I heard?" Mama asked when I went in with the tea and medicine. "Why didn't you invite him back? Lord knows I need someone to talk to. No one else in town has even bothered calling. We could have been dead out here."

"Well," I said, "the phones are down, so that would explain it."

Mama rested her head back against the cushion. "Maybe a game of cards would help steady my poor nerves. I haven't been this upset since the tragedy. This storm has about worn me out."

I sat through three distracted games of Rummy and another pot of brandy-laced tea before I got her off to bed. Then I snuck back down to the library and plopped into Grandpa Watson's mahogany swivel chair, contemplating the desk drawer and trying to figure out where he might have hidden the key to the glass first edition cabinet.

Twenty minutes later, I'd searched the whole room and was no closer to finding it. But it had to be somewhere.

I started all over again with the Georgian desk, and this time I took everything out of the drawers and patted down the sides and tops and underneaths. Grandpa Watson had been a tricky old bastard, especially after Lula left. He learned his lesson the first time, apparently, and wasn't about to leave anything valuable and portable lying around to provide Mama with the means or temptation to leave herself. Maybe that was also why he'd wasted every little bit that was left of what had once been the Watson fortune.

Searching the left-hand bottom drawer of his desk, I heard a faint click. A small indentation on the side gave way when I pulled my fingers back, and the end of the drawer swung open revealing a hidden space.

My breath caught on a wisp of hope. For a moment, I let my mind play with what might be inside. Stocks, bonds, jewelry, silver . . . Leaning forward, I probed inside. My fingers closed around the cold brass of a small key, and I took an extra breath before I dared pull it out to look if it was even the right size to open the leaded glass cabinet in the center of the wall of bookshelves. It was, and I was so relieved I almost closed the drawer before checking to see if there was anything else.

There was also a small packet of letters wrapped in string. The paper was brittle and yellowed. I slid the string off and removed a sheet of stationery from an envelope someone had already slit with a letter opener.

"Dear Pru," the letter began, in a flamboyant, sloping script. "I don't know what to think since you haven't answered any of my other letters. Either the old devil hasn't let you see them, or you don't want to hear from me. I can't exactly blame you. I'm not certain I could forgive either, if I was still standing where you are. All I knew at the time was that if I didn't get out, I was going to shrivel and die in that house, and if you had tried to talk me out of it, I wouldn't have had the courage to leave. It doesn't matter that corsets went out of style back when Grandma Dupree was a girl. In Watson's Creek they are always going to be in fashion. A bird can't spread its wings to fly if it can't fill its lungs to breathe. Can you understand that at all? I hope you can. I flew, Sister, because I had to. As it happens, I didn't get very far. There was an accident, and while I lay in bed recovering, I kept hoping all the platitudes about time healing all wounds might come true. I'm not done hoping yet, so don't feel sorry for me. Don't feel obligated either, but if you have any forgiveness in your heart, I would like to see you. The old man made it clear I will never be welcome back at Watson's Landing. You'll always have a place here with me, if you want it. Isn't it odd how you only miss a place after someone tells you it's off limits? Ever yours, Lula."

My hands shook as I read the letter. Tears blurred the handwriting, but I felt as if I knew Lula Watson from her words, as if I could have written them myself. My chest ached with the heartbreak of waiting for Pru, my mother, to write back, to say something, anything.

Reading through the rest of the letters, I realized Grandpa Watson must never have let Mama see them, any of them. It didn't surprise me, really. That was just the kind of sour, self-righteous, stubborn bastard Grandpa Watson had been. I knew he'd gone to his deathbed and never once said a word about these letters from Lula. As far as I knew, he had never spoken her name after the night she left.

I swiveled in the chair and studied the portrait of Grandpa and his wife, Eugenia, hanging above the fireplace. Eugenia Mae Tatinall Watson, who I was named after, looked like she might have once had a spark of life in her, too, before Grandpa snuffed it out. I remembered the old man as a source of terror, his loud voice jumping out at me as I tiptoed down the hall to run out and play, asking had I completed my homework, had I practiced my piano, had I done my drawing, and had I done it right? Maybe he was the reason I painted my landscape in shades of blue, mixing realism with sweeping abstract curves and thick blots of paint instead of the careful, precise still-lifes Grandpa thought were suitable. As if dead pheasants and rabbits and bowls of moldering fruits and cheeses suited anything except a bad case of indigestion. Probably it was Grandpa Watson's ghost that still clung to the dark, damp corners of the house and filled them with the stifling, claustrophobic sense of obligation.

I wondered what had happened to Lula. Had the broken bird ever flown again? Turning over an envelope, I peered at the San Francisco address. Had clear across the country been far enough to fly? Had she been happy all these years? Was she even still alive?

I wondered how different Mama's life, Mama's personality even, would have been if Lula had stayed in Watson's Landing. Wondered if Mama might have ventured a little farther out of her shell if Lula hadn't strayed quite so far.

I went to sleep that night still wondering and woke up with

thoughts of Lula running in my head. Why hadn't she ever tried to get back in touch with Mama? Grandpa Watson had been dead almost fifteen years now. Did she even know that? Or had she stopped caring, stopped thinking about Mama and Watson's Creek so long ago that it didn't matter. If I left, and Mama told me she would never speak to me again—which she was likely to do—how long would it be before I stopped caring? Never probably.

But the alternative was staying here, slowly selling pieces of the past to survive the present, something most of the rest of the South had given up on fifty or sixty years ago. If I stayed, I would spend the rest of my life working at the library and painting sweet, insipid murals for the Sunday school classes and backdrops for high school productions of *Peter Pan*, *Thoroughly Modern Millie*, and *High School Musical*.

I wished I had Aunt Lula's courage. Maybe I could borrow a little of it.

When Joe came by that afternoon, I took advantage of his being around to keep an eye on Mama. I drove to Charleston with a first edition of Robert Penn Warren's *All the King's Men* and, the jewel of Grandpa's collection, a signed first of *The Catcher in the Rye*. That should have been good enough for a roof all by itself. With change left over to fix the crumbling chimney.

The way to the shop on King Street had become so familiar, the car seemed to know the way all by itself. In the odd way storms can, the hurricane seemed to have passed Charleston by with a light brush of wind that only dropped branches and leaves on the streets and washed away the summer dirt from the houses. Inside, C. Birleigh's & Co Fine Antiques looked the same as always. Hepplewhite sideboards rubbed elbows with Chippendale chairs and Sheraton dressing tables, all of them loaded down with Sheffield silver and crystal decanters.

"Back again, Ginnie?" Shoulders stooped and footsteps brisk, Charles Birleigh strode around the corner in his customary blue oxford shirt and yellow bow tie to shake my hand, the top of his scalp gleaming in the brilliant light of the Czech crystal chandeliers hanging on display.

"How are you, Charles? How is it an extra birthday actually made you younger?"

His eyes twinkled behind his bifocals, and he stood a little straighter. "Now you know I haven't aged a day since I turned eighty-five, young lady. Don't intend to either."

"I brought you a very little something." I handed him a small canvas wrapped in silver paper.

"How many times have I told you, there's no need to butter me up? For you, I'll always give a good price." But he smiled with pleasure as he took the package to the counter.

My stomach twisted, and my palms started to sweat. I'd thought I was ready, but I hadn't been.

It took him too long to unwrap it. He stood even longer silently looking down at it. "Is this one of yours?" he asked me finally.

Heat pricking my cheeks, I set down the parcel of first editions and carefully began to remove the multiple layers of plastic bags and wrappings. "Yes," I said.

"You know I can't accept it," he said, gently.

The room blurred, and the floor seemed to wiggle under my feet as I stepped over to take the painting back.

"It isn't in my ordinary style at all, I'll admit," he continued. His voice was soft, and he raised my chin with his fingers so that I would look at him. "But it's lovely. Truly amazing, really. With the indigo wash you've used over everything, the mood should be dark. Somehow you've captured hope in the blue of possibility."

Tears swelled in my chest and rose up to clog my throat. For the first time in what felt like years, I could almost breathe again. "Oh, I'm so relieved. And I want you to have it. Happy belated birthday."

"I'll tell you what," he said, "I'll hang it here in the shop and point anyone who asks about it back to you. Then I can enjoy it for however many years I have left without feeling guilty for taking advantage of you."

"Speaking of which . . ." I pushed the two first editions toward him.

He nudged his glasses up his nose and bent over. His eyes widened. Putting on a fresh set of surgical gloves from under the counter before picking it up, he examined the Salinger first. The slight flare of his nose and the miniscule, acquisitive tightening of his fingers on the book were the only signs of his excitement. He set the book down and picked up the other without saying a single word.

"Regretfully," he said, when he eventually put that down as well and turned back to face me, "I can't take these either." He held up a finger to stifle my protest as I grasped at the edge of the counter. "But I will pass them on to a friend at an auction house who can do a better job with them."

I closed my eyes and took a breath, uncurled my fingers. "How fast?"

"How much do you need to get by?" he asked, taking my shaking hands in his own.

"Enough for a deposit on a new roof." I pushed the words past a tongue made awkward by guilt and pride and a hundred other emotions bred into my blood by generations of stubborn Watson ancestors. "On the condition that you'll take a commission for passing them along."

"Done," he said, and I got the impression as I left that he was happier with the transaction than I was. I'd been selling off pieces of Watson's Landing so long that somehow he'd become a friend.

I drove to the library with his check in my pocket, and I didn't feel any better about that than I did about this next errand. Despite my lack of certainty though, even without the lack of Internet and electricity back in Watson's Creek, it was best handled here in Charleston. At least here, every move I made wouldn't be known and dissected over Sunday chicken and biscuits at half the houses on Harper Hill. The last thing I needed was any of it getting back to Mama.

The one good part of searching for Lula, she wasn't hard to find. No need to wade through four-hundred-and-eight thousand Google entries. Even in a city the size of San Francisco, there was only one Lula Elizabeth Lucas Watson.

The car accident was one of the first references. The load on a logging truck driving ahead of her down the highway had come loose, and Lula had broken her back, both arms, and her right leg. She had kept quietly to herself since then, if the lack of mentions in my Google search were any indication. She was credited on the boards of various charities and as a sponsor of the opera and the ballet, but there were no pictures of her, and nothing at all about children or a husband. There was also no address, only contact information for an attorney on Fremont Street.

I couldn't bring myself to do anything with that. Nothing I had found, after all, told me anything personal about Aunt Lula, about who she had become.

I drove home on auto-pilot and discovered that Joe's Mercedes was still parked out front at Watson's Landing. I left my worn-out Volvo in the sagging converted carriage house and followed the sound of a chain saw until I found him in worn jeans and a plain white cotton T-shirt, slicing through a fallen cypress tree out near the edge of the creek.

"I didn't mean for you to come out here and work yourself to death," I said, my nose wrinkling at the tang of fresh cut wood.

His face was flushed, or maybe that was the result of being out in the sun and the wind all day. It made the blue of his eyes stand out like indigo. I wondered, since evidently I'd started down the dark road of introspection, how much my obsession with the color had to do with Joe and how much was due to my own history. One of my distant ancestors had planted the first of the seeds that transformed the indigo industry in the Colonies. Eliza Lucas Pinckney saved three Lucas family plantations and countless others with the crop, and she was only seventeen. She'd been younger than me when she helped lay the foundation of what I was now selling off. No wonder I felt blue so often.

"You would die sooner than ask someone for help," Joe said, pulling off his gloves. "Even if they're willing to give it." He wiped his face with a red bandana. "Now your Mama on the other hand—"

My hands clenched. "Oh, lord. Has she been out here talking your ear off?"

Grinning, he tucked the bandana back into his pocket. "Caught me as I was going back to the car. Took me inside for a glass of tea, talked my ear off about you, and gave me my marching orders."

"Marching orders?" I fell back a step.

"Nothing dire." His eyes locked on my feet. "Just about what all needs doing around here."

My heart squeezed at the look on his face. Sometimes, the thought of leaning in and kissing him was almost beyond resisting. Kissing him the way I used to be able to kiss him, back when things hadn't been so complicated. Back when he and I would go down to the creek with our friends and dance to music from someone's CD-player, swing out on a rope from the bank, and drop down into the middle of the current. Joe would stay under long enough to make my heart stop. Then he'd surge up from the churning depths, shaking the water and hair out of his eyes, skin gleaming in the Carolina sun and dappled blue cypress shadows.

I shook my head. "Mama had no right to tell you to do anything—"

"She knows I want to help," Joe said. "And you know I'd rather stay on her good side than catch the wrong end of that tongue. Not to mention she'd be on the phone with my daddy before my car hit the highway."

"You're a grown man—"

"Yes, I am," he said, taking a step closer. "Sometimes, it wouldn't hurt you to remember that."

Sudden streams of warmth spread through my veins, and my lungs squeezed down to nothing. Maybe the lack of air was what made the blood all head south out of my brain. I mumbled something incoherent and ran back the way I'd come, Joe's bark of laughter ringing in my ears.

It was still ringing when I let myself into the house and heard Mama calling. "Is that you, Ginnie Mae?"

"Yes, Mama." I followed her voice into the drawing room and found her on the couch glaring at her daily Sudoku. She was firmly convinced doing them would keep her brain sharp. Trouble was, she'd been at it so long, she'd worked past the hard levels and was now deep into Monster territory. According to Joe, Monster should have been familiar ground for her, except it suited only when she could be the one to dish it out. Ever since she had graduated up from Extremely Difficult, the Sudoku puzzles had become a love/hate relationship.

"And where have you been all afternoon?" she asked as soon as I stepped over the threshold. "Without so much as a single word to let me know where to find you."

"I knew Joe was here."

"Good thing, too." Her expression changed, went as sly as a cat ready to pounce. "He's turned into a good man, that Joe Beaufort. Wish you'd develop some common sense before he changes his mind about you."

I fought a sigh. "Can't you ever leave it alone?"

She dropped the Sudoku book and pencil into her lap and wagged her finger. "Don't you think you can talk to me like that, just because I'm In Bad Shape and Stuck Here in the house most of the day on account of my Heart and Nerves—"

"Can I get you some tea, Mama?" I asked. "I see the electricity is still out, so I'll need to be creative for dinner."

"Mind you ask Joe to stay," she called after me as I turned into the hallway. "After all he's done, it's the very least you can do."

I stood in the kitchen a long moment with my arms wrapped around my waist trying to ignore the sound of the chain saw outside and Mama's bulldozer voice still running through my head. Then I made her tea and escaped again to take a pitcher down to Joe. Feeling guilty, I invited him to dinner after all. I made a summer tomato salad, and a plate of cheeses and cold cuts, and set them out on the porch to take advantage of the fact that the hurricane had swept most of the mosquitos away. They would be back with a vengeance in a matter of days as the floodwaters hatched the dormant eggs.

Sitting in the white wicker porch set that needed another coat of paint, we ate and talked a while about not much of anything. I tried to ignore Mama's blatant early good night, which left me alone with Joe by candlelight under the big, gold moon.

"There's a bat," Joe said, pointing toward a fast-flying shape winging past one of the live oak trees. "See it? First one I've seen since the storm, and here you are wearing white."

"Yes." I nodded distractedly.

"Good thing you're already halfway to insane then," Joe said. "At least it won't matter as much if the bat tangles in your hair."

"What?" I jerked my attention back.

His rough chuckle shivered down my spine. His hand brushed mine as he reached to take my empty glass and set it down. "A dollar for your thoughts," he said.

"Is that inflation? Or do you really want to know?" I twisted my ring, resisting the urge to start clearing plates away.

"A lot of both."

I watched the bat fly, let my head fall back against the chair, and thought about Lula and Mama. Thought whether I should say anything. Do anything.

"What would you say if I found a letter Aunt Lula sent to Mama that she has never seen?" I said eventually.

Joe leaned forward slowly and picked up the sweaty tea pitcher. It looked small in his hand. I noticed all the cuts he'd gotten out there chopping my wood today, despite the gloves he'd worn. One of the cuts was still lightly weeping.

"You ought to take care of your hands," I said.

"Have you told your Mama about the letter?" My glass clinked as Joe carefully set the lip of the pitcher against it, refilled it before he refilled his own.

"Not yet. I'm not even sure I'm going to. I don't know what she would say."

"That's probably wise." Joe nodded.

"I know where she is though." I looked up and met his eyes, and suddenly felt a little breathless, and more than a little guilty. "I'm thinking of tracking her down."

"Why?"

I watched the Adam's apple fall and rise out of the open collar of the shirt he had carelessly thrown back on after he finished cutting the wood. "Because in the letter, she sounded lonely and sad," I said. "And she missed Mama. They were twins. You don't get over losing a twin."

"She was the one who walked away," Joe said in his careful lawyer voice. He leaned back into the deep, white wicker chair.

"It wasn't Mama she meant to leave. Only Watson's Creek."

"Sometimes it's one and the same thing, isn't it?"

Later, I lay in bed with the warm breeze blowing through the window and the yellow gauze curtains swaying, and I thought about his words. Thought about him.

The next morning, I told Mama I was going back to Charleston to check on the electricity and on one of my paintings I had left with someone. My cell phone was working again, but the land lines were still out. What I wanted to do was best done in person anyway.

"Don't know why you think anyone would be interested in that so-called art of yours," Mama said from the wingback chair in the morning room, sniffing as she peered up at me over her needlepoint. "It's almost as embarrassing as those erotic romances Arnell Mitchel's oldest girl is writing."

"I wouldn't worry. I promise I'm not painting anybody naked."

I drove back to the Antique shop and asked Charles if I could borrow his email account. Then I wrote a long note to the address of Lula's San Francisco lawyer.

"Would you call me if you get anything back from them?" I asked Charles after hitting send.

He'd been shamelessly reading over my shoulder the whole time, and now he straightened. "You know I will," he said.

"And one more thing?"

He gave me a long, searching look. "What now?"

"You honestly thought the painting was good? You weren't just saying so?"

He smiled and turned me by the shoulders to look up above the cash register where he'd hung the painting in pride of place.

Relief bloomed in my chest. Combined with the sending of the email, I felt about twenty pounds lighter than when I first walked into the shop that morning.

"I honestly know the painting is good," Charles said.

The next question was even harder. "Do you have any connections to galleries here?" I rushed on. "You know how I've talked about going to New York, well all this time, I guess I've been thinking it was an all or nothing situation. That I'd have to go up there, and study, and make connections before I could even think about selling my work or showing it to anyone. But if I could sell a painting or two now . . . It would make things easier."

"You'd feel safer," Charles said slowly. "Nothing comes with guarantees. But if I know anything about what people prize, you could sell a busload of your work to the tourists alone. That indigo effect, there's something hypnotic to it, and it speaks of the South."

"Would you mind asking around?"

"How many more paintings do you have?"

"A sanity-preserving shed full," I said. Not one of them meant a thing to me compared to the idea of having the chance to get out of Watson's Creek. Or at least of having the freedom to choose to stay.

I drove home overflowing with a burst of energy. It made me wish for a convertible so I could throw back the roof and appreciate the sun and the wind on my face.

The feeling drained away as the days went by. It was replaced by a heaviness inside me that mirrored the thick, indigo air and the swell of humidity as the floodwaters burned off and soaked into the moss and the trees and vegetation, until everything was heavy and oppressive once again. The phone and the electricity came back on. Charles called to say he had set up three meetings for me to show my work the following week. But that only added to my sense of wondering and smothering and waiting.

I convinced myself the appointments weren't going to translate to sales. I convinced myself Charles was being kind. And I finally admitted Aunt Lula clearly didn't want to have anything to do with us since she hadn't written back in response to the email I had sent.

My temper was short. With Mama, whose own temper already frayed too easily, and with Joe. He stopped by three times, and finally left with a determination in his step that made me miss him even before the soles of his departing wingtips crunched on the gravel of the drive. When the doorbell rang an hour later, I assumed it was him coming back.

I opened the door with my heart beating fast and an apology on my lips, and discovered it wasn't Joe at all. A long, black car with a driver stood waiting in the drive at the bottom of the steps. My eyes had to drop to waist level to find the woman in the wheelchair who had rung the bell. She had my Mama's eyes.

My fingers tingled, and my breath caught. My voice coming out in a cracked whisper of surprise, "Aunt Lula?"

The woman smiled broadly. Her lips twisted around an old scar that bisected her face from mid-cheek to chin. "You're the spitting image of your mother, child. Aren't you going to invite me in?"

I stepped back, not knowing what else to do. At a nod from Lula, the driver rushed up the stairs to lift the wheelchair over the threshold into the foyer. Dimly, I realized that had to have been the way she had gotten up there in the first place. The fact that she'd asked him to leave her to wait at the door alone told me worlds about her, and made me feel even smaller.

"Who's there?" Mama called from the parlor. "Is that Joe Beaufort coming back?"

"No, Sister," Aunt Lula shouted back. "It surely isn't."

Mama emerged from the parlor faster than I'd seen her move in the three years since the Tragedy. "My God! Lula is that you? You've come back?" One hand on her heart, she clutched at the wall, but the fact her knees were buckling didn't stop her from hardening her spine and raising her voice. "No, wait just a moment now. Don't you think you can go playing on my Good Nature, Lula Elizabeth Watson. You turn that chair right back around and go back wherever you've been hiding these thirty years. This is about the last place you'd be welcome after you left with never a word to me. And taking Great-Grandma Amelia's good silver into the bargain."

"I wrote and wrote and wrote," Aunt Lula said, "and if the old devil didn't give you my letters, that certainly wasn't any fault of mine." She rolled the wheelchair forward with her chin stuck in the air higher than strictly necessary to look Mama in the eye.

I knew that expression well.

Mama set her hands on her hips like a five-year-old child. "You did not!"

"Did so," Lula said.

"Did not."

"Yes," I said, finally stepping forward, "she did. I found the letters in the back of Grandpa's bottom desk drawer."

Both women turned to face me, and the hot air all went out of Mama as if she'd been poked with a pin and deflated. It was only when they both stopped shouting that I could see the trembling of Lula's hands and the tears leaking down her cheeks.

"Is it really you?" Mama whispered, turning back to her sister.

"Yes," Lula said hoarsely. "It's me."

"Your poor face. And your legs. What happened?" Mama collapsed to her knees in front of the wheelchair.

Both of them wept, clinging to each other as if the rubber band that had connected them from birth had finally snapped them back together and brought them back to life like the smack of a doctor's hand against a baby's bottom. In the midst of it, the driver came back up the steps with a couple of suitcases in either hand.

"Where do you want me to put these?" he asked, looking at me.

I started to open my mouth, but they both answered before I could.

"I'm staying," Lula said defiantly

"You're staying," my Mama said, in that tone of hers that said she wasn't taking any arguments. "We'll put you down in the drawing room, and I'll have Ginnie call over to Chandler's Construction to put in a ramp, and we'll get Joe over to bring down the bed from your old room . . ."

I smiled and started eyeing the suitcases with a proprietorial eye about halfway through that litany, right about the time Aunt Lula started chiming in with her own instructions. Fifteen minutes later, they were both in the parlor arguing about Great-Grandma Amelia's silver over a fresh pot of tea, which was probably the closest they were ever going to get to saying how much they'd missed each other. Both of them were too stubborn to admit they were happy, but I could tell.

The scent of tea and brandy, lavender and baby powder, had doubled in the parlor, and two women, old before their time, were happy to be arguing together again. The bird had flown and come back.

With Lula here, Mama wasn't going to be lonely anymore. Maybe it was time to see how far I could fly myself.

I thought of Joe and my paintings up in Charleston, of hope and indigo blue in the air, and suddenly, I wasn't sure I would be gone forever. Maybe it wouldn't be for long at all. I might even hate New York. But that was the nicest thing about having wings, I decided, as I watched Lula and Mama with their heads bent close.

Maybe it was never too late to fly south and come back home.

Lavender In Blue

Deedra Climer

"Welcome to Our Neck of the Woods"

The red letters painted on the cabin mailbox were well over three decades old and barely legible. As I turned on to the driveway, the hum of tires on asphalt changed to the crunch of rocks and red clay.

That sound always woke the children, no matter how tired they were.

But, there hadn't been any sleeping children in my backseat for decades. Now, it was just me. I maneuvered my Malibu around the curves that made our cabin seem further removed from civilization than it really was. Usually, trips to the cabin meant quiet relaxation, but this trip was different. Today, "our neck of the woods" was a million miles away from anywhere I wanted to be.

Will and I had bought the cabin on our honeymoon, with money his parents had given us as a wedding gift. A hand-lettered sign pinned to a cluttered corkboard just inside the entrance of the only grocery store in town had read "We Can't Stand the Heat—Moving North—Cabin for Sale."

On the way out, I'd balanced the grocery bag on my hip and ripped the phone number from the bottom of the page.

Will crinkled his forehead and looked at me.

"What?" I smiled at my new husband. "It's worth a look, isn't it?"

In spite of the milk getting warm in the back seat, we drove to the cabin. Standing on tiptoes, we peeked through the thin, ruffled curtains on the bathroom window at pine plank floors and a tiny claw-footed tub.

The last owners "must have" lavender, planted near the gate, came on a breeze—a sure sign from my grandmother that I should spend summers here, raise children here, get old here.

The next day, Will feigned meaningful questions to the agent, kicking boards and commenting on the roof. I followed them around the house, saying nothing. I was already imagining myself on the beach, reclining on Will's chest, watching the stars.

Will's parents were furious that we had squandered their gift on a wood-shingled cabin. His mother said the money was for a house—one we could live in, with a garage and a mortgage.

"So we'll stay in the apartment a little longer." Will had knelt beside her and taken her hand in his. "You always said you wished you and Daddy had a place to get away. Don't you wish you had done this when you could?"

There'd been no arguing with those dark, dreamy eyes.

"At least it's paid for," she'd said. "Fill it with love."

And, we had.

I turned off the engine and sat with both hands on the steering wheel, suddenly rethinking my decision to come here alone. My oldest daughter, Meaghan, had wanted to come along "to help carry things," she'd said. I knew better.

She'd sat on her daddy's side of the bed and stared at a framed picture of our wedding day. The comforter hadn't been pulled down on that side in almost three years.

"It's too sad, Ma," she said as she ran her finger over the silver filigreed frame. "You shouldn't be by yourself."

I threw another pair of chinos in my duffle bag and checked out my nightstand, deciding which book to take. "I'm coming with you. We all think . . ."

"No, you're not." I stopped her, knowing where the conversation was going. "I need to do this by myself." The truth was Meaghan hadn't seen me cry at all since her father died—neither of my children had. After three years, I wasn't going to break down in front of her now.

Meaghan gave a heavy sigh of resignation, and I squeezed her hand reassuringly. "I'll clean out the cabin and be back by this evening. Meg, I'll be fine."

I'd hoped Meaghan was convinced. I sure wasn't.

Sitting in front of the cabin now, I gripped the steering wheel tightly.

When did my hands get so old?

The plump pink hands that had diapered babies, baked pies and weeded the garden were now crinkly and dry. An old lady's hands. I twirled the braided gold wedding band around my finger and wondered if I'd ever be ready to take it off. A ridge was worn around my finger where the ring had been. I heard Will's voice say, "I told you. You are stuck with me, woman."

I opened the car door and pulled in a lungful of stale southern air, heavy with humidity and lavender now grown out of control. Gulls cawed, waves crashed, and children screamed, "Watch this Mama!" from the beach. The screen door slammed behind me as I entered the cabin and stood in the empty space that had been once the center of our family. Except for the pile of my belongings neatly stacked in a corner—the things no one else knew what to do with—the cabin was empty: A straw beach hat. Will's cane. A white wicker chair with yellow and blue flowered cushions and dog-chewed legs. My summer journal.

Thirty-five summers reduced to a pile in the corner.

I picked up my journal and sat down—the wicker chair creaking from my weight. I kicked off my sandals, opened the paisley cover and disappeared into my past.

July 26, 1976

We're here! Our first summer vacation in the new cabin! I was so excited, I packed everything last night so we could leave the minute Will got home from work. I love the simple magnificence of this place—even if it does smell like old people (laugh). I'd like to do some cleaning, but Will insists on a walk on the beach before bed. Tomorrow, I'll cut lavender and open the windows to help with the musty smell. I hope I can sleep with all this dust . . .

Will and I had gone to the cabin every time we could those first few years. Long weekends were filled with red wine and dinner on the beach. We made love and fell asleep in the sand and stumbled back to the cabin to make love again just as the sun was coming up. Will read me stories by candlelight while I soaked in the tub and talked about our future . . . the places we'd visit when we could finally afford to travel (Ireland was first on our list). Whether to name our first born after his father or mine (James or Walter).

We never left each other's side because too much of Will had never been enough for me.

March 29, 1985

I have every window in the cabin open, and I'm still hot. Will has been wrapped in Mama's quilt and huddled in the corner of the couch since he got here. I, on the other hand, haven't been comfortable enough to read in ages. I would go lay in the tub, but I'm afraid I wouldn't be able to get out. There is no room left in my body for this child to grow anymore, and I have no idea how I'm going to make it through the next three weeks . . .

I'd gotten pregnant with our first child at the cabin over the Fourth of July holiday after watching fireworks on the beach and drinking too much rum. It wasn't a momentous event. We'd made drunken love—short and sweet—and drifted off to sleep without even saying goodnight.

Now, mere weeks before I was due to deliver, I wanted nothing more than to be in my cabin. Every smell of the city made me wretch, and I longed for the lavender-filled breezes. Will had been working long hours ever since we'd found out about the baby, and I was lonely and afraid.

I'd left Will a note that said, "You know where to find me" and made the three-hour trip alone.

No person in their right mind would have gotten in the water before Easter. But, my body—overstretched and overheated—needed each wave like it needed oxygen. I was still sprawled out at the water's edge when I heard Will's truck door slam at the cabin. I smiled to myself. He really did know where to find me.

Pots clanged, cabinets opened and closed, and then Will appeared beside me on the beach with two glasses of tea. "I stopped for groceries and took next week off."

He removed his shoes and socks and rolled up his pants legs. Settling into the sand beside me, he added, "Even brought a bottle of wine in case you decide to take the doctor's advice to have a glass."

"My hero," I'd mumbled from under my beach hat.

April 1, 1985

Looks like I won't be making it three more weeks after all. My water broke early this morning (no contractions though), so Will is packing up to drive us home. The next time I write I will be a mother—a strange and somewhat surreal thought. I guess it's too late to say I'm not ready for this, isn't it?

We'd lived the life every young couple dreamed of. After Meaghan was born, I decided to stay home. In between diaperings and feedings, I freelanced for a few local newspapers. Will worked at the bank and brought me flowers every payday.

Our second child arrived in February when Meaghan was four. Will and I had timed it so Meaghan would have us all to herself until she started kindergarten. Once she was in school, we'd be able to focus on another child without taking away from her. Now that the time for her to go to school was drawing near, I wished I had waited a little longer. Meg was ready for kindergarten, without doubt. She had the vocabulary of a college freshman and could build an argument to rival any Greek scholar. In my eyes, Meg was still a baby herself in so many ways. I saw it in her dark eyes when the other kids on the playground didn't want to play with her. And, I saw it when Molly came home from the hospital.

"I can't nurse anymore, right Mommy?" Meg crawled up in my lap and snuggled in beside her baby sister who was slurping away at my breast and smacking her lips in delight.

"That's right, sweetie. It's Molly's turn to nurse now. You're able to eat vegetables now," I said. Then added, "And cookies!"

"I got too big, didn't I?" Her words were more a statement than a question. Then Meaghan had laid her head on my chest and stroked her sister's pudgy hand while Molly blew milk bubbles.

July 12, 1990

When I lose it, I'll plead temporary insanity, and any judge who has children will let me off. Coming to the cabin with a five-year old and a seven-month old is pressing the boundaries of what any sane person can manage. Coming a week after getting a new puppy is downright demented. Shannon is so cute though—I can't keep my hands off of her. The baby isn't bad either (ha!) . . .

August 25, 1992

We only got one day on the beach before the rain hit. They say

Andrew is headed this way. Shannon is running in circles and barking her head off, so I believe it. Will boarded up the windows and put sandbags around the cabin (don't ask me what good he thinks that will do). The kids are whining like crazy, but what can you do? Mother Nature made other plans, and apparently she didn't consult my children . . .

I'd sat at the kitchen table and picked at the plastic place mat. Will had paced and scribbled on the back of an envelope, Shannon a few steps behind him.

"How does this sound," he said. "'Patrick David Mason, fifty-three, died in his home on October 23, 1995. He is survived by his beloved wife, Ramona, and his son Randall, fourteen. In lieu of flowers, please send donations to the Disabled American Vets.'"

"Sounds perfect." I held my tongue, not telling him to spell out the word Veterans. I wanted Will to be done with this. To think about anything other than his brother's death for a while. He had sprung into action four days earlier when the news came that his brother died and hadn't slowed down since.

"I think beloved wife is too much."

Shannon barked in agreement.

I nodded. Ramona was a drunk, more concerned with stirring up drama than parenting her son. She opted out of most family gatherings, which disappointed no one. The day she'd married Patrick, Ramona had told her new mother-in-law that she'd raised a "Mama's Boy. " "I'll spend the rest of my life undoing what you did."

No, "beloved" wasn't a word that came to mind when I thought about Ramona. "Might be a stretch," I agreed and took a swig of my coffee.

July 14, 1998

Meaghan brought her friend Jessica with her this trip, and the poor girl can't take her eyes off Randy. You'd think that skinny boy was George Clooney the way she looks at him. Of course Randy is so interested in fishing with Will he hasn't even noticed her (Thank Goodness!). By next summer, I'll have to figure out how to have teenaged boys and girls sleeping in the same house without "problems."

Tonight, Will crept up behind me while I was washing dishes, put his arms around my waist and kissed me on my neck. I turned my face into his and stood still, afraid that the slightest move on my part would end the moment. Alas, the kids walked in and yelled, "Gross! Get a room!" I bit my tongue not to tell them that this was our room! They would die if they knew half of what had gone on in this cabin . . .

Will had enjoyed his work and gave it all he had. He went into the office before I rolled out of bed in the mornings and got home most nights well after the girls were asleep. I'd wait up for him whenever I could, desperate for a few minutes of adult conversation and a foot rub. But, on the weekends, he'd been all "family man. " Saturdays I'd sleep in and almost always woke up to the smell of breakfast cooking and the sound of the girls giggling at something silly their father was doing.

Over time, the long hours and cancelled vacations had started to wear him down. I don't think anyone else had seen it but me, though. Once the girls had started to have lives that only included their parents' funding rather than energy, Saturday mornings provided sacred sleep for Will. Sure, I worried, but he'd assured me that everything was fine.

"The old gray mare, ya know . . ."

"A mare is a female horse, William."

"You know what I mean. I'm just getting old. You're going to have to put me out to pasture."

"With all the other mares, huh?"

August 30, 2004

We are settled in for the long weekend—just Will and I. Meg is settled into her dorm, and Molly would rather spontaneously combust than hang out with us anymore. I'm finally feeling like I have my husband back to myself after all these years.

I gathered wood hoping for a fire, but it's way too warm. Will still isn't feeling good, so I put him to bed. I've had lavender drying for ages, so I guess I'll bake tomorrow if he's still not up to snuff . . .

Shortly before Molly graduated high school, Will had been diagnosed. A few weeks later, we found out that the cancer had already metastasized. Will decided not to undergo treatment. He'd rather spend his days reading with Shannon lying at his feet.

Seeing Will so peaceful, it was hard for me to be upset.

"You can cry if you need to, love." Will stroked my hair. I was cuddled under his arm on the couch . . . Will with his book, me with mine.

"Why would I need to cry?" I asked.

I put down my book and looked up at him. "I've lived the past thirty years with my best friend by my side. That's more than most people can say."

"When it's time . . . when you feel like it. It's okay to cry."

"I will. If I feel like it." I looked back down at my book. I meant it, too. My life was full of joy and love. I knew I was blessed.

And, if I had let myself think about waking up a single day without him next to me, my world might have fallen apart.

March 29, 2005

Will wanted to see if the crocuses were out, so we drove in this morning. I've got him set up by the front window looking out over the water. He says he's reading, but I haven't seen him turn a page in days. Mostly he looks out at the water. We tried to go for a walk on the beach, but he's just too weak. I took a bucket down and brought some sand back for him to stick his feet in while he "reads". . .

The sun was going down, and it was hard to read the tear-splatted pages. I closed the journal and looked around the empty cabin, taking a final deep breath of lavender and must. "Well, there you go, William. I guess I finally felt like crying," I said aloud.

The wicker chair barely fit in the back of my car and gave a protesting moan as I closed the hatch. I pulled back down the curving drive, stopping before I hit asphalt.

I pushed a "For Sale" sign into the dry, red dirt under the mailbox that read "Our neck of the woods" and drove away.

Chasing Sunset

Darcy Crowder

Going. Going. Gone.

I pulled my knees up and rested my chin on the warm denim fabric of my jeans as the last, glowing curve of the sun dipped below the worn edges of the Appalachian foothills.

"Good night, Momma."

Ignoring the persistent buzz of mosquitoes, I sat quiet, surrounded by the scent of night jasmine and honeysuckle, as the colors in the sky faded from brilliant pink and orange to the soft blue gray of night. If I closed my eyes and concentrated, I could still remember the warmth of Momma's side pressed against mine as we'd sat on this very same rock perched over the deep waters of the Tennessee, sharing sunsets and secrets.

Momma once told me that if you kissed your true love at the exact moment the sun dipped below the horizon that you would have a lifetime of love and happiness. It was exactly the sort of promise that immediately captured my childhood imagination, and truth be told, lingers still.

But that night, years ago, she must have seen a look of skepticism on my face, because she nudged her shoulder against mine and laughed. "It's true, Rosie, cross my heart. I kissed your daddy on this very same river the night he asked me to marry him—at sunset—and we've been happy in love ever since."

I'd slipped my hand into the warmth of hers as we watched the sun go down.

After that it was like a special secret we shared. Sometimes she'd wink at me and say, "Look Rosie, another perfect sunset. Let's go watch." We'd climb out to my favorite perch over the river and watch in silence as the Good Lord put on a show just for the two of us.

Of all the places in the world I may one day travel to, I don't imagine I'll ever feel closer to God or Momma, than sitting on this rock suspended over the lazy, deep waters of the Tennessee.

For Momma, life was a garden, and my sisters and I were her most cherished blossoms. Like the master gardener she was, she knew how to love us in that special way that spoke to who we were.

She took long walks with my sister Aster, a bundle of energy who never seemed to be able to just sit a spell and talk, but was always striving to move forward in everything she did.

With Lily, Momma would cozy up among all the colors and textures in Lily's room and chat, admiring as Lily dabbed and stroked another vision of beauty onto her canvas.

But with me, with me it was always sunset. Momma used to tell me she thought the reason I felt at home sitting on my rocky ledge suspended above the river was because I had my feet on solid ground, but my head in the clouds. Not to worry, though, because one day I'd figure it all out, and that everyone should remember to reach for the sky.

She always knew just what to say to make me feel better.

I stared down at the letter I held in my lap, wishing she was here now, wishing she could tell me what to do.

The paper, worn and soft from carrying it around in my pocket, fluttered in the night breeze. This would be the last letter. After three years in the war, my best friend was coming home tomorrow.

Jake was coming home.

I took a deep breath and finally gave voice to the secret I held closest to my heart, the words drifting into the growing darkness. "I've fallen in love, Momma."

I couldn't say exactly when it happened during these letter writing years, but the *first* time I fell in love with Jake was the summer he moved into the old Cooper place across the cove. Jake was just a boy of thirteen, and I was all of ten years old. And Momma was still with us.

My sisters and I grew up living at Piney Cove Marina, passed down three generations on my daddy's side. But Daddy also had a calling early on to be a preacher and took over the care and spiritual feeding of the Harvest Bay Baptist flock when we were just little girls. It often fell to Momma to run the family business when Daddy was doing the Lord's work.

So Aster, Lily and I learned the marina business inside and out, and the value of a good day's labor. It never felt like work, though. At least not to me. Growing up outside in the sunshine on the banks of the Tennessee was nothing less than a blessing.

After Jake moved in across the cove it didn't take long for him to discover he was always more than welcome to come over and hang out with the other boys and fishermen who frequented the place. I've often thought a rod, reel and the purr of an outboard are like a siren song to teenaged boys.

In my case, the lure of the open water came right on the heels of learning to walk.

Being the middle child, I was always looking for a way to define myself, to stand apart from my sisters.

Aster, the oldest, sturdy and practical like the flower she was named for, has always been a more common sense kinda gal. Momma and Daddy knew they could always count on her to be responsible when they weren't around.

And Lily, the youngest, has always been the artist. Gentle and soft, content to do what is expected of her, she lives for those quiet moments when she can be alone and create.

I too have my practical side—I know my way around a boat engine better than most—and a creative side—I enjoy making up stories whenever I'm alone out on the water or watching the world from my rock ledge. But it was in my love of the water, of swimming, fishing, sailing, any adventure really, that I found my way to be different.

Jake overheard Daddy call me Rosebud one day and took it upon himself to start calling me Bud, just to get under my tomboy skin. The summer I turned twelve, I put an end to his teasing when I used his fishing boat as a launching pad for an early July 4th fireworks show and inadvertently caused it to sink about twenty feet off shore.

Of course, this led to all manner of pranks between us which I chose to interpret as a sort of pre-teen mating ritual, which came to an abrupt halt when he discovered Aster had bloomed right beneath his nose. With the simple act of asking my sister on a date, Jake had ripped my heart out from my prepubescent chest and stomped on it.

I never let on, though. In fact, that was the year I seriously thought about joining the drama club, I'd developed such a talent for hiding my true feelings.

Jake and Aster only dated that one summer, but it was enough for me to decide he'd never look at me as more than just a little girl at best, or maybe worse, his kid sister.

The tomboy tendencies I'd thought helped define me had only kept me hidden.

The next morning, thoughts of Jake's imminent arrival firmly placed in a box and labeled Do Not Open, I tip-toed into the kitchen and snagged a fresh slippery peach wedge from the heaping bowl next to Aster.

"Stop that!" Aster slapped at my hand as I popped the fruit into my mouth. "Those are for tonight's cobbler."

I wished I was like those other girls who couldn't eat a bite when they were anxious about something. Not me. I had a healthy appetite come rain or shine. Determined not to let on just how nervous I was, I shrugged as I licked peach juice from my fingers and reached for the coffee. "I thought you were making blueberry cobbler?"

"I am." She brushed hair from her face with a flour-smudged wrist. "I figured I'd make both since Mrs. Branson practically invited the whole town for the welcome home party tonight."

Nonchalant was not something I did well. And I knew it. I stuffed my free hand into my back pocket to keep the tremble from giving me away and rubbed my finger over Jake's last letter. I'd been carrying the darned thing around like some sort of talisman or good luck charm, I don't know which. That single page telling me my true love was coming home at long last had the power to calm me and practically make me sick with nerves at the same time.

A high-pitched screech, followed by excited chatter, filtered in through the open window above the sink where we stood. Aster, hands deep in a ball of dough, shot me a worried look as I pulled back the lace curtain to peer outside.

The activity across the cove in Jake's backyard resembled the frenzy of ants on a broken hill. Mrs. Branson had recruited a small army of neighbors and church ladies to set up for the party. Some of whom were at this moment scrambling to right a fallen ladder under poor Mr. Thompson, recognizable by his unnaturally white hair and protruding belly, as he dangled from the lower limb of a large sugar maple.

As we watched, Daddy came to the rescue, hefting the ladder under Mr. Thompson's flailing legs, then kindly taking over the job of stringing tiny lights in the tree.

Crisis averted, Aster turned back to her cobbler, but I sipped my coffee and continued to study the chaos across the water. How was I going to pull it off? How was I going to look Jake in the eye when he came home tonight and not give away my feelings?

It wasn't that I didn't ever want him to know I was in love with him. But neither one of us had ever written those three little words to each other. Sometimes, when he seemed especially homesick, it felt like he came close, but I always managed to talk myself out of believing there was anything more than just friendship on those pages.

Turns out, the walls built by the tender heart of a twelve-year-old were made of pretty sturdy stuff.

"Everything's going to turn out just fine, you'll see." Aster slid the heavy ceramic dish full of peaches into the oven and shut the door.

I turned my back to the window and smiled before taking another sip of coffee. "I'm sure it will. Mrs. Branson wouldn't allow anything to be less than perfect for her one and only son."

Aster made a face as she turned back to the sink and began washing blueberries. "I'm not talking about the party, that's a given." She glanced at me from the corner of her eye. "I'm talking about you."

Heat crept up the back of my neck. Was I really that transparent? I grabbed my tote off the back of the kitchen chair and began sorting through it, making sure a fresh pad of paper and my favorite pen were inside.

Leave it to Aster to get right down to business. Well, I wasn't about to have this conversation. Voicing my feelings alone in the dark to memories of Momma was one thing. I wasn't going to risk admitting anything to anyone in the light of day—not until after I'd seen Jake.

And after that, depending, maybe never.

"Yep, everything I need is right here." I patted the sack as I slung it over my shoulder. "I'm sure you're right. The article will turn out just fine. You know how nervous I get before each deadline."

Her words chased me out the back door as I headed for Jake's place. "Go ahead. Pretend you don't know what I'm talking about. But anyone with two eyes and a lick of sense knows you're in love with Jake Branson."

The little smile I allowed myself at Aster's expense—she hated being ignored—faded with each step I took along the worn dirt path leading to Jake's. It was a short cut forged over many years of circling around the deep cove between my house and his, and the street he lived on which led directly into town.

Not only did it work as a quick route for the local boys to get to our marina on foot, but when we were old enough, my sisters and I used it for the well-earned trip to the general store for ice-cream or maybe a matinee.

That it ran right alongside his place and offered the occasional chance to see what he was up to was a bonus. I'd offer every chance I got to run into town for Momma, hoping to catch another glance of Jake.

Pathetic.

Sometime during my early years of high school Jake had started working summers at the marina. That's when we'd slipped into an easy friendship over our mutual love of all things water related. But then, as I'd started my junior year of high school, Jake joined the reserves and was deployed to Afghanistan.

The only thing worse in my young life was when we'd lost Momma the year before.

One thing I'd learned about myself during those years of letter writing was that I did, in fact, have a way with words. So I joined the yearbook club and the high school paper and decided to study journalism when I entered community college. Mr. Smythe had even given me a part-time job covering local human interest events for the *Harvest Bay Herald*.

Today my assignment was to cover the story of a local boy returning home from war.

I shifted my tote to the other shoulder and sighed. I'd like nothing better than to turn around and spend the day hiding on my favorite perch over the river until Jake got home. If what Aster said was true, about everybody being able to see the truth of my feelings for Jake, how was I ever going to make it through today?

"Momma, I wish you were here."

I took a deep breath and stepped from the woods into the fray around me. Better to face my problems head on.

"Oh, there you are, Rosie." Mrs. Branson marched up to me with a basket full of party lights and gave my wrist a squeeze. "Can you believe it? My baby's coming home."

Before I could utter a word of response, she shoved the basket into my hands. "Be a dear and take these down to your daddy. He's draping them around the dock for me."

She turned away, never doubting for a minute I'd do as she'd asked. Her normally perfect hair looked a little frazzled, as did the blouse pulled out from one side of her lemon yellow capris. Despite her usual bossy demeanor, I couldn't help sympathize with her great need to make every last detail perfect for Jake's homecoming.

Half way across the lawn I spotted Lily sitting at the large wooden picnic table working diligently on a flower arrangement, swatches of colorful summer blooms scattered all around her. She caught my eye and waved.

Sidestepping a stack of bright green and white, plastic chairs no doubt meant to encourage party goers to sit outside and admire all the lights, I made my way down the walk to the dock. "Hi Daddy."

"Hey there, Rosie girl. How's the article coming along? Any good quotes?" Daddy swept off the ocean blue ball cap he wore, revealing a wild crop of brown curls dusted with gray at the temples, and wiped an arm across his brow before settling the cap back in place. "Thanks," he said, taking the basket from my hand.

"No, I haven't started interviewing anyone just yet." I settled onto the sun-warmed wooden planks next to him. "I wanted to talk to you first."

"Well." He scratched his chin. "I'd have to say that I always knew Jake Branson would make us proud. That boy has a good head on his shoulders. A real asset to the community." He chuckled. "I guess that should read man, instead of boy."

I grabbed my pad and scribbled his comments, then nibbled at the eraser. "Thanks, but what I meant was, I want to ask you something."

Daddy sat back and gave me his full attention, a virtue that made him all the more loved by his flock. "Go ahead, Sugar, what's on your mind?"

The words rushed out before I was even aware of what my question was. "How did you know you were in love with Momma?"

A startled look came over his face, but he quickly covered with a smile as he gazed out over the water. "Now that's a fine question, Rosie. A fine question. I suppose I could say it was the first time I laid eyes on her, but I'm not exactly sure when that was. We grew up in town together, and it seems like she was always a part of my world."

Memories clouded up behind his eyes. He cleared his throat, pulled another string of lights from the basket and began to wrap them around a post. Then his hands stilled. "Or I guess I could say it was the night of our senior prom, when she came out of her room to stand at the top of the stairs, looking down at me like a pure angel from heaven. Her blond hair swept up in curls and her cheeks the same pale pink of her dress."

I closed my eyes, picturing the way Momma must have looked at that young age.

"But to tell the truth," he bent back to his task, "I'd have to say I knew I was in love the day she put salamanders in my bait can."

My eyes flew open at his words, and he laughed. "Yep. Your momma was some kinda girl all right. She wasn't afraid of anything, and mischief was never far away." He winked at me. "Kinda reminds me of someone else I know."

He took off his hat again and ran a hand through his hair as he warmed up to the story. "Apparently she felt the need to make me pay for some slight or another. She knew my habit of fishing early on Saturday mornings, so she talked one of her girlfriends into helping her round up some of those little lizards that live in the rocks. They snuck over to the marina while I was getting my gear together, dumped out my worms and replaced them with about a dozen or so of those poor frightened critters."

He grinned from ear to ear. "I can still remember Hank, my fishing buddy's scream when I opened that can, and all those salamanders went every which way. Hank jumped up and fell overboard trying to shake them off."

Daddy paused to look back out over the water. "I stood there in that boat, Hank flailing about in the water, and watched your momma and her friend on the riverbank practically rolling with laughter." Daddy looked me in the eye. "I knew right then I was gonna marry that girl one day."

This was a different side of Momma than I'd ever heard of before. I tried to picture the proper pastor's wife I knew, the consummate southern lady I loved, picking up lizards and shoving them into a can. It couldn't be done.

"You're teasing. Momma never told us any stories like that."

Daddy handed the other end of a string of lights to me, and we began working together. "Well now, she sure didn't need to go planting ideas in you girls' heads. Especially you, Rosie. You were never at a loss for making your own kind of mischief." He laughed. "I still remember the look on Jake's face as he stood right here on this dock and watched his old fishing boat sink to the bottom of the cove under a blaze of fireworks."

I bent to hide the blush I felt rising to my face.

He reached out to cup my cheek. "You're just like her, you know. Even more than your sisters."

"I always thought Aster—"

He chucked his knuckle under my chin. "Aster was born knowing what she wanted in life, same with Lily. Your momma had to fuss and fight her way into her skin. Just like you."

I swallowed back the lump in my throat and wrapped my arms around his neck. "I love you, Daddy."

He rubbed his big hands across my back. "You're gonna be all right, Rosebud. You wait and see." He pulled away to look me in the eye. "I have it on good authority."

The day sped by in a blur of activity, but I had a good head start on my article for the paper. Everyone had been more than ready to share stories about Jake, though it was a miracle I could concentrate at all. By midday all the decorating was done and the food prepared. I'd had just enough time to shower and change and get back to the Branson's before Jake was due to arrive.

Everyone's nervous anticipation was sucking all the air from the room. Jake had instructed that he didn't want one of those public airport scenes, so he intended to take the bus from Knoxville to Oakridge and have his daddy pick him up at the station and bring him home. Each time a car drove by, Mrs. Branson's eyes would tear up.

I slipped out the back door, intending to wait out by the water's edge where I could breathe. Before I realized where my feet were taking me, I had followed the worn dirt path leading from Jake's house back to mine. I stood on our boat dock staring up at my rock ledge.

What was I doing?

Sudden laughter and music drifted across the cove. Jake must have finally arrived home. Sooner or later someone would wonder where I was, why I wasn't there welcoming him alongside everyone else.

For some reason, the idea, the sanctuary of climbing out onto my favorite spot above the river chafed at me. I couldn't hide from this any longer. I had to face him. I had to risk him seeing the love I knew I wouldn't be able to keep from my eyes.

Even if he didn't love me back.

Jake was my best friend. If that was all I would ever have, it would have to be enough.

My thoughts drifted with the current back to the last conversation Momma and I had sitting high above the river. The last time she'd found the strength to watch the sunset with me. And to my everlasting shame, how I'd asked her if she'd felt cheated of her sunset promise.

"I thought you were supposed to have a lifetime of love and happiness," I'd said.

Her fragile hand gripped mine and brought it to her lips where she placed a fierce kiss on the back of it. "Rosie, God promised me a lifetime of love and happiness, and He made good on that promise." She patted my hand. "Yes, He did. A lifetime's worth."

The reflection of the lights in the trees across the cove blurred and shimmered on the water like a million fallen stars. Wishing stars, Momma had called them. I blinked back unshed tears and took a deep breath.

A lifetime of friendship with Jake. Would that really be enough?

I glanced down river. The sun lay cradled on the ridge, darkness was coming fast. I'd learn to make it enough. After all, I was my momma's daughter.

Urgency, not dread this time, propelled me into action. I had to get back to the party and find Jake. With any luck I might even make it before anyone realized I'd slipped away.

As I turned from the water's edge, a shadow stepped out from the woods. My pulse skipped for just a moment until I realized it was Jake. He'd grown taller, it seemed, in the years since I saw him last. More muscular, more imposing, more . . . everything.

I steadied myself against the deck railing half convinced this was a dream, half afraid it wasn't.

He stepped onto the dock, his blue eyes fastened on mine. "I've been looking for you."

Everything I should have said, everything I wanted to say, bottled up in my throat. "I've been right here."

He stepped closer. Really close. He still wore his fatigues and smelled slightly of buses and strangers, but also warm cotton and rich Tennessee earth, as if he carried home with him wherever he went.

Home. Jake was finally home for good.

I couldn't seem to find something to do with my trembling hands, until he tucked them into his own and pulled me just a little bit closer still.

"There's something I've been wanting to say, to tell you, in my letters. I . . ." He swallowed, and suddenly I realized he was as nervous as I was. Hope stole its way into my heart. "Something I should have said before now." I think I heard him mutter "Oh, hell," as he pulled me up against him and kissed me like I've never been kissed before.

I don't know how long we stood there letting our hearts and lips say all the things we each needed to hear, but I did manage to have the presence of mind to peek open one eye and catch the sun just as it dipped over the worn edge of the Appalachians.

Going. Going. Gone.

The Authors' Favorite Recipes

Martina Boone

Confetti Chicken Salad

Ingredients:

4 cups chopped cooked chicken breast
¼ cup finely chopped sweet onion
¼ cup finely chopped celery
1 cup quartered, red seedless grapes
¾ cup finely chopped toasted pecans
4 slices finely chopped crispy bacon
¾ cup mayonnaise
½ cup sour cream
1 tablespoon Dijon mustard
½ tablespoon chopped fresh tarragon
½ teaspoon sea salt fresh ground black pepper to taste

Preparation:

Combine chicken, onions, celery, pecans, grapes, and bacon. Mix in a large bowl and refrigerate.

Whisk mayonnaise, sour cream, mustard, tarragon, salt, and pepper together in a separate bowl. Add to chicken mixture and serve on lightly toasted sourdough bread with bread and butter lettuce, or over romaine lettuce as a salad.

Deborah Grace Staley

Sausage Puffs (Toasty Balls)

Ingredients:

2 containers of crescent rolls
1 (8 ounce) package of cream cheese
1 package of breakfast sausage, any kind

Preparation:

Preheat oven according to package directions on crescent rolls and spray a cookie sheet with non-stick cooking spray. Brown sausage, breaking up meat so it will be crumbled. Drain grease, then reduce heat to low and add cream cheese in chunks. Stir until cheese is melted and well mixed with sausage. Remove from heat.

Spread crescent roll dough out on pastry sheet or waxed paper. Press together perforations. Cut dough into 2-inch squares. Spoon sausage mixture onto dough. Pull up edges of dough and press together. Place dough balls onto cookie sheet.

Cook 10-15 minutes, until dough is golden.

Jane Forest

Famous Adaptable Potato Salad

Ingredients:

6 to 8 medium potatoes (I prefer Yukon Gold)
4 eggs
¾ cup mayonnaise
½ cup chopped onion (I prefer Vidalia onion)
¼ cup sweet pickle relish
¼ cup finely chopped celery
2 tablespoons white vinegar
1 tablespoon mustard (yellow or Dijon)
¼ teaspoon garlic salt

Preparation:

Boil the potatoes until done, rinse in cold water, when cool, peel and chop into small chunks. Sprinkle with the two tablespoons of white vinegar, stir gently and refrigerate. Boil the eggs, peel while hot, and refrigerate to cool while you fix everything else.

Chop the onion. If you're lucky to get Vidalia in season, use the whole ½

cup or more, if not, reduce the amount of onion to your family's taste. Chop the celery. I like to mince my celery very fine.

In a large bowl, mix the mayo, onion, relish, celery, mustard, and garlic salt. Stir well. Chop and add the eggs. Last, stir in the potatoes. Adding them last keeps them from getting as mashed up.

Here's some adaptations depending on what flavors your family likes and what you have in your refrigerator and on your spice shelf:

¼ teaspoon celery salt
1 clove of garlic, minced
¼ cup black olives
¼ cup bacon, crumbled
¼ cup green olives

¼ cup cheddar or other cheese, shredded
¼ cup Ranch dressing (reduce some of the mayo)
¼ cup chopped dill pickle (reduce or eliminate the sweet pickles)
¼ cup green onions
2 tablespoons chives
2 tablespoons chopped banana peppers (or chili peppers if you like things hot)

Salt and pepper to taste
Sprinkle a little paprika on the top, for pretty

Kathleen Watson

Chicken Salad

Ingredients:

2 ½ cups shredded, cooked chicken meat, chilled
½ cup golden raisins
½ cup coarsely chopped cashews
2 tablespoons chopped fresh parsley
Salt to taste
1 cup mayonnaise
¼ cup heavy whipping cream (not Cool Whip)

Preparation:

In a medium bowl, whip cream to soft peaks.

Combine meat, raisins, cashews, parsley, salt, and mayonnaise with whipped cream. Chill.

Valerie Keiser Norris

Slow-cooker Brunswick Stew

Brunswick Stew can require a lot of preparation, but not this version. And it's the closest version to my favorite barbecue restaurant's recipe I could find!

Ingredients:

1 medium onion, chopped fine
2 (14 oz) cans petite-diced tomatoes (chunkier tomatoes if you prefer)
2 (10 oz) cans barbecue pork
1 (10 oz) can barbecue beef
1 (10 oz) can chicken
1 (14 ¾ oz) can creamed corn
1 (15 oz) can whole kernel shoepeg corn, drained
¼ cup barbecue sauce
½ teaspoon ground black pepper
½ teaspoon salt
½ teaspoon granulated sugar
1 Tablespoon vinegar

Preparation:

Place all ingredients in a 6-qt. slow-cooker and stir until combined. Cook on low for 6-8 hours.

Valerie Keiser Norris

Malinda's Sweet Potatoes

Ingredients:

1 cup sugar
dash salt
½ teaspoon cinnamon
½ cup water
1 tablespoon butter
4 medium sweet potatoes, peeled and sliced in ¼-inch thick slices. (Malinda uses a ripple cutter which makes beautiful slices. Everything Malinda does is beautiful.)

Preparation:

Mix dry ingredients in a medium saucepan. Add water and butter and cook over medium heat until syrupy. Add potatoes and cook approx. 20 minutes.

Malinda's recipe includes this note: If syrup cooks away, make another half batch and pour over. I've not yet had to do this, but the instructions must be in there for a reason!

Valerie Keiser Norris

Pumpkin Pudding
(Pumpkin "Stuff," according to my family)

This recipe is the reason my husband never gets to have sweet potatoes for Thanksgiving. The rest of us love Pumpkin Stuff, and it's too similar to mashed sweet potatoes to serve both. He loves us anyway.

Ingredients:

For Pudding ("Stuff"):
½ stick butter (4 tablespoons)
1 pound canned pumpkin. Do not use pumpkin pie filling
1 cup sugar
2 eggs
½ cup flour
1 teaspoon vanilla
½ teaspoon salt
¼ teaspoon baking soda
1 cup canned evaporated milk

For Topping:
¼ cup sugar
½ teaspoon cinnamon

Preparation:

Heat oven to 375 degrees. Spray 2 ½ qt. baking dish with non-stick baking spray.

Melt butter in baking dish. Mix the remaining pudding ingredients with an electric mixer and pour into the dish.

Mix topping ingredients. Sprinkle on top of pumpkin mixture.

Bake for 30-40 minutes or until firm.

Misty Barrere

Granny's Chocolate Wonder Pound Cake

Ingredients:

2 sticks butter
3 cups sugar
½ cup shortening
5 eggs
3 cups all-purpose flour
½ teaspoon baking powder
1 cup sweet milk
1 tablespoon vanilla flavoring
¼ cup cocoa

Preparation:

Be sure to use shortening to grease your bundt pan & flour to coat it—none of this spray-on stuff. Love, Granny.

Cream butter, sugar & shortening, add eggs one at a time, add dry ingredients alternate with milk, add flavoring.

START IN COLD OVEN

Bake 325 for 1 hour and 10 min. in dark bundt pan. Do not open door until done. Test with tooth pick.

Love, GRANNY.

Willis Baker

Southern Summertime Strawberry Ice

Ingredients:

2 cups buttermilk
1 pint fresh strawberries
1 cup Sugar
1 egg white

Preparation:

Combine buttermilk, strawberries (slightly crushed) and sugar.

Pour into 9 X 13 dish and place in freezer until mushy. Beat egg white until stiff, then fold into strawberry mixture. Return to freezer until firm.

Clara Wimberly

Shaker Lemon Pie

Ingredients:

2 large lemons
4 eggs, well beaten
2 cups sugar
2 (9-inch) ready-made pie crusts

Preparation:

Slice lemons as thin as possible, including rind. Add sugar and mix well. Let stand at least two hours, blending regularly. Add beaten eggs and mix well. Ladle the mix into one of the nine-inch pie crusts, making sure that the lemon slices are evenly distributed. Top with the second pie crust. Cut several slits near that crust's center. Bake at 450 degrees for 15 minutes. Reduce heat to 375 and bake for about 20 minutes or until a knife inserted near the edge of the pie comes out clean. Cool before serving.

Darcy Crowder

Caramel Chess Pie

Ingredients:

1 stick margarine
1 ½ cup brown sugar
1 cup sugar
4 tablespoons flour
½ cup milk
4 eggs
1teaspoon vanilla
1 cup nuts (optional)
2 pie shells

Preparation:

Cream butter, sugar, flour. Add milk. Beat eggs separately before adding. Add vanilla.

Pour into pie shells. Sprinkle nuts over top.

Bake at 350 degrees in preheated oven approximately 45-60 minutes.

Susan Sipal

Homemade Butter

Butter is extremely easy to make at home, even without a churn. After experimenting with an old daisy churn (oh! my arms!), a blender, and a food processor, I've decided that I like the food processor the best.

If you're fortunate enough to have access to fresh, raw cream—lucky you! But you can also use cream from the store.

Let the cream come to room temperature for a couple of hours, then put it into your food processor. You'll want to only fill your processor about 2/3 full because the cream will expand as it is whipped. As the cream blends and thickens, you'll hear the change in tone. After it has thickened considerably, then it will start to subside. At that point, you'll notice little globules of butter forming. Keep blending until these globules come together in lumps, probably about 30 more seconds or so.

Strain off the milk (buttermilk), but leave the butter in the processor. This buttermilk can be used in any recipe calling for cultured buttermilk, but will need to be used within a couple of days.

To the butter that is left in the processor, add enough water to cover it and turn the processor on for about 15 seconds. This whips any remaining buttermilk out of the butter so that it will not spoil. Drain this liquid, add more water, and repeat for another 15 seconds. Your butter should now be ready to place into a mold or form into a ball. Add salt as desired.

You may also want to consider experimenting with cultured butter. The process is exactly the same as above except you use cultured cream. Simply add about 1/4 cup of cultured buttermilk to a quart of cream and let it ferment outside the refrigerator for about 24 hours before processing. Use the best quality buttermilk you can find for this. The cream once cultured is a type of sour cream known as *creme fraiche*.

Kimberly Brock
Not Your Mama's Pot Roast

Ingredients:
1 chuck roast
2 tablespoon vegetable oil
Water
Salt
Pepper
Garlic powder
1 sweet onion
8 carrots (sliced)
12 Small red potatoes

Pour vegetable oil in a large pot. Season roast generously with salt, pepper, and garlic salt. Brown on both sides in hot oil. Cover the roast with water and turn heat down to a high simmer for three hours, refilling the water to keep the roast covered. Add onion and carrots, salt and pepper to season, and more water to cover. Simmer another hour. Add potatoes and simmer until all vegetables and meat are tender, about thirty minutes.

Tom Honea

Cochon-de-Lait: (whole pig roast)

A Cochon-de-Lait is basically a Cajun pig roast of a whole young pig. The pig is slow roasted for ten-to-twelve hours: an event rather than a meal.

Ingredients:

25 to 100-pound young pig
Injecting marinade (see recipe below)
Cajun seasoning mix
Several heads of garlic
Cooking shed
Lots of wood

My expert advisor, a good friend of mine, starts with several bottles of good red wine and at least a couple of cases of beer. This is for the cooks, you understand . . . not the recipe. When the beer cooler is empty, the pig is most likely done: a Cajun-meat-thermometer.

Cajun Seasoning Mix:

A Cajun seasoning mix is used in many Cajun recipes. It is basically salt with a variety of spices. There are many commercial seasoning mixes on the market. Below is a seasoning mix recipe if you would like to make your own. Experiment with every batch until you have the spice combination you like.

Ingredients:

Table salt, 26 oz.
Cayenne pepper, 5 tbs.
Black pepper, 3 tbs.
Onion powder, 3 tbs.
Garlic powder, 3 tbs.
Chili powder, 3 tbs.
Thyme, 1 tbs.
Sweet basil, 1 tbs.

Bay leaf, 1 tbs.

Mix Seasoning:

Add all the seasoning, except salt, in a blender. Cover and blend to a fine consistency. Don't breath the dust: you'll be sneezing the rest of the day.

Mix the blended spices with the salt until you achieve a uniform color.

Use as you would salt.

Preparing the Pig:

Obtain a young pig. We usually cook about a 70-80 pound pig. The largest we ever cooked was about 115 pounds, which fed some eighty people.

The pig needs to be butchered by scraping and not skinning. The skin needs to be on the pig so the meat does not dry out.

If you do not want the little fellow looking at you while it's cooking, then cook it without the head. Personally, I consider having the head on part of the presentation of a Cochon de Lait. But by all means, remove the eyes.

Prepare a sturdy frame to spread and skewer the pig. You will have to partially split the backbone of the rib cage from the body cavity side in order to spread the pig flat. The pig needs to be supported for its full length, or else it may fall apart when it gets tender.

My friend lays out the whole hog on a sheet of plywood, rubs every nook and cranny of the pig. Then lets it rest for an hour. This is a good time, beverage in hand, to chop onions, bell peppers, and celery: the Cajun Trinity. Peel 25 cloves of garlic.

We take a paring knife, punch holes in the thick parts of the pig, stuff the holes with the Cajun Trinity and garlic cloves. Then, if you are a real Hog Cooker, it is time to shoot-up your pork.

Seasoning the Pig:

This is the most important part. The pig needs to be injected with a marinade, stuffed with garlic, and coated on all sides with a seasoning mix.

Inject Marinade: About a quart of marinade is injected into all parts of the pig. Use an injector needle that has holes on the side. I have never made the same marinade twice, but it is always a mixture containing a Cajun seasoning mix, garlic powder or juice, onion powder or juice, hot pepper sauce, Worcestershire sauce, and sometimes butter. For starters, try the following turkey injecting recipe, without butter.

Injecting Marinade:

Liquid garlic, 6 oz.
Liquid onion, 6 oz.
Liquid crab boil, 3 oz.
Worcestershire sauce, 6 oz.
Your favorite hot red pepper sauce, 6 oz.
Cajun seasoning mix, 6 tbs.

Makes about 28 oz.

(Note: My friend insists on adding a bottle of Shiraz to the mix.)

It's now time to get the Cajun Microwave fired up. This is Cajun invention is the ultimate device, used from Thibodeaux all the way out to Eunice and Abbeville, is the best device to cook a fine piece of pit! The preferred cooker is a 24 x 36' cypress box lined with sheet metal, and a sheet metal lid, 5" high and with two handles.

You build your fire on top of the metal lid. The oak wood fills the box with heat and smoke. You cook your pig low and slow.

Cooking the Pig:

Place the pig in the box. We usually leave the head on. But, if you don't want him looking at you, this is not necessary. Replace the lid back onto the box.

Start the fire in the back of the shed. Let it burn until you have a good bed of coals.

Keep enough wood on the fire so it's hot enough so you can only stand or hold your hand a foot away for 5 to 10 seconds. I have no idea what temperature that would be, but I'm guessing about 180 to 200 F. It's not a bad idea to start out with a pretty hot fire to get the outside of the pig up to temperature quickly, then let the fire die down a bit for the rest of the cooking period.

Now comes the easy part. Pull up a log or a plastic lawn chair. Sit back, drink a cold beverage, throw some wood on the fire every now and then, tell some bad jokes, and enjoy the company of your friends. Crank up some Jo-El Sonnier on the sound machine . . . do the Cajun two-step. "A good time was passed by all."

Cook the pig until the skin is golden brown, starts cracking, and the meat starts drawing away from the bones. This can be anywhere from 10 to 12 hours, depending on how hot you kept the fire and the size of the pig.

If you like, you can insert a meat thermometer into the hind quarter to check the internal temperature. Cookbooks indicate a temperature of 170 F is desired for pork. However, the only time I ever measured the internal temperature, it never went above 155 F, yet the pig was cooked throughout and the meat was falling off the bones. Go figure.

When the last cold beer is pulled from the cooler the lid comes off the cooker, revealing a golden crusted pig. Bowls, platters of dirty rice and white beans appear: Candied yams, bread pudding, etouffee, pork boudin.

Carving and Serving:

Lay the cooked pig on a flat surface, skin side down. Filet the meat off the bone and away from the skin.

Enjoy the feast!

About The Authors

Kathleen Watson

Kathleen decided she wanted to be a writer when she was twelve years old, so took the most natural path towards that goal by studying chemistry. The people inside her head, however, were not to be silenced and after hiding her dream for years, she came out of the closet as a writer and has been pursuing the dream ever since. Along the way, Kathleen has won numerous writing awards, including the Romance Writers of America Golden Heart for Romantic Suspense, earned her Master's in Technical Writing and is working on a Masters in Forensic Drug Chemistry. A mad scientist by day and fiction writer by night, Kathleen also juggles the life of mom to her daughter, Maggie, a 16-year-old heroine-in-the-making and aspiring writer in her own right. She currently lives in the suburbs of Cleveland, OH and can be contacted at Kwhodges@aol.com.

Misty Barrere

When she was little, Misty Barrere's parents gave her a bedroom with a walk-in closet so she could read during the night without keeping everyone awake. Now that she's older (and still an insomniac), she writes stories and teaches creative writing at a women's shelter. She lives north of Atlanta with her husband and three kids. She'd love to hear from you at mistybarrere@gmail.com and please visit her blog at mistybbarrere.com

Valerie Keiser Norris

Valerie Keiser Norris moved south 25 years ago. She won first place in a South Carolina Writer's Workshop fiction contest, and Honorable Mention twice in Writer's Digest Fiction Competitions. A novel excerpt *("Satan's Lingerie")* won a scholarship to the Lost State Writer's Conference and was published in *The Petigru Review*. She's had short fiction published in *Golf Digest, Southern Golfer* and *Mother's Manual,* and articles and short humor in small magazines. She works with a critique group through the South Carolina Writer's Workshop, and hates beer. You can find more of her brand of humor at valerienorris.blogspot.com.

Darcy Crowder

Darcy Crowder is the author of *Chasing Sunset*, a short story in the anthology, *Sweeter Than Tea*, from BelleBooks. Other publications include a short story in *Homecoming in Mossy Creek*, also from BelleBooks, and a short essay published in *A Cup of Comfort for Weddings*, from Adams Media. Darcy is a member of Romance Writers of America, the Women's Fiction chapter of RWA, LRWA, and has served on the board of Georgia Romance Writers, where she continues to be an active member. She is also the proud recipient of The Laurie Award from The Rocky Mountain Romance Writers. She lives in a log cabin in the woods, surrounded by family, nature, and endless inspiration for her novels. Darcy and her daughter, author and screenplay writer, Brenna Lauren, co-host the blog It's Only a Novel.com

Kimberly Brock

Kimberly Brock is the acclaimed author of THE RIVER WITCH, a 2012 novel that has been praised by Terry Kay, Sharyn McCrumb and Joshilyn Jackson. Her writing has appeared in anthologies and magazines. After studying literature and theater, she earned a degree in education. She lives north of Atlanta where she is a wife and mother of three. Visit her at kimberlybrockbooks.com for more information and to find her blog, *Tales of a Storyteller*. You can also find her author page on Facebook at Kimberly Brock, or tweet her: @kimberlydbrock. She is currently at work on her next novel.

Clara Wimberly

Clara Wimberly always wanted to be a writer. When she took early retirement from the U.S. Forest Service she began writing full time to pursue the dream of becoming a published writer. The influence of Victoria Holt and Phyllis Whitney, as well as southern writers fueled her interest in atmospheric historical writing. The South is a favorite setting for Clara's novels. Her first book, *The Emerald Tears of Foxfire Manor*, a Gothic Romance, was set during the Civil War in North Carolina. That first book won an honorable mention in Georgia Romance Writers' Maggie Awards. Since then she has published more than 20 books in a variety of work, from gothic to historical, mainstream, suspense and southern nostalgia. She has written for publishers Kensington, Zebra, Pinnacle, HarperCollins, Silhouette and BelleBooks. Several of her books appeared on National Best Seller lists and two placed in Georgia Romance Writers' Maggie Awards. Wimberly's books have been published in Russian, Chinese, Spanish, Italian and German and have appeared in over a dozen different countries. She is the mother of three adult children and the grandmother of 7–3 boys and 4 girls. Her interests include American history, herb gardening, counted cross stitch, genealogy, traveling, collecting vintage teapots and of course reading.

Jane Forest

Jane has been working as a Youth Services Librarian for the last fifteen years. She likes finding just the right book for a person, as well as helping adults on the computer, planning programs, running the summer reading club, and playing with puppets at story time. Her previous careers have included teaching K-8 and directing resident camps. She currently enjoys vegetable gardening and being a copyeditor for BelleBooks. This is her first published story. She lives in Memphis with two spoiled Siamese cats and stacks and piles of quilts in various stages of completion. Friend her on Facebook: Forest Jane Jacobson, or visit her blog: www.forestjane.blogspot.com

Deborah Grace Staley

Deborah is a life-long resident of East Tennessee. Married to her college sweetheart, she lives in the Foothills of the Smoky Mountains in a circa 1867 farmhouse that has Angel's Wings in the gingerbread trim.

In addition to being an award-winning author, in her spare time, Deborah enjoys watching her son play college baseball and recently received a Master of Fine Arts degree in Creative Writing from Goddard College in Port Townsend, Washington. She now writes full-time and teaches. Deborah loves to hear from readers. Please contact her at: P.O. Box 672, Vonore, TN 37885 or via her website at www.deborahgracestaley.com.

Willis Baker

Willis Baker's literary essays have appeared in newspapers and the World Wide Web, his short stories in anthologies, and his poetry in distinguished journals such as the Appalachian Journal and Poem. He recently released *Mourning Tide*, his first book of poetry. Being a true 'Son of the South', his book of inspirational essays, *"Songs of the South; Musings on Faith, Family, and Growing Up in the South"* is to be released in July, 2012. Dr. Baker is a member of the National Association of Scholars (NAS) and Knoxville Writers Group. He is a retired corporate executive, theologian, chaplain, and maintains an inspirational website www.jesusisstilltheanswer.com.

Deedra Climer

Deedra Climer is a transplanted Southerner living outside Ann Arbor, Michigan with her German Shepherd, Ezra. Deedra's stories are inspired by things every girl learns growing up in the South—race, food, death, poverty and gender roles—and how to make peace with your past.

Tom Honea

Tom Honea is a true son of the deep south. He grew up in the 1950's on a working dairy farm in rural south Mississippi, Magnolia. There were no paved roads or telephones for much of that time, and certainly no television! There were, however, story tellers a-plenty, on front porches in the summer and around the fireplace in winter. Athletic ability got him off the farm and into college. After college came a stint in the US Marine Corps. Then some number of years as a successful football coach and teacher in Florida, North Carolina, and Memphis. Tom's second vocation was a dozen years in construction management. For the past twenty years he has been owner and manager of a marble/granite fabrication company in the western North Carolina mountains. He plans to spend his 'fishing year' writing.

This is his first published work. He has a completed novel, southern literary fiction, and is deep into a second work: set in the Hampton Roads (Virginia) region during the WWII years. Tom is an ongoing member of the Great Smokies Senior Writers group, a part of the University of North Carolina Creative Writing Program, a by-invitation-only group.

Martina Boone

Martina Boone writes fantasy and magical realism for adults and young adults when she isn't writing web site copy, and resides in Virginia with her family, a therapy dog, two black cats, and as much wildlife as she can coax into taking up residence in the yard.

Susan Sipal

Published in fiction and non-fiction through essays, short stories and a novel, Susan Sipal lives in rural North Carolina with her husband, two children, one dog, three cats, and too many squirrels for the dog to keep up with. She has presented multiple workshops, both at home and abroad, to help writers develop their craft as well as analyze the mysteries of Harry Potter. You can follow her on Twitter @HP4Writers, or on her blog at HarryPotterforWriters.blogspot.com.

CPSIA information can be obtained at www.ICGtesting.com
Printed in the USA
LVOW122101101012

302362LV00002B/5/P